# ESPERANZA STREET

# ESPERANZA STREET

*Niyati Keni*

LONDON · NEW YORK

First published in 2015 by
And Other Stories
London – New York

www.andotherstories.org

ISBN 9781908276483
eBook ISBN 9781908276490

A catalogue record for this book is available from the British Library.

# ESPERANZA STREET

*For Radha Ann Keni Smith, my beloved*

# ESPERANZA STREET,
# MAY 1981

The rain came down. On Esperanza Street the hot-food vendors, already prepared with tarpaulins, called to one another in mock dismay as the rain hissed on their braziers and broke the crowds. A layer of steam rose from the ground and clung to the leaves of the cheesewood hedge that separated Aunt Mary's boarding house from the commotion of the street.

I stood at the boarding-house gate and watched as the rain emptied Esperanza Street. Generally, our people didn't run too hard to escape the monsoon rains; only the tourists, for whom such rains were a novelty, sprinted happily for cover. The rest of us knew that at the height of the season, over the course of a day, the chances of staying completely dry were slim, even with an umbrella. Later on, when the rains grew less frequent, people might work a little harder to avoid getting wet.

At the top of Esperanza, where it joined Salinas Boulevard, the fish vendors stopped pouring cups of water over lines of crab and milkfish and groupers and rolled back their canopies, if they had them, to let the rain wet their wares.

Nearby, a ripple of activity passed through the muddle of tricycle and motorcycle rickshaws grouped at the junction. The trike riders, all men, turned up their collars against the light wind that drove the rain along and reached down to unstrap umbrellas that were fastened to the cycle frames. Straightening up, they slotted the umbrellas into place and opened them out, securing the fabric domes with string. The men checked the lines for tautness with their thumbs before sliding back into their saddles or lounging in the sidecars, apparently asleep, but with eyes on the street, waiting for the fares the rain would inevitably bring.

I knew the rhythm of this street by heart. On the nearest corner, within eyeshot of our gate, Johnny Five Course would be wedging an umbrella into the boughs of the frangipani tree and leaning back against the trunk, his feet up on the wheels of his food cart. On the corner opposite, Abnor, short for Amos Balignasay Junior, sixty if he was a day, would be flipping up the wooden wings of his tea cart and sliding his stool underneath before slipping into the doorway of Primo's store to share a cigarette with the man himself, perhaps making his long-considered move on the chess board atop Primo's counter. Half a block along, in the direction of the sea, Cora would be hooking the sunshade down over the chairs in front of the Coffee Shak. At the bottom of the hill, Colon Market would be blossoming into a patchwork reef of awnings and umbrellas. And down at the jetty, my father and Jonah and the rest of the boys would sit it out under any shelter to be had or, if there was none, would squat on the sea wall, their shirts pulled over their heads and, laughing at each other, turn their faces up to the sky.

*Esperanza Street, May 1981*

Esperanza, one of the oldest streets in Puerto, its heart-beat made up of thousands of smaller pulses, lulled us all with its apparent constancy. Yet even then, unknown to us, in a bright, air-conditioned office as close to our street as it was distant, a new and remorseless beat was gathering.

# SPANISH COLONIAL ARCHITECTURE

I was eight when my father brought me to one of the big houses at the top of Esperanza Street and left me with Mary Morelos. Aunt Mary, as I called her, though we weren't related, was from a good family, well known in the neighbourhood. At one time her family had owned much of Esperanza and the surrounding streets as well as estates up in the hills. However it was common knowledge that her late husband had been something of a gambler. Thousands of acres of sugar plantations and coconut groves were lost to the other landowners who formed Uncle Bobby's poker crowd, until all that remained to his wife was the house and its garden and the freehold to a couple of stores further down Esperanza.

Relieved of her inheritance, Aunt Mary ran her home as a boarding house, the only one in Esperanza that charged per night; all the others had hourly rates, too. And she was fussy about whom she let stay: unmarried couples were acceptable; single women, Filipino or foreign, were usually welcome, but single foreign men, especially the older ones, especially the quiet older ones, she didn't much like. She wasn't above asking them to leave before they'd even settled in if she got a hunch about them. Her foreign guests were mostly Germans or Swiss with the occasional American. When she was younger she'd spent time in Europe and the States and so seemed at ease in almost any foreign company.

The Morelos house was a three-storey building constructed during Spanish times: coral stone for the ground floor, hardwood for the two above. It stood, at a slight angle, behind the neatest garden in the street. The garden, thick with greenery, was formal in design, planted in a European style but with the waxy, wayward leaves of the tropics. The trees and bushes were cut as standards, with caverns of cool, shadowed earth beneath them. Arching over the verandah, fingers of bougainvillea twitched in the rain.

My father brought me to the house with a small bundle of my things; nothing much – a change of clothes and some schoolbooks. I had on an old pair of slippers that had belonged to my brother which were too large for my feet, treacherous to walk in. I didn't even have a toothbrush.

We called at the back door, by the kitchen. Aunt Mary asked my father to bring me into the sala, where she scrutinised me. She didn't ask us to sit down and remained standing herself. My father removed his cap.

'I haven't the time to fix broken wings,' she said. 'Does he have any trouble with discipline?'

My father glanced at me before answering. 'No, the boy can work hard when he puts his mind to it.'

I stood motionless in the centre of the room. The shutters were open but the cane blinds were lowered and the inside of the house was cool. The room smelled of dust and flowers and camphor. Aunt Mary frowned at me. 'Do you have another pair of shoes?' she said. I shook my head.

'I'll bring some,' my father said hurriedly, as if my ill-shod feet might break the deal, but she waved his offer away.

'Leave him here,' she said.

I was sullen that day and for much of the first month, but I did work hard and with care. Just to make it clear that I was there to work, Aunt Mary set me to polishing the wood in the house straight away, and there was a lot of it: stairs and balustrades, and the heavy narra-wood furniture. She made me polish everything but the piano; she wouldn't let me touch that at first. Everything was dusty; her previous houseboy had left over a week ago, heading back to his native village to cultivate the quarter-acre his father had left him and look for a wife.

Aunt Mary bought me new shoes and a toothbrush and tyrannised me into cleaning my teeth twice a day. In the evenings I was expected to do my schoolwork like her own boys. At night I slept next to America, the housekeeper, on a mat in the kitchen. America's children and grandchildren were a long distance away, in a village to the west. She missed them and I suppose that worked out well for me because she clucked over me like a mother.

On my first day Aunt Mary called me over to her and said, 'This is your chance, Joseph. Do you understand?' I said yes because I didn't want her to think I was ignorant. I expected I could mull it over in my own time and work out what she meant. Much later, it seemed so obvious. Puerto was a working port and a market town. It had its share of tourists, but they didn't usually stay for long, preferring the long stretches of white beach to the north and south of town.

The foreigners passed through now and again to renew their papers, visit banks or hire motorcycles on which to explore the hinterland when they tired of white sand and the sound of surf breaking out over the reefs. Some, usually men, came to stay for short stretches in the inns behind Salinas Boulevard, close to the shanties behind the Basilica de Nuestra Señora. There was something faded about these men, something careful and deliberate. They arrived in town, hired a room for a week or so, sat with warm beers at the Chinese bars, wilting behind sunglasses. From the sidewalk tables outside the bars, they faced outwards, towards Greenhills, glimpsing the nakedness of slum kids in the alleys. After a while they would leave for the beaches, sometimes with a local kid in tow. At first I envied these kids, imagining them fetching beer and folding laundry and being repaid for a few weeks' work with training shoes, video-game consoles and money.

Our neighbour's daughter, Elisa, disappeared for a fortnight once, and when she returned she had new clothes, new shoes, a bag full of music cassettes. Her family's house seemed quiet for a while after that; there was no celebration of her safe return. Then her father bought a new TV set and things seemed to return to normal. Elisa was sulky after her reappearance, though, and clicked her tongue at me like I was just a stupid baby. I was only a year younger than her and took it badly, avoiding her in spite of her new-found wealth and independence.

Later that same year I got a job bussing tables after school and at weekends at one of the Chinese bars, but it didn't last for more than a day. A neighbour saw me there, and my father came from the jetty in the middle of the day, a Saturday, and dragged me away by my ear. I'd thought that he, a stevedore who knew the meaning of hard work, would have been pleased. The following weekend he took me to Aunt Mary's.

The month after my arrival some women came to the house to help in the kitchen. My mother was among them. I'd seen her only twice since I'd left home and I was looking forward to it. She'd grown thin but I didn't think anything of it; I was young and she was my mother. It was the day before All Saints' Day and a picnic was to be held in the cemetery the next evening. The cemetery housed Aunt Mary's family crypt, where Uncle Bobby was buried, and she wanted a roast suckling pig and chicken and all manner of sweets.

My mother interrogated me as she split coconuts with a knife longer than my arm. 'Have you behaved yourself?' she said sternly.

I nodded.

'You're sure you've not given Aunt Mary any cause for complaint?'

I shrugged and said I didn't think so.

'I don't want her thinking ill of our family,' my mother said. Then, more softly, 'It's quiet at home without your hollering.'

Elisa had disappeared for a second time, though she was now back home. Her mother, Bina, had taken to her bed for a week afterwards and had not responded to any of my mother's enquiries. Elisa's father was drinking again. My mother didn't tell me any of this directly. The women discussed it among themselves in soft voices, ignoring me mostly, taking their dismay out on the suckling pig and the chickens as they rubbed in spices and stuffed the skins with herbs.

I loitered, listening to their talk, until America, uncertain how to give me orders in the presence of my mother, set me to cleaning the rice. She was on edge at the intrusion in her kitchen, but enjoying hearing gossip from a part of the neighbourhood that fell outside her usual territory.

'Poor Bina,' one of the women said. 'No one wants to marry a horse.' My mother's face tightened. She started talking about another neighbour whose skin had turned silvery and scaly by degrees. The man could recollect no change to his routine, no unusual events. His wife believed he had been cursed by a local woman who worked in the fish market but who everyone *knew* was a sorcerer. The women seized on this new topic immediately. Several times America and my mother crossed themselves in unison at some new revelation.

They were discussing this when Aunt Mary came into the kitchen to see how things were progressing. She was carrying a bundle of bed sheets. The women paused in their work, if only for an instant; somehow, a pile of laundry still seemed out of place in Mary Morelos' arms. Aunt Mary had studied a lot but never had to work before the death of her husband. She'd studied piano at a place she called the *conservatoire* and had been to university in Manila and Paris. After Uncle Bobby died and the well-wishers had drifted away, the reality of keeping the house emerged. She had Vincent, her old houseboy, but the added work when it became a guest house was too much for him and America alone. Bit by bit Aunt Mary learned, and she wasn't afraid of the work, though in front of certain people she preferred not to be seen doing it. For this reason, the women spoke about her in a different tone than the one they used for the women of the other big households at the top of Esperanza Street.

The women stopped talking now, though they continued to sing at intervals as they worked. Aunt Mary walked through the kitchen and into the laundry room at the back. 'He was so handsome,' one of the women said. The others, including my mother, exchanged glances and smiled down at the meat and the piles of scraped coconut. My mother threw me a warning look. I was too young then to guess the colour of the story. Aunt Mary was already thirty when she married Captain Bobby Morelos, and even then she was plump, with a round, plain face. Uncle Bobby was much younger and beautiful to look at, a favourite among the young ladies of the neighbourhood, but bar his navy commission and the clothes he wore, had little to offer. Of course I never heard any of this from Aunt Mary herself. She always remained tight-lipped about private matters.

When Aunt Mary came back into the kitchen the women fell silent again. I was sitting on the floor, sifting the rice for stones. She watched me for a while. Then, to my mother, she said, 'I've interrupted your discussion.'

'One of my neighbours is sick,' my mother said. 'Nothing unusual.'

The women nodded, smiling at Aunt Mary. Aunt Mary looked relieved. 'I trust you and your families are all well,' she said.

'Yes, ma'am,' my mother said, the unofficial spokeswoman.

Aunt Mary inspected the suckling pig and the row of stuffed chickens. 'On schedule?' she said, to no one in particular.

'Ahead, if anything,' my mother replied.

The women stood back to let Aunt Mary examine the food. They were all from families that had some connection with her, though not by blood or marriage. Perhaps she'd lent them money once or used her influence for them in some way. Their help today and on other days like it was a part of whatever bargain had been struck. From that time on, the existence of a connection with her, though never the details of it, was happily and widely acknowledged by these women, whose *level* otherwise was understood by both sides to be far below Aunt Mary's own.

Aunt Mary sniffed the air. It was heavy with the smell of garlic and onion. 'When the sheets are done,' she said to me, 'hang them outside.' Aunt Mary usually preferred the guest house laundry to be hung indoors, invisible to the town. 'Yes, ma'am,' I said, to impress my mother. A nod was usually sufficient acknowledgement for Aunt Mary; there was something about her home that encouraged silence. Even my mother and her friends were not raucous here like they might have been elsewhere.

Aunt Mary smiled at my mother and left; it was well known that she didn't enjoy neighbourhood gossip and so no one was offended.

The conversation foundered now as little remained to be done. Before she left, my mother said, 'I hope you're taking care to wash your privates properly.' I wish she hadn't, for it turned out to be the last thing she ever said to me. As the rest of the town worked excitedly through All Saints' Day to prepare for a night of festivity, my mother started bleeding and less than a week later she was dead.

# RICE AND CHOCOLATE

I hadn't been established long enough at Aunt Mary's to find it strange when my father came to collect me unexpectedly in the middle of the week. He waited in the sala while Aunt Mary called me in from the yard. I had barely started my chores and came into the room dragging the broom behind me to find him perched on the very edge of a chair by the doorway, nervously rubbing the back of his head with one hand and holding his cap in the other. I thought he might have been sitting that way, the chair taking hardly any of his weight, because he wanted to leave as quickly as he'd come, or because he couldn't make up his mind whether to sit or stand. I realised later, when I thought back over the day, that it was because he was afraid of dirtying the chair, as if the marks of a hard job at the jetty shouldn't be left in a house like this; I remembered also how he'd stood just outside the edge of the rug the day he first brought me here.

He wouldn't tell me why he'd come, but I knew from his face and from Aunt Mary's that it was something important. He said nothing as we walked down the hill. We'd turned off Esperanza, passed the Espiritista chapel and were almost at the street where we lived, when he said, 'Your mother was unwell.' But he couldn't bring himself to say anything more, and it wasn't until we reached our door and Aunt Bina came out to meet us that I learned my mother was dead.

He told me that, in the end, it had been quick, merciful. I couldn't understand what he meant by that. What was merciful about dying, about having so much taken from you?

Her body was lying on the bed. She looked asleep, pale, barely like the person she'd been and, for a while, I hoped it wasn't her, hoped that somebody in their grief had made a mistake and that my mother would return to demand an explanation for the presence of so many strangers in our apartment.

Aunt Bina helped my father to wash and dress my mother's body while Elisa took me outside to play cards in the hallway. We played Pusoy even though there were only two of us, and Elisa talked and talked, about nothing perhaps, for later I couldn't recall a single thing she'd said. The only time she was silent was when she was dealing the cards, and then I heard soft sounds from the apartment, which might have been a man crying.

My mother lay in the apartment in a simple coffin for a day and a night while people came to see her. It was November and the rains had stopped and the days and nights were slightly cooler. It was still warm though, and Aunt Bina opened all the doors and windows and pressed my mother's face and chest gently with ice, bought from the store downstairs, that she'd wrapped in a towel. I heard someone say, 'At least she won't puff up like a balloon like the Magpulong boy,' and I imagined a boy blown up into a taut sphere, skin stretched to bursting and I giggled, but only for a moment before my father shushed me angrily.

The apartment slowly filled with people. I recognised only a few of them, but they all knew who I was and looked at me with pity. The women sat by my mother's body and the air rang as they chanted. My father smeared oil on my forehead with his thumb and then on his own and on Elisa's and so on round the room. He swayed a little; he'd been drinking. Aunt Bina lit incense and candles.

Jonah and the jetty boys came. The boys stayed in the kitchen, playing cards and sipping from the same bottle as they passed it round, curling their fingers round the rim to keep their lips from touching it. Jonah came through into the main room and, though I saw him glance towards the kitchen several times, he stayed by the coffin, by my father, for the entire afternoon.

Elisa, helping out, disappeared and reappeared constantly. Deep into the afternoon she arrived again by my side, her eyes broad, astonished. She touched my fingers lightly and leaned into me, whispering in my ear. She'd overheard her mother say that Jonah had paid for the funeral. I felt ashamed as she told me but annoyed too, with her and with Aunt Bina. I looked at my father but I didn't know how to ask him. I went with Elisa to find her mother. Aunt Bina was outside in the hallway. She spoke authoritatively, like a teacher, as if a vigil was for her an everyday event, although I couldn't remember another in our building. 'To start with, he refused to accept any repayment from your pop,' she said. 'But you know your father. Dante wouldn't take the money except in loan, so Jonah's agreed to take instalments. He won't charge any interest on it though. Almost came to blows over it,' she added with satisfaction, though she broke her eyes away from mine as she said it. *Interest, instalments.* I wished Elisa hadn't told me at all.

Elisa held my hand through most of the evening and I let her. She squeezed my fingers every now and then. Her hand felt dry and rough. She seemed older, smarter, and I wondered more than once how it was that she too seemed to know what to do when it was *my* mother who'd died, when I felt like a visitor in my own family's apartment.

My brother and sister returned for the vigil, arriving together late in the evening. Luisa brought with her two small children I'd never seen, laying them down to sleep, amid all the noise and the passage of people, on a mat under the dining chairs that had been pushed back against the wall for want of room. Her husband didn't come with her. My father asked after him but seemed barely to hear her answer. Luisa had married young but reasonably well, at least that was what everyone said at the time. Her husband was considerably older and had a steady job with *prospects*. She'd done well enough, my mother had once said, for a girl who never finished high school. Behind her, my brother Miguel took his cap off as he came through the door and stood next to my father, his face serious, his back straight like a soldier's. He watched me for a minute, as if wondering who I was. Soon after they arrived I was sent to get some sleep in Bina and Elisa's apartment. The next morning as we stood by the grave Miguel rested his hand on my shoulder all the way through the eulogy.

After the funeral my father told me to wash and, as I stood at the tap in the yard, he came over to me and scrubbed my hair roughly with soap, holding my head down as he sluiced pail after pail of water over me to rinse the suds away. When he stopped and I looked up at him in astonishment, I saw his eyes were wet. He turned away without a word. Elisa came out with a towel and wrapped it round me, rubbing the ends of my hair with it, gently.

Luisa stayed for a couple of days, making sure our father ate and keeping the place swept and clean. Miguel left straight after the funeral. Before he went, he pushed some coins into my hand and said, 'If Pop asks, it's for Our Lady, but if you want to get some candy, that's ok too.'

It wasn't much but I slipped the coins into my father's bedside drawer, leaving them on top of his Bible, before I set off back to Aunt Mary's; all but one, which I clung to, the metal growing damp in my palm in the heat. In the street outside our building I waited for America, who'd come to collect me and pay her respects, though she'd barely known my mother at all. My father stood with his back to me, in the stairwell, talking to Pastor Levi while America talked to Aunt Bina and waited to catch my father's eye to tell him she was taking me back to the boarding house.

On the ground floor of our building, to one side of the street entrance, there was a small general store. It was owned by our landlord, who owned most of the building and one or two others in the centre of town. The store was open and I thought of what my brother had said. I bought a handful of Juicy Fruit candies and some chocolate and three hard sugar cookies, one each for my father and America and one for me.

When we were ready to leave, after Pastor Levi had gone, I pulled the cookies and some of the candies out of my pocket and offered them to my father. I thought he might take one, or maybe shake his head and leave them for me but, his face alive with rage, he swiped at my hand and scattered my offerings across the sidewalk. I was stunned. America said nothing to me but put a hand on my father's arm and said, 'Think what you want the boy to remember about today.' My father pulled his arm away and glared at her, but he watched us as we walked away through the alley towards Esperanza. When we got home, America made coconut cakes and *champorado*, rice cooked with chocolate, and let me eat only sweet things for the rest of the day.

# STEVEDORES

Aunt Mary gave me every Sunday off, but after my mother died, I lost the greater part of these to God, fidgeting silently beside my father in the chapel while he prayed. Sometimes I prayed too, mostly that my father might decide to skip church the following week, but my appeals were never answered. Afterwards we'd return to his apartment for lunch, where he'd try to make conversation to stretch out the afternoon, turning a cup round and round in his hands while I watched him from across the table, the dirty plates stacked between us. Eventually we'd end up back at the jetty, though Jonah always saw to it that my father had Sundays off too. As soon as we got there, my father seemed to relax. It never struck me as strange; somehow the jetty was the proper backdrop for him. Even now, when I think of him, the first image that arises is always of a man balanced on the cross-pole of a newly moored outrigger, his hard brown feet curved round the bamboo, one hand on his hip, the other on the boat's canopy.

The jetty was always a relief after the sobriety of the boarding house and the chapel, and every Sunday I found myself straining my eyes towards it as we walked down the hill.

*

As always, Jonah pretended to be surprised to see us. 'You're getting big,' he said to me. 'How old are you now?' Though he knew very well.

'Fifteen.'

'Can't tell you apart.' He made a show of looking from me to my father and back again, and I was pleased, even though I knew it wasn't true; I took after my mother. My father rolled his eyes.

We settled ourselves on the sea wall. As usual for the hour, business at the jetty was slow. In the shallows, under a hard blue sky, two of the jetty boys splashed ashore with bunches of flustered chickens like sprays of flowers. Behind us, near the road, two more heaved pigs one by one into the trailer of a waiting motor rickshaw, the animals screaming as they were lifted by ears and tails and swung over the side like sacks. In the shade cut by Jonah's office, three of the boys were shooting hoops at a basket nailed to a palm tree, watching out for any signal from Jonah in between shots. The rest sat along the sea wall, perched like gulls, retreating under the visors of caps, eyeing the line of boats that rocked in the swell.

Jonah patted his belly absent-mindedly. On a clear day, I could distinguish him from the rest of his boys from as far back as the crest of the hill by the bulge of his belly, out of proportion with the rest of his wiry frame. He referred to it as his *pregnancy* and said, with slightly exaggerated joviality, that it just went to show he didn't need a woman. Jonah's wife had left him a couple of months before.

With little else to do, the boys on the sea wall started up a noisy game of poker, tossing single cigarettes into the centre as stakes. We watched them for a while. Then Jonah said, 'Well, she came back.'

'Who?' said my father, his eyes on the game.

'Margie. Long enough to get the *armoire*. Some antique her grandmother left her.'

'Is it so bad to just do what she wants?' my father said. Then, softening, unwilling perhaps to sound critical, he added lightly, 'She leave you with *any* furniture?'

'You heard about the note?' From the way my father smiled, I guessed he already had, but he sat quietly, attentively, as Jonah told it again. Jonah started off as if it were just another of his anecdotes. 'A man gets home after a hard day at work to find his wife gone. She's left him a note at least, but she's made him a ham sandwich and impaled the note in the middle of it with a toothpick. Like the sail of a boat, you know. A joke maybe about me belonging at the jetty? Only this time, unlike all her other departures, the note was real short.' And he said in a high voice, mimicking his ex-wife, '*It's just not enough anymore.* What does that mean, anyway? This time she didn't even bother to cut the sandwich in half. Now, I like my sandwiches whole anyway. Whole and square, not cut into little triangles with the crust trimmed off like the First Lady's expected round for tea.' He crooked his finger daintily. 'You think she did it so I could finally have something my own way? A last kindness for the condemned man?'

My father shrugged; Jonah didn't expect answers. He carried on, he was just warming up. 'So I get a beer and take the sandwich through to the TV. No point wasting food. My parents are watching *Kuwarta O Kahon* – they love that show, never miss it. Every week they talk about what they'd do with the money if they won. Or about Pepe Pimentel's hair. So we sit there, no one saying anything; I guess they figured she'd be back, like before. Then Pop says, "He's my age, but he's got a better head of hair." And my mom says, "He's younger than you, and anyway it's a wig, Dexter." "*Pepe?*" my pop says. "A *wig*? No way!" And they're arguing about Pepe Pimentel's hair when I notice some photos are missing from the cabinet. Can you believe it, she left behind our wedding photo but she took the one of Enrique, her dead Pomeranian. And now whenever I think of Margie, I can't help but picture Pepe Pimentel. I've even imagined the two of them together, you know, *together*,' and he said the last word carefully, with a glance in my direction. I saw my father's jaw tighten as if he were stifling a laugh. Jonah's ex-wife, Margie, was easily the most glamorous person I'd seen in Esperanza – not the sort of woman I could imagine with Jonah. I'd seen her a few times at the jetty and she seemed wrong there, like she'd arrived by accident – taken a left when she should have gone right. Her presence had felt strange, like an intrusion, and even though I didn't know her, I'd wanted her to leave. She'd seemed startled when my father brought her a chair, eyeing the seat for dirt before she sat down.

'She says the jetty's days are numbered. That we can't *stem the tide of progress*,' Jonah's voice rose to a peak, 'That only an idiot *clings to the past rather than embraces the future*.' He swept his arms out in a grand gesture. 'I mean, do I look like an idiot?' My father clicked his tongue, drew his legs up, dropped them down again. Margie's father ran a freight company and her uncle owned a fleet of jeepneys. It wasn't the first time, my father told me later, that Jonah had declined to work for either of them, preferring to make his own way. After Margie left, her family insisted they hadn't seen her.

'That's what happens when you bite your own finger,' my father said.

Jonah threw his hands up. 'Ah, who needs an armoire?'

The jetty boys erupted loudly as another poker player folded. The nearest, Subong, often to be found in my father's orbit, was a boy too simple and too open to bluff well at cards. He pulled back from the group now, groaning. My father glanced up at him, a half smile on his face. Subong walked a few paces along the wall, his arms folded above his head, berating himself. He stopped, looked up at the sky for several seconds, then he turned round and walked back to the group. The boys dealt him another hand. Subong sat down again, one leg dangling over the seaward edge of the wall, the other leg bent, cards propped against his knee. He eyed the growing pile of cigarettes hopefully. My father shook his head and then, catching Jonah's eye, started to laugh, quietly at first and then more deeply, until his whole body was shaking. His mirth infected Jonah who wiped his eyes and slapped a hand again and again on the concrete coping of the wall.

I stared at them, at my father, at the unexpected spectacle of his pleasure. I would have liked to laugh too, to share the joke, but instead I watched and, without really understanding why, I felt rebuffed.

# A HOUSE ON WHEELS

The last boats always departed earlier on a Sunday and they waited now, surging gently, loaded up and ready, for anyone who might fill the remaining seats. While the light lasted, the boatmen would hang on for as long as they had the patience, regardless of the official timetable on the notice-board outside Jonah's office. I knew my father wouldn't leave until the last one had been pushed out into the waves, and so I sat, quietly, savouring the grainy lilac light that washed the jetty, the soft flare of boat lamps.

Along the sea wall the jetty boys stirred suddenly in the middle of a hand and I turned to see Subong, on his feet now, cards and cigarettes momentarily forgotten, pointing along the coast road. In the near distance a man pushed a cart along the edge of the traffic stream, a handkerchief tied across his face like a bandit to shield him from the road dust that swirled up around him. The occupants of the cart, a woman and some kids, waved in our direction and, seeing them, Jonah started whistling and waving back. Everyone craned to see. 'Trouble on wheels,' Jonah said, but loudly, as if for the new arrivals' benefit, though they were still far out of earshot.

'I don't want to hear later that you've been playing,' my father said to me.

31

Lottie and Lando's House-on-Wheels was a mobile casino and – though my father, Jonah and most of the boys enjoyed an evening spent at its tables – in deference to a promise he said he'd made to my mother, my father vetoed all such pleasures for me. The House travelled up and down the coast, returning every few months to Esperanza, moving on as soon as people started getting careful with their money again. Its usual stay was about a week. Lando had designed and built the House, which was really a cart, himself. It incorporated fold-away gaming tables that blossomed out like a lotus so that punters could bet on all four sides, though when packed up for the road it was no bigger than the watermelon vendor's cart, compact enough that Lando could push it by himself with Lottie and all the children aboard. When the tables were out, Lottie and her eldest daughter Lorna sat back to back in the centre of the cart with the number trays and the rolling balls and a feather duster to keep the trays clean. Lando kept an eye on the younger kids, whom he'd post at street corners to tout for gamblers and look out for cops, ready to close up and push the cart away at the first sign of trouble. Packing up was a smooth operation and they had it down to less than a minute. I'd seen Lottie and Lorna haul the tables back in as Lando pushed the cart at full speed, the kids running barefoot into the alleys to rendezvous around the corner. The House was, of course, unlicensed, and if they were caught unofficial overheads could run high, especially to keep Lottie or Lando – and now Lorna, who was fourteen and almost a woman – from being arrested.

The House-on-Wheels was also their home: they slept under it and washed beside it and kept their food and cooking pots in it. On top of the bedding and the cooking pots and the half sack of rice and the folded gaming tables, Lottie kept a tray of cigarettes, which she sold individually, and a shoe-shine kit.

Of the children, Lorna was the eldest, thin and small for her age as they all were, followed by Luis, Lenora, Luke and finally Buan, because their parents had tired of the joke by then. Lorna had left school after elementary, though the younger children continued to attend sporadically.

The House-on-Wheels drew closer and I saw that since its last visit Lando had added foot-rails along both flanks of the cart and carved a design like coiling snakes along its top edge. The youngest children stood on the rails, clinging to the sides as the cart rolled along, too big now to all fit inside it.

'He could probably make anything,' I said, eyeing the snakes.

'He really has some talent, eh?' Jonah nodded.

'Talent's nothing without money,' my father said, and there was a murmur of agreement.

'Kids keep you poor,' Subong broke in. 'That's what my mother says.' Subong was only a few years older than me. He lived with his mother and some nights he didn't go home, sleeping down by the jetty on the floor of Jonah's office or, at the height of summer, in the shadow of the sea wall. He always wore a cap with a neck guard but never wore a shirt.

'Sex keeps you happy,' said someone else. 'Blame the Pope.' There was a ripple of laughter.

The House-on-Wheels pulled up and Lando helped his wife and elder daughter out of the cart as the younger kids slid down to sit on the foot-rail and inspect their surroundings, already bored. The jetty boys fell silent for a moment, for Lorna, at fourteen, though she barely looked that, was pregnant.

'Congratulations,' said my father, but it came out sounding like a question. Lorna flushed. The boys all tried not to look at her belly.

'Made your fortune this time?' Jonah said to Lando.

'What do you mean?' Lando said hotly.

'I didn't mean . . . ' Jonah glanced at Lorna.

'He's just being nice. He doesn't mean anything,' Lottie said. 'It's Jonah.'

Lando licked his lips and looked round the jetty boys. There were some new faces since the House had last been in town.

'Aw, they're all right,' Jonah said. Lando nodded. Lottie patted her husband's back and then rapped her knuckles on the wood of the cart and smiled round at the boys. 'We bought our mansion, but we prefer life on the road,' she said.

'Really?' Subong said.

Lottie threw him an incredulous look. I looked at the House kids. Their clothes were grey from the street and patched. Lorna's dress was thin, the print faded. She'd left it partly unfastened at the back to accommodate her pregnancy. Lottie, ignoring Subong now, turned to Jonah, who said, 'We didn't expect you back so soon.'

'We don't stay so long in each place now. Better to move on before we get conspicuous,' Lottie said.

'There's always someone who notices when somebody's making a little money,' Lando said. 'Last night we were down near the ferry terminal. You know, close by the twenty-four-hour café.'

'Eddie Casama's place,' Jonah said.

'Sure, him. There was talk. About this place being demolished. Some big development. You heard anything?'

Jonah puffed his lower lip out, gave a harsh sigh. I imagined his Margie: *You can't stem the tide of progress.* And almost immediately I imagined Pepe Pimentel and then, for no reason, a Pomeranian with Pepe Pimentel's hair.

'Drinking talk maybe,' Jonah said hopefully.

'Maybe. We didn't stick around to find out. Lottie didn't like the look of a couple of the customers. Drunk, you know. Looked like they'd be happy to find trouble.'

'Who'd we go to if anything happened?' Lottie said. 'The police?'

'They probably were the police,' Subong said. My father hissed under his breath.

'Got enough to worry about right now.' Lottie stared at her daughter, who pouted and looked away over the water. 'Who'd know to miss us?'

'It's a big ocean,' Subong said. Everyone shot a look at the horizon. 'Full of secrets,' he added and giggled self-consciously.

My father looked at Lorna's belly and frowned at Subong. 'It's not good to talk like that around unborn children,' he said. There was a silence while people considered, perhaps, what kind of mischief might come as a result of careless talk in the earshot of foetuses.

'So, any new ideas for that house you plan to build?' Jonah said at last to Lando.

'Some,' Lando said. 'Still saving up for the land right now.'

'Been saving for that for a *long* time,' Subong said earnestly and whistled through his teeth. My father made a grab for Subong's cap and, as he ducked away, caught it by the neck guard, whipping him with it softly before tossing it back to him.

'Cheaper out in the country,' Lando said doubtfully, but somehow I couldn't imagine him and Lottie in a field, pulling up sweet potatoes or picking beans. I could only see them in the House-on-Wheels. 'Maybe next year,' he added. He slapped the side of the House and said, 'I was thinking of renaming her "The Las Vegas". What do you boys think?'

'American,' added Lottie. 'Better for business.' My father snorted. Apart from Sam Cooke and maybe Elvis Presley, he was unconvinced about most things American.

'How about "The Full House"?' Subong said, looking at Lorna. My father reached an arm out towards him but this time Subong ducked right away and my father's hand grasped at empty air. 'It's a gambling term,' Subong protested.

Lorna threw him a look and moved to the cart to wedge herself in among her younger siblings on the foot-rail but, unable to get comfortable, rose to her feet again and stalked down to the water's edge. Her defection seemed to break things up and now Jonah set one of the jetty boys running around to look for mats and sacking so the kids could make up a bed for themselves later on his office floor. Lottie dispatched her sons to the water pump in the market with pails and a kettle and dire warnings of what she'd do to them if they dawdled. Lenora went down to where her sister kicked at the surf as it rolled in and the two girls squatted down and washed the road dust from their arms and faces.

My father, Jonah and Lando seated themselves on the sea wall. Lottie pulled a pack of Champions out of the depths of the House and tossed them to her husband. Lando fanned out a handful, offering one to each of the jetty boys in turn. Except for my father, none refused. Lottie watched, nodding as if counting the boys, the cigarettes, weighing perhaps the cost in cigarettes against the goodwill and safety they might buy; extra pairs of eyes were always useful. Lando offered me one too, his eyes curious, as if uncertain whether he'd seen me before. My father clicked his tongue and shook his head before I'd even had the chance to refuse.

Lando drew his knees up and propped his elbows upon them, stretching his arms out, hands flopping, his cigarette pointed at the water. Everyone smoked silently, and when they were done, the boys eyed the cart hopefully. But Lottie had already put the packet away and was shaking out the bedding. The boys looked at Jonah, my father and Lando on the wall and, understanding, started to disperse, to shove the last boat into the swell, to light the lamps in Jonah's office or just to sit, further along the wall, for a final game of poker before leaving for home to eat and return later. I stayed next to my father on the wall, but he never turned to include me.

The sun sat low on the horizon. Now, with the jetty quiet, the sea's voice reasserted itself throatily. I could hear again the slap of water against the wooden posts of the jetty. The last boat grew small over the water. 'Yard's opening up later,' Jonah said. Lando looked past him to the freight yard gates; one of the yards doubled as a makeshift cockpit once a fortnight, the afternoons when my father seemed more impatient than usual to return me to the boarding house. I looked in the direction of the yard. Men were already gathering, carrying their birds like babies, tenderly. I looked at my father, hopefully.

'You have any school work left to do?' he said.

'No,' I lied.

'Let the boy come,' Jonah said.

'He's big enough to stand a little blood,' Lando said.

My father shook his head. 'Carmela never liked it.'

I wanted to hang out at the jetty that evening. Lando and Lottie had a way of bringing colour with them; I knew the jetty would be a lively place tonight. I wanted to watch the cock fight, stay up late, drink even one shot of rum or *tubo* with them, place a few bets at the House tables. Especially now that my father had said my mother's name, and a few drinks might loosen his tongue further.

'Just one fight, Pop,' I said. 'I've never seen one.'

'Time to get you back,' he said tightly.

Jonah clapped a hand on my shoulder and said, 'You're getting to be a fine young man. Managing that big house by yourself for Mary Morelos.' I knew he was just saying it so I wouldn't look like a kid being dismissed.

As I turned to go, I noticed a woman standing further along the sea wall looking out to sea, at the boats dwindling in the half-light, at a group of boys relaxing in a rowboat, fishing lines tied to their toes. Every now and then the boys jiggled their lines and lit cigarettes from each other's, red points of light bobbing up and down over the darkening water. The woman stared out, her hands behind her back holding a chicken by its feet as easily as someone might hold a newspaper. I was startled but only for a second. She was the same height as my mother and as slender. My mother used to gaze into the distance, or at nothing, for what seemed like hours at a time. I remembered how, after her funeral, we'd returned by a different route from the cemetery to dissuade her ghost from following us back to the house.

Perhaps aware of being watched, the woman roused herself from her thoughts and walked away. I watched her go and when I turned back to my father he was watching her too. My eyes sought his, and when I found them he flushed angrily. He looked away and even when I said goodbye he didn't look up.

# SNAPSHOTS

Aunt Mary had two sons. The youngest, Benny, was only a few months my junior and commandeered me as a playmate soon after my arrival at the boarding house. We played together after school and at weekends, in between my duties and his piano lessons or his math and Spanish tuition. The games were his inventions and he managed to press entire worlds into fragments of time. We were time travellers, sailors, ninjas, flailing manfully at each other in the garden. Benny was always the Admiral, the Master. I suppose I minded it, but I knew my place, and besides, these were adventures I could never have created by myself.

One summer we made amphitheatres in the yard out of stones and trapped insects to battle in them. The smaller, more sluggish creatures were invariably mine, though they mostly just crawled away so there were no actual victories and it became simply which bug could break out of captivity first. When I was called in to work, he continued to play. I watched through the window as the arenas became more elaborate, with galleries, moats, drawbridges and pennants. I saw how the building became the pleasure and the insects were forgotten.

Over the years, as my duties increased and Benny's

interest in drawing and komiks developed, we played together less, but we remained comfortable in each other's company. Sometimes he sat and read in the kitchen, folded like a seabird on an old stool, his back against the stone wall, reading out loud while I washed pans or ironed clothes. Other times he sketched me as I worked, asking me to stay in a pose until my limbs ached and he was still only half done.

His brother, Dub, was four years older than us and the age gap was enough to make him mysterious. Dub had always been good-looking, but there came a point in his late teens when something inside him just switched on and after that it was hard not to look at him. He filled out, held himself differently. In a room full of people, he was often the centre. 'Like his father,' America said, eyeing the girls that had started to dawdle by the gate on the way back from convent school. 'More cream than coffee.' If Dub noticed, he didn't show it. He spent most of his time with a guitar, writing the songs that he was sure were going to make him famous.

When he was sixteen he learned to ride a motorcycle, which caused quite a ripple in the household, impressing Benny and I but dismaying his mother, even though it was a mosquito in comparison to the one he exchanged it for later at Earl's garage when he turned eighteen and came into a little money. After the bigger, better bike, and after his schoolfriends left for university, Dub's crowd changed and he started hanging out with the bikers that gathered at Earl's. They called themselves the Wolf Riders – Dub's idea, from some komik Earl had brought back from the States for Benny the year before. At nineteen, Dub started working at the garage and the plan for him to go to college just fell away. It happened in a roundabout way, after Earl came back from the States with an electric guitar.

It was the first time Earl had been to the Bougainvillea. I'd never seen him up close before. I knew him by sight, had seen his pale body bent over an engine in the dark interior of his garage, his baseball cap backwards over his greying blond head. He was bigger than I'd expected and white from several months back in his home town. He made the settee look small. 'Seattle,' he said, looking straight into my eyes, 'is our rainiest city. Period.' He made a cutting motion with the flat of his hand.

Earl's manner was open; when he talked, he looked at each of us in turn. If he made any distinctions between us, it wasn't apparent. I struggled to meet his eyes when he was talking to me, but I was sure it only made him stare at me for longer.

Aunt Mary greeted Earl politely and sat in the sala while he and Dub talked. Earl was a kind of American she wasn't so familiar with. 'An ex-USMC mechanic, ma'am,' he said, and I thought he sounded rueful. 'I went home after my discharge, but kind of drifted back and wandered round your fine archipelago for a few years before finally running aground here.' He slapped the upholstery, at which Aunt Mary looked alarmed. 'In Puerto,' he added and stretched his arm out across the back of the seat again. Aunt Mary smiled at him. There were a lot of Earls in the Philippines. They often ate and drank in the same places and could be overheard sometimes complaining about how Puerto wasn't like Pittsburgh or Reno because you couldn't get this or that.

Earl leaned forward and pushed the guitar towards Dub. 'The exact same model,' he said. It was a beauty. A second-hand Stratocaster; warm, dark wood with a high gloss. I would have loved to touch it. It was that sort of object, asking to be picked up to complete itself, but I knew it was off-limits to me. It wasn't like the piano, a piece of furniture that required polishing; it was a part of the body. I'd never seen anything like it, but when Dub picked it up it looked to me like he'd always held it. I watched him as I served out the coffee and calamansi juice, loitering afterwards in the doorway as Benny ran a careful, supervised finger along the guitar's neck.

'It was very expensive, Earl?' Aunt Mary said doubtfully.

'Sure,' whistled Earl. Then, understanding, he said to Dub, 'You can work it off at the garage.' He turned to Aunt Mary and, smiling, said, 'He's not bad with a spanner. A little training and he could make a career of it.'

Aunt Mary laughed carefully. Dub said, 'You bet,' his fingers already forming chords, picking quietly at the strings.

'Dominic is due to go to college soon,' Aunt Mary said.

'Just till I've paid Earl back for her, Mom,' Dub said without looking up. Aunt Mary folded her hands on her lap. This wasn't a negotiation she would attempt in front of an audience.

Dub didn't move from the sala for the rest of the afternoon and, in between my chores, I watched him. By the evening, he had a notepad in front of him and a pencil behind one ear, and he sang softly to himself as he scribbled things down.

He started to grow his hair long, down to his shoulders. He'd run his hands through it when he took off his motorcycle helmet, or smooth it down with the shell-handled comb that he kept at the ready in his jeans pocket. Other times, he'd lean over and shake the entire top half of his body before throwing his head back to let his hair fall into place. One day Aunt Mary, tired of reminding him to trim it at least, turned her attentions to mine instead, at which America sat me down firmly on a kitchen stool and took the scissors to it. 'Not too short,' I said as she wrapped a sheet round my shoulders.

'You want me to leave it longer *here*, maybe a nice *fringe*?' she said, and I knew she just meant to cut it as short as she could so as to leave the longest interval before she had to do it again. She pushed my head forward and I felt the cool metal of the scissors at the nape of my neck. From the sala came the sound of Dub singing. His voice was a little rough at the edges. Maybe he sang that way on purpose because the music he liked best was what was *huge* in London and the States, he said, and it was called *punk*. It was unlike anything I'd ever heard before. In our house, my father had mostly played Sam Cooke, Rey Valera, Elvis Presley.

'You like that?' America said, waving the scissors in the direction of the sala.

I hesitated. 'Sure.'

'What do you know? You never had any taste. That's why you don't know that your hair suits you short.'

We didn't have to endure Dub's *punk* for much longer. A month after he started work at the garage, he took to writing love songs.

# A VIEW OF PROSPERIDAD

Earl's garage occupied the corner of Esperanza and Prosperidad, only a couple of blocks from the jetty. Prosperidad was an old, narrow street, shabby but still respectable, where the bustle of Esperanza was abruptly curtailed by dense wooden apartment blocks just like my father's, within which lived families whose children might become kindergarten teachers, factory foremen, tour guides. After Dub started work at the garage, I found myself there often, dispatched by America with another of his forgotten lunch parcels or a message from his mother.

It was late morning, the sun high, as I made my way there yet again, America's reheated fish and rice warm in my hands. I walked quickly. I was due at the curandero's afterwards to deliver payment to him for treating America's latest ailment and I was looking forward to it: the curandero's shop was interesting; his daughter, Suelita, even more so. Besides, he'd also known my mother and, unlike my father, talked about her freely when we met.

When I arrived at the garage, Dub was on the forecourt talking to a woman. I couldn't see her face; she was wearing a headscarf and sunglasses like the middle-aged rich women at the top of Esperanza. Dub was smiling, but a little uncomfortably, so I figured she was giving him a hard time over her car repairs, reminding him that she knew his mother. My thoughts were full of Suelita, and it wasn't until the woman spoke that I realised she was young. 'You think you're Jimmy Dean?' she leaned forward, looking over her sunglasses at Dub. 'You know who Jimmy Dean is, right?' Her voice was like water on a hot day.

Dub didn't reply. He just stood there staring at her and, because I felt affronted on his behalf – even I knew who Jimmy Dean was – and because her voice made me feel like an intruder, I thrust the food parcel at him and said quickly, without thinking, 'Your mother sent lunch.' He looked at me as if he'd only just seen me and reddened.

'Mommy's little boy, huh?' the woman said. 'She cut the crusts off too?'

'Fish,' I said, feeling the need to defend Dub, 'and rice. No crusts.'

The woman smiled at me, a little uncertainly perhaps, and I felt like I'd been wrong-footed. Dub made no move to take his lunch parcel. I waited for a signal from him that would let me leave but he was looking at her. 'So when will the car be ready?' she said.

Dub recovered enough to ask, 'Will you be coming every day to remind me until it's done?'

'Will it make any difference?' she asked.

'Well now,' he said smoothly, 'it'll take a whole lot longer then, my lady.'

Earl came out looking for Dub, but when he saw the woman and the look on Dub's face he retreated, smiling to himself. After a minute, he came out again and said, 'A little help.' Maybe he'd decided Dub could flirt on his own time. Dub walked back inside, but from the way he moved, every step as soft as a cat's, I could see he was conscious of the woman's gaze.

The woman watched him go. Still holding Dub's lunch, I turned to follow him, but she started talking. Even as she talked, she stared into the gloom of the garage, to where Dub and Earl were bent over a bike. 'I moved in two weeks ago,' she said, pointing to the building opposite. 'I told Eddie I wanted the top floor. It's always cooler on a top floor, right? I get two rooms, a kitchen, my own bathroom. And a balcony. I leave the balcony doors open all day until I have to close them in the evening to keep the bugs out. I open them again later, when the bugs are gone, to let the night air in. I don't like to feel like I'm in a box. Anyway, fresh air is healthy, don't you think?' I looked up at her balcony. She had a clear view of the garage forecourt. Recently Dub had taken to working out there with his shirt off. I wondered why she was talking to me; did she think I was his brother? I stood up a little straighter in what I wore: Benny's old jeans and a t-shirt that said *Sampaguita Chemical Corp*, a present from one of Aunt Mary's friends.

'It's a good kitchen,' she continued, 'I get it all to myself, but I don't get to use it that much – only the refrigerator. Meals are sent over ready-made most times. Eddie arranges it. I know when he's coming because he sends over double, or more if he's not alone.' I wondered if Eddie was the name of her husband. I thought if I had a wife that looked like that, I'd be home every night. She said his name as if he were someone familiar to both of us, a mutual friend. 'It's mostly from the same restaurant,' she continued. 'Rosaline's. Not real expensive as you might expect with Eddie. He took me there for our first proper date. When I saw it, I thought he was testing me. He said he used to wash dishes there and sweep up when he was a kid. I guess he wanted me to see that part of him.' I knew the place she was talking about, though I'd never eaten there. It was near the jetty, one of a line of noodle joints and eateries. It had been there for as long as I could recall. I couldn't imagine a woman like her in it. 'It's a rat-hole really, but Eddie says he'll miss it when it has to close for the first phase. He imagined when he was a kid that it would always be there. But it's like he always says: change is inevitable. He says he'll have to make sacrifices like everyone else.' I didn't know what she was talking about but I didn't care to ask; looking at her, it was hard to think straight. She carried on, her voice low, conspiratorial, eager to fill any gaps. 'I'm a village girl,' she said, but I didn't believe her; she looked nothing like the village girls that came through Esperanza on market day. 'When I first came, I slept on the floor of my friend's room. There were four of us just on the floor. We had to go for a walk when her boyfriend came.'

When it became clear that Dub wasn't coming out any time soon, she said, 'He thinks he's Elvis, right?'

'He plays the guitar,' I said, 'and sings.'

'Who doesn't?'

'I don't.'

'You want to?'

I'd never really thought about it. I tried to picture myself holding a guitar and singing, and it made me laugh out loud. She seemed to like that. 'What's your name?' she said.

'Joseph.'

'Maria Luisa. But I get called BabyLu.'

I looked at her smooth brown face, her arched brows that made her eyes look as if they perennially harboured a question. 'He has long hair.' I said.

'Elvis?'

'Dub.'

'What kind of a name is Dub?'

I shrugged. 'He's a musician.'

She started laughing. She was still smiling as she crossed the street back to her apartment. I watched her go. Even after she'd disappeared into the building, her scent hung over the forecourt.

Dub came back out. 'Did she ask about me?' he said.

I held his lunch out and he took it automatically. 'She said you looked like Elvis.'

He stood looking at her apartment block for a couple of minutes until Earl came out and said, 'I gotta do all the work by myself today?'

After Dub had gone back inside, I turned to leave and, looking up, I saw BabyLu on her balcony. She waved at me and I waved back. *Lucky Eddie*, I thought.

# GIRL IN THE HATCH OF
# A *SARI-SARI* STORE

'What are you, a Champion or a Pall Mall man?' Suelita, the curandero's daughter, leaned across the counter of her mother's *sari-sari* store, her head framed by packets of Crispy Pops and chicharon. Her elbow on the counter, she held up two cigarettes, as if she was displaying a deck of cards, inviting me to choose one. She was weighing me up; was I a big spender or a cheapskate? Already, she'd hijacked our interaction far away from the one I'd rehearsed as I walked down Esperanza to the curandero's alley, confusing me almost immediately by smiling as I approached. It was an expression she wore infrequently, even less so when serving in the store. Unfortunately her mother, Missy, was also the local midwife, and so Suelita was left to man the store often and at short notice.

She was still smiling as she held up the cigarettes. Her smile was difficult to interpret, as enigmatic as most of her expressions seemed to me, but she wasn't about to give me time to analyse it; she expected an answer. Champion or Pall Mall? I looked at the cigarettes in her hand, then at the hand itself: slender, tapering fingers but broad at the palm.

A hand that might lift sacks, keep children in line, play the piano. I looked at her other hand flat on the counter and she slid it away from me as if conscious of the scrutiny. The movement made me look up at her face, which still contained the question. I didn't smoke, had never learned to, and besides, Aunt Mary hated it. For a moment I felt relieved that I didn't have to name my brand when I couldn't know what Suelita, with her singular way of appraising the world, might make of it.

'I don't smoke,' I felt slightly ashamed as I confessed. Her smile returned, deepened as she shot a closed look at the boys who lounged on the benches to the right of the hatch. Rico and his boys. I knew some of them from school. They were all smoking. 'Uncle Bee in?' I said.

'Sure,' Suelita said in English. 'He's treating a man for importance.'

She watched me closely as she spoke, a spark in her eyes that waned as quickly as it had flared. Then she said, 'He'll be out in a minute,' and I thought she looked disappointed. For the briefest moment I considered the unlikely possibility that her disappointment might have been because I'd come to see her father, not her. I stayed where I was, wondering how I might revive the conversation, but she picked up a pair of scissors and started snipping at a pile of old newspapers, turning her shoulders so gradually against me that it took me several more seconds to realise I'd been dismissed.

Suelita was seventeen and her mother had plans for her to go to nursing school. She could have been anything she wanted; I was sure of it. Watching her now, as she cut out individual words from the newspaper and spread them out over the counter, a bored expression on her features the whole while, it occurred to me that perhaps the reason why she always looked so discontent was because the best she could hope for was nursing college, when maybe what she wanted was something else entirely.

I looked around to see where I might wait. Rico and his boys stretched out a little, closing the gaps between them. I was glad; the store had a liquor license and they looked like they'd been here awhile. I moved round the corner away from the hatch and sat down on the front stoop.

The curandero's shack squatted in the alley that ran from Primo's store all the way to the basilica and the Chinese bars that skirted it. It was a single-storey wooden structure that Uncle Bee's grandfather had built with the help of his neighbours when Esperanza Street was still young; when the older, richer houses perched wide apart on the hillside with a clear view of their lands, the docks and the ocean beyond.

The shack, like countless identical buildings in the neighbourhood, or like the nipa huts that were scattered through the backcountry, had an ageless quality to it. Whenever I saw it, it seemed to me a thing that lay close to the heart of our street, not its geographical heart but its essence. The bones of buildings just like it lay under ever-newer structures like the Coffee Shak with its rain-marked concrete and plate glass, or the forecourt of Earl's garage, or my father's apartment block.

Uncle Bee had added the *sari-sari* store and a consulting room to the shack himself, though he hadn't had to rebuild anything to do it. Both were just part of the main room that he'd fenced off with nipa panels and were separated from each other by a partitioning curtain. The consulting room contained a fold-down bed and floor-to-ceiling shelves packed with herbs, bundles of dried leaves, dried fruit, oils and balms, cigarette papers, candles. From the rafters, long strips of Sunsilk shampoo, hair conditioner and laundry-detergent pouches hung down like creepers.

From the back of the shack came a chorus of voices and electronic noise. Suelita's younger brother Fidel and his boys were in. I watched Uncle Bee through the small front window, heard him talking, going over something once, twice, pausing for a response. I couldn't make out the words.

Beng Beng Bukaykay had been a curandero, a healer, since his teens. He wasn't really my uncle. Before I went to live at the Bougainvillea, I'd come to his house sometimes with my mother, and so now, whenever I passed that way, the place took on the colour of memory.

Uncle Bee told me when I was a kid how he came to be a curandero. He said that one by one he'd discovered the secret nesting sites of all the birds including, finally, the *daklap* owl that lays its eggs on the beach. And it was on account of the owl that he'd been given his powers. He told me how he'd stumbled upon her nest as the sun was setting and she'd begged him not to reveal its whereabouts as her children had yet to hatch safely. He promised never to breathe a word and, in return, the spirits gave him his powers on the understanding that if he ever went back on his word he would lose them. That, at any rate, was his story for the children. I liked his version and demanded to hear it every time I saw him, even after my mother told me that Uncle Bee's grandfather and great-grandfather had both been curanderos and that he'd learned the trade from them. She also said that Uncle Bee's father alone had broken with tradition and tried to make it big as a musician in Manila, the Big Apple. He'd come back a shadow, she said, fond of his drink, and married Bee's mother but died not long after Kokoy, Bee's younger brother, was born. That part she didn't tell me, but she discussed it with her friends, forgetting, as usual, that I was there to hear it too.

Uncle Bee did a pretty good trade; he was the only curandero in the barrio. From the bottom end of Esperanza almost everyone came to him, apart from Pastor Levi and Father Mulrooney, who both preferred the attentions of the real doctor in the health clinic on Salinas Boulevard. Pastor Levi could afford a real doctor because his brother, Cesar, was a solicitor who worked for Eddie Casama. Father Mulrooney was a foreigner and didn't trust Uncle Bee's remedies. At the top end of the street, most families, including Aunt Mary's, had their own physicians in the centre of town – guys that had trained in Europe or the States and charged by the hour. For everyone else, Uncle Bee could always be relied upon to offer a cure.

Uncle Bee accepted payment in many forms and it wasn't unusual to see rice, or eggs, or a pile of sweet potatoes left on his stoop. For a long time, I'd wished to be ill enough to be treated by him, an illness so life-threatening I imagined the white-coated doctor on Rizal Avenue at a loss to diagnose it, my only hope being the curandero with his jars of tree barks and dark, oily pastes and Latin prayers. But Aunt Mary would never have heard of it, and so it wasn't until America came out in a rash and refused to see anyone else that I had a chance to see inside Uncle Bee's consulting room again.

I was lost in these thoughts when the door opened. I stood up and moved out of the way as a woman came out. I'd expected a man, an important looking one. I glanced in the direction of the hatch where Suelita was chiding Rico as he rapped on the counter with a coin for another cigarette.

Uncle Bee followed his patient down the steps, clapped a hand on my shoulder. 'Joseph!' he said. 'I see you walking past but you never stop by.' Uncle Bee was of a breed of men whose appearance never seemed to change; he would remain the same weight and young in his face forever. He was a good advertisement for his herbs.

'Aunt Mary sent payment for America.'

'Straight to business? No time for a drink even?' He twitched his fingers, palm up, motioning me indoors after him.

When he built the house, Uncle Bee's grandfather would have slipped some money into the hole for each corner post, as was customary, to ensure prosperity. He must have stuck some bills down there rather than small change because his grandson was doing well for himself. Outside, the house was shabby from season after season of monsoon rain and inside it was cramped, but squeezed in among the furniture were a TV and hi-fi equipment and a new Frigidaire.

Fidel was playing a video game with his friends. They were perched everywhere like birds in a tree. Fidel lay across the armchair, languidly, as if he were holding court and slightly bored with it. Fidel was nice enough, an average kid, not especially bright or athletic, but the video game had made him popular. I was in the same class and had heard about the game console that Uncle Bee had bought him for his birthday, bought second-hand from one of his patients, but nevertheless one of the first in the barrio. Even Benny didn't have one, though not for lack of asking. I could still hear Aunt Mary's voice explaining why he wasn't going to get one: 'Just how is a thing like that going to help your *development*?'

'Atari Twenty-six hundred,' Fidel said to me, briefly lifting his eyes from the screen. I nodded as if this meant something significant; it was certainly a phrase that had some effect on our classmates. He shifted his legs along the armrest. I sat down lightly on it and he handed me the controls, like a king bestowing honours, enjoying his own generosity. 'Pac-Man,' he said. I was immediately inept. He took the controls from me again to demonstrate, smiling as he did so at my momentary reluctance to let go.

Behind the partition, I heard Uncle Bee moving crates around. He emerged from the store with a Pepsi in each hand, jerked an invitation with his head for me to follow him out onto the stoop. 'Big mistake buying that thing,' he said. 'House is never quiet anymore.'

'See you, man,' Fidel said as I left, but he didn't look up.

In the alley, the recent rains had turned the ground to slurry. I watched passers-by pick their way around the edges of puddles. 'You're almost a man,' said Uncle Bee, settling himself back against the doorpost. 'You ever think about where you're heading? What you want?' I'd heard Aunt Mary ask the same of Dub and Benny, but unlike them I was unprepared with an answer. All I could think of at that moment was going back inside and having another turn at Fidel's video game, joking around with the boys, feeling for a while like I had my own crowd, maybe having the highest score when Suelita's shift was up and she passed through the room on her way to help her mother in the yard. I didn't say anything. Uncle Bee watched me but he didn't press for an answer.

From inside the shack a clamour erupted. Fidel and the boys were hollering in victory. From somewhere out back Missy Bukaykay yelled, 'Oy, oy!' The boys quieted. A few seconds later a jaunty series of beeps was followed by a more subdued murmur.

Uncle Bee tipped his head in the direction of the back yard. 'Wearer of the Pants,' he said grandly, as if it were a ceremonial title.

He leaned in to me and said softly, 'You know Eddie Casama?' His eyes flitted to the corner of the shack round which Rico and his boys lounged.

'Sure. Who hasn't heard of him?'

'Mary Morelos have any dealings with him?'

'I guess she knows everyone round here, but he's never been to the house.'

'She or America hear of anything *big*, you'd tell me, right?' I looked at him and he held my gaze until I looked away again. 'Cesar Santiago's been working long into the night for months now. Walking around with a haunted look in his eye,' he said, his voice low, close to my ear. 'Wouldn't even tell his brother why.' Cesar Santiago: Pastor Levi's brother and Eddie Casama's lawyer. I sat a little looser on the stoop, arms resting on my knees, drink in hand, mimicking the way Uncle Bee sat, like a man rather than a kid, talking about bigger matters than whether it was ok to make chicken three nights running. 'Levi finally got it out of him yesterday. Application was submitted to redevelop this place.' I looked up at the eaves of the shack. 'Not just my place,' he said and thrust his chin out in a wider arc. I looked up and down the alley. Uncle Bee settled back and watched me. He looked like he had more to say but he waited. I guessed some kind of response was required of me first.

'Hard not to tell a thing like that to your brother when he's asking,' I said.

Uncle Bee shook his head; I was missing the point. 'For some, money beats blood. They filed the application in February.'

I took this in slowly; it was hard to keep a little secret in Esperanza – a place where everyone knew who was more interested in their brother's wife than their own, or who'd lied about their son's school grades, or sold their neighbour's dog – so to keep a thing like that quiet for months took some cunning. 'Just after the Pope arrived,' Uncle Bee said. 'I guess they figured it would go unnoticed with all the excitement.' I thought back to the Pope's visit. Even in Aunt Mary's house it seemed like the TV had never been switched off. 'That boy Rico,' Uncle Bee said. 'Friend of yours?' I shook my head. 'Good. The kind of boy your mother used to call *bulok*.' Bulok, rotten. She'd used that word often, for people she'd wanted me to stay away from.

Rico was my age but he'd dropped out of school a long time ago, so I saw him only occasionally, hanging out with his *barkada*, his gang: street-corner boys. They called their gang the Barracudas. The Barracuda *barkada*; I guess somebody thought it was funny. It was no secret that Rico ran errands for Eddie Casama, which was as close, I reckoned, as he was ever going to get to real wealth. The rest of the time he and his boys made it their business to keep order in the barrio. In their own way, Rico's family were as well known in the neighbourhood as Aunt Mary's; if trouble broke out, it was widely assumed they knew more about it than most.

Rico's brother, Caylo, ran some pool tables, pinball and mahjong in their yard. His cousin Rolly – after the bodybuilder Roland Dantes; I never knew his real name – ran a gym and Rico and his boys worked out there for free after closing time. In front of the store this afternoon, Rico had left his shirt wide open and anyone could see the working-out was paying off. Rico's association with Eddie Casama had given him a kind of surly confidence. 'Been strutting round like a prizefighter for weeks now,' Uncle Bee said. 'Like he knows something we don't.'

'I could ask Aunt Mary if she knows any more,' I said, dropping the pitch of my voice to match his. I wouldn't ask her, of course. I'd ask America instead and she'd probably just tell me off, like she always did, for being inquisitive.

'Naw. You keep it close to you just for now, ok?'

'Sure,' but I was disappointed, a kid again.

'Levi's going up there this week to check the facts.' He nodded uptown. 'Maybe it's nothing, eh?' But he said it too carefully.

'I hear anything, I'll let you know.'

Uncle Bee smiled. 'Ok, tough guy,' he said.

He told me to wait and called to Suelita to wrap a couple of biscuits for me. After a minute we heard her knock on the counter to let us know they were ready. I stood up and reached out to shake his hand. He smiled at me again, raising his eyebrows when Suelita rapped, more loudly, a second time. He shook my hand, placing his other hand on my shoulder. It felt affectionate, easy, the kind of thing a father would do when his son might feel too old to be embraced.

At the hatch, Suelita held the parcel out to me without so much as a glance in my direction, continuing to stare down at the newsprint clippings spread over the counter. She'd knotted her hair back, secured it with an array of pencils. She tapped the handle of her scissors against her lower lip with her other hand, pouting slightly as she concentrated. I took the parcel and her hand folded in again like a *makahiya* leaf touched by rain. I stood there a little too long after taking the biscuits, imagining unfolding the newspaper to find a message from her, decoded slowly from the words she'd cut away – nothing obvious or sentimental, but something that would make me feel like an accomplice. Of course I knew the paper would contain no such thing, but I also knew I'd check anyway and consider keeping the paper, if only because she'd thought to press the top of the parcel into a handle. Then, for no reason, I pictured her handing a secret message to Rico instead and I flushed. She chose that moment to look at me, and gave me a questioning look: *why are you still here?*

I turned to go, stuffing the biscuits self-consciously into my mouth like a child. I crumpled the wrapper and pushed it into my pocket, to keep for the boarding house trash can, Aunt Mary's voice in my head reminding me how uncouth it was to drop litter. I thought I caught Suelita's smile as I started off but when I looked back she'd turned away again and was frowning down at her newsprint words, the luckiest scissors in the world tapping her plump lower lip.

# HEN-COOPS AND FISH BASKETS

The curandero's alley split in two as it moved away from Esperanza Street. To the right, it widened and finally grew a sidewalk before leading to the basilica, the Chinese shops and restaurants and, eventually, the expensive apartment blocks higher on the hill. To the left, the alley led into the heart of Greenhills, so called by the inhabitants, though it was the colour of dirt and was flat, in mockery of the circumstances in which they lived: in Manila, Greenhills was where the rich lived; in Puerto it was a slum. If one continued walking through Greenhills in the direction of the sea, one came to Colon Market, quiet only at night, its stench declaring its presence long before and after its boundaries.

At the spot where the alley split stood the Espiritista chapel. Uncle Bee's grandmother had established the chapel in the 1920s. The congregation had grown steadily since then but the chapel, hemmed in by wooden double storeys, had stayed the same size. To accommodate everyone, the rough wooden pews had been moved outside to line the courtyard in front of the chapel and the services were now all conducted standing. Even after mass, when the worshippers lingered awhile in the courtyard, people remained standing for there was nowhere left to sit, the pews having gradually accumulated ranks of potted plants: flat-leaved palms or succulents in empty paint cans, rusty pails, gallon vegetable-oil canisters with the tops cut jaggedly away. In one corner of the courtyard, empty fish baskets and firewood were stacked. In another stood a hen-coop, its inhabitants noisy, ruffled by the presence of the congregation. After everyone had left, the chickens would be let out to scratch and shit. Or if it was late, they'd settle where they were while Nening, Uncle Bee's sister and the Espiritista priest-ess, swept the yard clean.

People came to the Espiritista chapel from a distance sometimes. In the alley, some evenings one might see a car that didn't belong – a BMW or a Mercedes – its owners in the congregation, searching for something money couldn't buy. The cars always drew an audience, children mainly, who were watched in their turn by the chauffeurs that leaned against the bonnet smoking or singing along to the hymns that drifted out into the evening. Most of the congregation, however, were from Greenhills or from the lower half of Esperanza, people whose skins were dark from working long days under the sun.

I attended the Espiritista church once with America, but only the once, for Aunt Mary made it clear afterwards how much she disapproved. It was two years after my mother died and I'd heard America talk about the Espiritista priestess contacting the dead, drawing power from them to heal the sick. I was ten years old and couldn't resist; I pleaded with her for weeks before she agreed to take me.

We went to an evening service. In the chapel yard, the air was heavy with incense and the scent of night jasmine. Standing behind America, I watched the chickens squabble

in the hen-coop and the lizards slip between the plant pots.
Inside, the chapel was like a shop, with a counter but nothing for sale. It wasn't what I'd expected at all. I'd pictured
Nening in a flowing white robe and behind her a high arched
chapel, its shadows filled with echoes. She came out to meet
us, a plump woman – brown arms bleached a European
white in patches by some skin ailment – wearing a faded
skirt printed with orange flowers, a pale-green shirt, rubber
sandals. Perhaps she'd half read my mind, for she said to
America, 'I'm the High Priestess of fashion too, no?' And on
seeing me, 'Yours?'

America said, 'Naw. This is Joseph. Dante Santos' boy.'

'O-oh,' said Nening. I didn't like the way she stretched
the word out, as if my identity was quite a revelation.

The service was to be at nine o'clock. The congregation
started arriving around half past eight but by nine they were
still drifting in through the gate, no more than forty of them
in total perhaps, and Nening didn't call for everyone to be
silent until about twenty past the hour.

I stood close by America. A girl, not much older than I,
came to the front and sang the national anthem in a thin,
high voice, first in Tagalog, then in English. The people
were silent; some looked about to see who else was present.
I looked about too, but America squeezed my hand and I
turned back to the girl. *Thy banner, dear to all our hearts, its sun
and stars all right, never shall its shining feel be dimmed by tyrant
mice.* I grinned up at America. She gave me a stern look.
From all around us came a murmur of approval, scattered
claps. The girl slid back into the crowd.

Nening stepped forward again and led the worshippers into a hymn. There were no song sheets or books. The

congregation sang 'Abide with Me' and 'Come Holy Ghost'. I didn't know all the words and joined in intermittently, worrying the whole while that my efforts might not be enough to draw my mother. After the voices had died away, Nening raised her hands for silence again. The worshippers, whispering to stragglers that had joined the group during the singing or fidgeting against the night insects, became still. A clamour arose from the chickens and a barrio dog, unseen and unheard during the singing, was spotted nosing around the hen-coop. A man – I recognised Uncle Bee – stepped forward and chased the dog away. He addressed the dog as *sir* while he ran it out the gate, which made me giggle. America clicked her tongue at me but even some of the adults had started laughing softly.

When people had subsided again and the chickens were some way to settling, Nening read from the Bible, a short passage about raising the dead, cleansing lepers, casting out demons. She started reciting a prayer. I tried to listen but it was late and her voice and the night air, sweet with flowers and sweat and putrefaction, conspired to make me sleepy. I yawned loudly, but America didn't notice. I looked up into the faces of the people around me; some were swaying as they prayed, eyes closed, trembling. After a while the voices of the congregation rose and the trembling for some became shaking. Nening called out for the Spirit Protectors to come and to keep away the evil spirits, those that might for their own reasons mean her flock some harm. She called for the Spirit Protectors to speak. The people pushed forward and one or two started to speak in Tagalog, but words that I didn't understand. I wanted to move forward myself, hear what was being said, but America, her lips still moving in prayer, gripped my shoulder and held me back. Then Nening, in a shrill and urgent voice, called out a name and someone in the congregation answered. One by one she called out more names and someone came forward and laughed or wept or cried out and I waited for the moment when she would call out my mother's name or mine. It never came.

We didn't idle in the yard after the service. America knew many of the congregation and she called to them in passing, pausing only to make me recite my thanks and a good night to Nening. The priestess winked at me cheerfully as she said, 'Your father came to mass here too. Once or twice only. After your mother died.' I was young and didn't know how to ask then if my father had found what he came for, or if he too had left disappointed.

I thought about my father at the Espiritistas all the way back to the boarding house. He'd kept his visits there a secret. After my mother died, he'd carried a vigilant look in his eye, as if he'd misplaced something that he might, without warning, come across again at any moment. It had taken a long time for that look finally to leave him and be replaced by a kind of dullness.

America pulled me home quickly. She'd not told Aunt Mary she was taking me to the Espiritistas. I'd worked hard all afternoon to complete my chores and my schoolwork and had assumed that Aunt Mary would have no objection, but I was wrong. She was even less pleased with America for taking me and I didn't attend an Espiritista service again, though Nening called out in greeting whenever she saw me.

# VILLAGE GIRL

Dub took to staying at the garage later and later, hanging around even after Earl had packed up and gone. I'd see him there as I passed by on my way back to the boarding house with whatever I'd been sent to fetch: candles or torch batteries, shrimp paste and powdered chilli – objects that demarcated the boundaries of my life. He'd wheel his bike out into the centre of the forecourt and polish it carefully, tinkering with it before revving it hard and cruising slowly onto Esperanza for the short ride home. He started strumming on his guitar during his lunch breaks, on a crate on the forecourt, his cap pulled low over his face to keep off the sun.

Whenever I saw him there, I looked up at the balcony of the second-floor apartment opposite and more often than not I caught the curve of her profile as she watered her plant pots or a flash of colour from her dress as she threw open her doors to the early evening air. To anyone else their presence at such times would have seemed nothing other than coincidence, but to me it was as if there were an invisible thread of electricity that ran between them, animating first his hands on the bike engine, then hers on the petals of her bougainvillea. They were utterly aware of each other at those times. Then, one day, I was sent to enquire of Dub whether he was ever going to sit down to dinner with his family again and, as I approached, BabyLu waved to me from her balcony and I waved back and in that instant Dub looked up and followed my gaze to her and there was no reason for him not to wave at her too. She was down on the forecourt within a few minutes.

'You're gonna polish that bike away to nothing, Elvis,' she said.

'I like things to look good, my lady,' Dub replied.

'Shallow, huh?' she said, leaving Dub chewing on air for an answer. 'Hey, Joseph,' she turned to me. 'I've seen you walking around. Are you well?' She'd remembered my name and I felt my face grow hot. 'Eddie sent lots of food today and then rang to say he wasn't coming. You two want to help me eat it? I hate to waste it. Still the village girl at heart.'

'I should get back,' I said, looking at Dub.

'Girl needs a chaperone, Joseph,' she said. 'You look like a gentleman, whereas *you* . . . ' she said to Dub. 'You look like trouble.'

Her apartment surprised me. I'd expected it to be full of new things but the furniture was old and heavy like the narra wood at Aunt Mary's. She had a dresser and an armoire and a long, dark dining table with six chairs. Every surface was crammed with things: vases with paper flow-ers, ornaments, glass decanters, stuffed toys and books. A lot of books. I'd imagined a hotel lobby, of the type I'd seen in some of Aunt Mary's magazines, but the place was more like a museum or maybe a library, and it was clean, no dust anywhere. I leaned in to study some of the titles, my hands clasped behind my back. 'They're *real*,' BabyLu pouted, but she was laughing. 'You can even touch them!' I picked one up: Thomas Hardy, an English author. Aunt Mary had a few of his books too. 'I've read quite a lot of them now,' she said. 'Eddie likes me to be in if he calls.' She shrugged. 'You can borrow it if you want.'

Dub moved around the room looking at things. He smiled at a figurine; it was not dissimilar to something his mother might possess. He moved over to an armchair and, lifting a pile of papers from its seat, flopped into it. He looked around for somewhere to place the papers but every nearby surface was full. He looked at the floor, at BabyLu and then at me, the pile in his outstretched arms. I affected not to notice, my eyes on BabyLu. She smiled at me as she turned away and walked into the kitchen. Dub placed the pile precariously on the chair's armrest. He sat back, studying the objects around him, his hands folded neatly in his lap like a boy waiting outside the headmaster's office. I eyed the pile of papers for a second or two and then stepped forward to retrieve it. I placed it on the dining table. Dub shot me an uncertain smile. BabyLu walked back into the room with a jug of water. She set it on the dining table, took glasses and plates out of one of the cabinets. 'It'll take a few minutes to heat things up,' she said. 'I'll be in the kitchen but I can hear you if you speak up.'

I felt like an impostor, invited to eat at this flat as if I wasn't Dub's houseboy, but his friend. I hesitated at the kitchen doorway, nodded at the parcels of food as she unwrapped them. 'I can do that,' I said, but she laughed at me and pushed me back into the dining room. She pointed at a chair like a schoolteacher. I sat down.

BabyLu wedged the kitchen door wide open so that we could hear each other more easily as she threw the food into pans. She talked as she worked. 'Most of the furniture was here when Eddie bought the flat. Belonged to the previous owner. A *professor*.' She peered round the doorframe at me, her eyes gleaming. 'Eddie wanted to get rid of it but I liked it. I didn't have anything much of my own anyway. Most of the books were here when I came too but some I bought myself. Eddie brings me books sometimes, but he only likes ones with a particular kind of cover.' She stopped stirring to count off on her fingers: 'Hard covers. Leathery. Gold lettering.' She picked up the spoon again. 'He doesn't care who writes them. He never looks.' I wondered about the kind of man who chose a book like he would an ornament, buying it for its binding, as if opening it to discover its real value was out of the question.

Dub was quiet but it didn't matter because BabyLu talked for all three of us, as if all the loneliness and boredom that besieged her in this apartment full of things had, while we were here, only a brief time to purge itself. 'I used to be Eddie's maid, but then his wife caught us fooling and gave him an ultimatum. He brought me here. It's ok I guess. I left the village when I was fifteen. I have nine brothers and sisters. I'm not used to silence. It's unnatural, don't you think?' She peered out from behind the doorframe again to solicit our responses.

BabyLu was talking even as she brought the food out, but while she served it she fell silent. She arranged the food carefully on each plate, her every movement reflected in the polished dark wood of the table, the bird's egg blue of her shirt becoming sky mirrored in water. Hers was the only movement or sound in the room then, for instead of picking up the weft and continuing to weave a conversation, Dub and I watched her work. BabyLu kept her eyes on the plates, but as we looked on her breathing quickened, and when she was done her colour was high.

The food was good and there was plenty of it. Dub picked at his plate and tried now not to stare at her. Still, she caught him watching her several times and glanced away quickly as if bashful, though I thought once that she looked pleased. She ate carefully, self-consciously, and when at last Dub witnessed her splash sauce down her chin, she blushed and, flashing a wounded look at him, cried out: 'Psychic surgery! Do you believe?' We stared at her, astonished. She pointed with her spoon at the pile of papers Dub had moved off the armchair earlier, that she had pushed aside to make room for the food. On the top was a flyer: *The Reverend Julio Orenia, World Famous Psychic Surgeon, Is Coming to Heal You!* I'd seen the same flyer just a few days ago. America had brought one home only for Aunt Mary to remove it, though it was soon replaced with another. They were everywhere, especially thick in the vicinity of the Espiritista chapel from where they'd no doubt originated. BabyLu wiped her chin stealthily, spoke in a rush. 'Such people are extraordinary, don't you think? He's restored eyesight and made people walk again. He's cured cancer! And all with the power of spirit. He doesn't claim it for himself.'

Dub studied the flyer, his full spoon poised near his lips. 'He calls it a prayer meeting but people will have to pay to go,' he said softly, cautiously.

'You'd pay to see any doctor,' she said hotly.

Dub started laughing. 'But he's not a doctor.' BabyLu's eyes glittered at him. He shot me a look but I stayed quiet.

'Well, I will be going! Eddie has promised to take me.'

Dub opened his mouth to say something, but thought better of it. BabyLu turned to me and said, 'Julio Orenia. His name sounds like a *proper* rock star. And he's coming *here*, to Puerto. Imagine this little place for a man of his reputation.'

Dub flushed. I looked back at BabyLu guiltily, searching for something to say. 'I've never thought of Puerto as a little place,' I said at last.

She stared at me for a moment and then unexpectedly she started to giggle. It was my turn to blush; seeing it, she laid a hand on mine and said, apologetically, 'I guess I try to think of everywhere like a place in a book. That way I don't miss it if I leave.' My hand felt hot under hers and my skin prickled with the weight and softness of her touch. Dub glanced at her hand and then away again.

BabyLu got up and started to gather the plates together. I stood up to help. 'Are you planning to leave?' I said.

'Sure, why not? Unless I find a reason to stay.' She fixed her eyes on me as she said this, but I was sure it was only so that her eyes wouldn't find Dub. I helped her carry the dishes through to the kitchen but BabyLu wouldn't let me wash them, slapping my wrist lightly as if telling off a child. She walked back into the main room, where Dub was still sitting at the table. She handed him the sponge. 'I'll talk you through it,' she said mischievously.

I stayed in the sala, browsing her collection of books, my thoughts punctuated by the splash of water, by their laughter. They took a long time to wash a few dishes. I became anxious to leave. When they emerged, they were still laughing. The front of Dub's t-shirt was sodden. I said awkwardly, 'Aunt Mary will be wondering.' The sound of his mother's name seemed to sober Dub suddenly; he'd had enough explaining to do before we even came up here, but now the street was dark and dinner at the boarding house would be over.

We waited by the door as BabyLu ran her fingers along the bookcase and pulled out the book I'd picked up when we first entered the flat. She held it out to me. 'Dub can drop it back when you're done,' she said. Then, looking at him askance, she added, 'That's ok, isn't it, Elvis?'

'Sure,' he said lightly.

She stayed in the passageway, half lit by the light from her apartment, till the elevator doors closed. 'Jesus,' said Dub as we were carried downwards, but it was all he said.

Out on Prosperidad I waited for him to retrieve his bike from inside the garage where earlier he'd locked it away, but he surprised me by starting towards the boarding house on foot. Perhaps he wanted to prolong the evening as much as possible, for he certainly walked leisurely, and of course while I walked beside him holding her book some connection to her remained. Whatever his reason, I was thrilled. Strolling along as his companion, comfortably silent together, I felt older, broader, more substantial.

As we came onto Esperanza a gold Mercedes rolled down the hill from the direction of Salinas. I watched as it slowed down and turned onto Prosperidad. In the back, his face in profile, was Eddie Casama. He stared blankly ahead, oblivious to life on the street. The Mercedes pulled up in front of BabyLu's building. *Eddie*, I thought and the thought was like ice. I looked back towards the apartment and she was there on the balcony watching us, watching Dub, walk away. I thought about all of the food we'd just eaten. Because of us, however briefly, Eddie Casama would once again, after so many years, face an empty plate. I quickened my step, quelling an urge to tug at Dub's arm, and he laughed softly at me, at my impatience.

# GIRL UNDER
# A YELLOW BELL TREE

Without warning, Aunt Mary was summoned to Manila by her mother. It wasn't unusual for Lola Lovely to make sudden demands on her daughter but Aunt Mary seemed more preoccupied than she might ordinarily have been before the trip. She was nervous of ferries anyway, refusing to travel by some passenger lines altogether or to travel at night. She left early, breakfasting soon after dawn, eating little. I heard her reminding America for at least the third time, as they settled themselves into the taxi, to make sure the boys ate.

America was to accompany Aunt Mary only as far as the jetty, where she planned to buy grouper and baby squid fresh off the boats. She preferred to run her errands early, before the sun grew strong enough to bring out her rash. With Aunt Mary gone, I knew she'd take her time returning. I'd noticed how she tired more quickly these days and had started leaving more of the work to me. The walls of the house seemed, she said, to want to close in on her, a feeling that only dissipated when she was outside. In the past month I'd come in more than once to find her in the yard, staring up at the sky. I didn't mind if she wanted to stay out; there wasn't that much to do. At dinner the evening before, our only guest had announced his plans to explore the backcountry for a few days on one of Earl's hire bikes. The boys weren't around either; Benny was at school and Dub had left early for the garage. So it wasn't far into the morning when I found myself completely alone.

I enjoyed the times when I had the house to myself; it was such a rare sensation of stillness and one that had been unknown to me before I arrived at the Bougainvillea. Even if the day was hot, if I found myself there alone I would shut the sala windows to dull the street noise and lower the blinds halfway so that the room yellowed. And then I'd sit at the piano stool and wait as every object around me, with nothing to intrude upon it, nothing to compress it back down, seemed to swell before my eyes until it occupied its space more fully.

For a long while I pretended the house was mine, that I'd just bought it, and I surveyed the downstairs rooms as if deciding which furnishings, which colours would change; how I might rearrange things. When that game became a slightly bitter pleasure, I pretended instead to be a guest, newly arrived and soon to depart. And when finally I tired even of that, I took to inspecting the contents of Aunt Mary's bookcases and then, more boldly, leafing through the family photograph albums that she kept in the sala.

There were two shelves of albums, containing generations of the Morelos and Lopez families: Uncle Bobby and Aunt Mary as a young couple, his hand at her elbow steering her to face the camera; Aunt Mary in school uniform playing jacks in the garden, the sun bright on her head; the boys as babies; and many more pictures of long-dead, un-named relations. In some of the images, landmarks of Puerto could be seen that, though old and much changed, were still recognisable: the passenger jetty, the basilica, the gates of the naval college. Over the years, I had looked through every album. I was fascinated by the pictures, returning to them again and again. There were so many. I possessed only one photograph, which was of my mother. And, like me, America also had only one, a group portrait of her family in the village, which she kept with her at all times, though she appeared in Aunt Mary's albums at least every few pages, usually with the boys as children. I hadn't thought so much about history, or heredity, till I came to the boarding house and first encountered these albums. I knew of course that everyone had to come from somewhere, that everyone had ancestors, yet the power of these photographs, the solidity they conferred, was undeniable. Aunt Mary, occupying her own place in this photographic lineage, could never have doubted she was *somebody*. It was a guilty pastime. I felt almost as if I were eavesdropping, as if I'd pressed my ear to the door of the past, but to someone else's past, not my own.

There was one picture in particular that I sought out now, which unlike the others remained unmounted, having been slipped into the back sleeve of one of the albums, as if it were not for display yet couldn't be discarded. I had found it quite by chance when I dropped the album at some slight noise, noticing as I picked it up again the protruding corner of the photograph and the slight ridge it made under the sleeve's fabric. Each photograph, like everything in Aunt Mary's house, had its place. Every album, every section, was dated. Many pictures were captioned: *Bobby and I in Singapore*;

*Mom and Aunt Elvie*; *Graduation*; *The De Souzas, London, 1972*; *Niagara!* The exclusion of this picture meant that I couldn't work out when it might have been taken, or whether it was someone Aunt Mary or Uncle Bobby had known when they were young, before even the boys came along. I imagined that I would come across the place left for it as I carried on looking, that I would restore it to its title: *Girl under a yellow bell tree*. It was an excuse, of course, to look.

The picture was of a young woman, at most a year or two older than I was now. She stood under the dappled shade of the yellow bell tree in the boarding-house yard. The picture had been taken at an angle, as if the photographer had knelt before her, so that about her face was a halo of blooms just starting to turn with, here and there, small seed pods already forming. She wasn't dressed up for the occasion of the photograph yet her attitude seemed formal, an obeisance to the camera. She held her arms stiffly, without grace or purpose, by her sides. She was pretty with an open brown face and long black hair that had been swept to one side to lie flat against her shoulder like a curtain. She wasn't smiling and looked, if not exactly unwilling, at least uncertain, unable to refuse. She didn't look like a Morelos or a Lopez; her eyes lacked the self-assurance of the other portraits. Rather, she looked like any other pretty village girl with clothes slightly too big for her, her likeness snatched without ceremony. There was only the one photograph of her and I knew exactly which volume it was hidden in. I went straight to it now. I remembered details like that easily; it was me who Aunt Mary asked to fetch things she couldn't find.

I was inspecting the girl's picture when the sound of a key in the front door cracked the soft, still ochre of the room and, startled, I made to push it under a seat cushion. America walked into the sala. She took in the albums stacked on the piano, the one open on my lap, my hand sliding out of the upholstery. 'Haven't I enough to do without you making more of a mess?' she said sulkily. She dropped the bag she had been carrying, pointed to it on the floor. I picked it up and carried it through to the kitchen. The bag smelled of fish. I unwrapped the grouper and baby squid and slipped them into bowls, covering them over with water. I left the bowls on the counter next to the sink. I was drying my hands when America burst through the kitchen door. 'Have you any business at all looking at these, Mister?' she said with unexpected ferocity. Her voice made me jump. 'Where did you find it?' She thrust a photograph at me, jerking it away again as I reached for it. The girl under the yellow bell tree. 'The boys see it?' I shook my head. 'Tell the truth now!' she shouted.

'They haven't been home all morning.' My voice sounded wheedling. America glared at me. She stalked over to the Frigidaire and placed the photograph on top of it, pushing it as far back as she could. She had to stand on her tiptoes to do it. I looked away before she turned round again. She moved over to the counter and tossed the baby squid roughly into the sink. She turned the tap on full. Water spattered her blouse. I lurched forward and turned the tap down, retreating again quickly. America grabbed a knife. One by one she stabbed each squid between the eyes and squeezed out the ink, plunging them into the water to rinse them before dropping them back into the bowl. When she was done she moved away. I slid a plate over the top of the squid to cover them.

'Who is she?' I ventured.

'I'll tell her I caught you snooping,' America said tautly without looking up. I didn't repeat my question. America carried on working in silence, clattering dishes once or twice when I glanced over at the Frigidaire. Pretty soon I stopped looking, though I remained conscious of its white bulk as I moved round the kitchen during the afternoon.

In the morning, when I checked the top of the Frigidaire, the photograph of the girl under the yellow bell tree had gone. I looked, of course, through the albums a few days later, expecting to find it back in one of the sleeves, expecting that switching albums might represent the limits of America's ingenuity. But I'd underestimated her, for there was no trace of it.

# A RIDE THROUGH THE
# BACKCOUNTRY

With his mother gone, Dub was scarcely to be seen at the Bougainvillea in the evenings. At first, America sent me out nightly to fetch him, but more often than not when I arrived at the garage it was locked, the windows dark. If Earl was still about, he'd profess ignorance even as he frowned up at the building opposite. At those times, I looked up at the balcony of BabyLu's flat and usually the doors were open, a light on, sometimes music floating out into the evening.

Dub brought back more of her books for me, his eyes eager as he dropped them onto the kitchen table in the mornings before he left for work, waiting till America was out of the room. He told me how BabyLu put them aside in a pile near the door so she wouldn't forget, as if he wanted me to think well of her even though we both knew she was Eddie Casama's mistress. I was flattered by the books, by the knowledge that she thought of me at all, though I also knew they meant he always had an excuse to return to her.

With better claims upon his time, Dub's bike grew dusty and even America remarked on the dulled chrome, the encrusted paintwork. She grew weary of worrying about him. She left it later and later before asking me to look for him, and then after a while she didn't ask at all. The last time she sent me down to the garage neither of us expected I would actually find him, but when I arrived he was on the forecourt cleaning down the bike. It looked like its old self again. He smiled when he saw me and shot a glance across the road and up to BabyLu's balcony. I followed his gaze to where she stood, watering her plants. 'She wants me to take her out on it,' he said. 'She wants to feel what it might be like to leave town, even if it's just to come back again later.'

I watched him work. He was careful with the machine, as he was with his guitar. I thought about how often Aunt Mary scolded him for shoving aside the antique figurines she'd brought back from Europe to make room for his drink, his keys, his helmet. I wondered how he was with BabyLu, whether he treated her as if she were fragile, irreplaceable.

We watched as BabyLu's balcony doors closed and her curtains were drawn. A minute later she emerged from her apartment building and slipped quietly across the street. She had on jeans and a light jacket and her headscarf. She looked like an American movie starlet. Dub laughed when he saw her and reached out to pull at the knot of her scarf. I was startled by the familiarity, as was she. She jerked her head away and reproached him with her eyes, glancing along the street. But she was smiling as she removed her scarf and pushed it into her pocket to grasp the helmet he held out to her. She fiddled with the straps for a while and then, giving up, winked at me as she lifted her chin to let Dub fasten them, his fingertips as delicate as if he were picking out splinters. 'Bye-bye, Jo-Jo,' she trilled as she climbed on behind him, her voice cloying and comical, childish. I watched them ride away, waiting till they'd disappeared from sight before I started back to the boarding house.

The following day, Dub recounted how their evening had unfolded. He had taken her along the coast road as far as Little Laguna. She'd pulled faces at him in the rear-view mirrors all the way. At Little Laguna they'd taken a rowboat out to a floating bar to sip cocktails while the sun set over the water. When they returned to shore, they'd continued down the coast before cutting through the backwaters to ride through the villages back to Puerto. They'd stopped a few times for a cold drink at a roadside shack or for her to take a picture or disappear into the bushes to relieve herself. Afterwards they'd sat together for a while on the wall of a bridge to watch *carabao* carts laden with sugar cane or bamboo roll by and, in the distance, people walking across rice fields towards narrow plumes of smoke that rose from behind the treeline. I wondered if he'd glimpsed BabyLu the village girl then, however fleetingly, but of course it was too tender a question to voice. Dub's first account of their evening stopped there and I thought he was simply being discreet. What he didn't say then was that when they returned, as the bike cruised into Prosperidad, they saw Eddie's Mercedes waiting in front of her building.

# STREET VENDORS

The sun, long depleted of its vigour, at last drew its uppermost edge down behind the buildings on the opposite side of Esperanza Street, its final glow outlining them thinly against the descending dusk. From the gate, I watched the street turn to velvet and everything become rich, convivial. In a line stretching from the brow of the hill down to the jetty, the lamps came on in clusters, their yellow light seeping through the smoke that layered upwards from the braziers. Into this haze, the night flowers had already started to release their scent. Behind me, the house lay quiet. It was time to close the gate for the evening but I lingered there thinking, as I often did, about how the falling light smoothing over the boundaries of the street endowed the scene almost with the illusion of freedom. I didn't want to go back inside just yet, and of course today there was no one to mind if the gate closed a few minutes late: Aunt Mary was still in Manila with her mother and America had already retired. Still, I hesitated, if only for a moment, before slipping out onto the sidewalk.

Johnny Five Course sat by his stall reading a book. Even from a distance I recognised the cover: *Bartlett's Familiar Quotations*. Aunt Mary kept a copy in the sala for the amusement of the boarding-house guests. Books of quotations and anecdotes were the only things Johnny liked to read.

Johnny's food cart was easily the most colourful stall on the street, and consequently was a magnet for foreigners. Johnny's sign said in English: *Five Corse Meals. Two Set Menues, Complimentry Tea and Coffee. Eat-In. Take-Out.* Today, as nearly every day, menu 'A' was *pinakbet, lumpia*, pork and egg noodles, coconut curd and tea or coffee. Menu 'B' was *pinakbet, lumpia*, pork and egg fried rice, coconut curd and tea or coffee. There were no chairs and *Eat-In* meant sitting on the low wall behind the frangipani tree, the food laid out on a banana leaf in front of you. For *Take-Out*, Johnny served the *pinakbet* in a polystyrene cup and the rest wrapped up in waxed paper packets enclosed in another banana leaf. From the roof of the cart, a hurricane lamp cast its gauzy light over a row of open pickle jars and bottles of soy and fish sauce. A ring of flies circled lazily over the jars. Others clung to strips of fly-paper strung like forgotten Christmas decorations along the cart's awning. All the while a small table fan taped to one of the posts arced uselessly from left to right and back again.

Johnny glanced up as I emerged onto the street. He looked pleased to see me and my heart fell; it meant he had news. He beckoned me over with his book. He looked different and he waited, smiling, while I appraised him. His hair had been teased into a quiff like the prow of a boat. I didn't say anything. He closed the *Bartlett's* and stood up, laying the book down on his stool. He smoothed his quiff with the palms of both hands like he was diving into a pool. 'Hey Joe, how are you doing?' he said. I wondered what response might result in the shortest conversation.

Johnny was full of schemes to make it out of Esperanza Street, out of Puerto, out of the Philippines. He was going places: 'The Mississippi River, man,' he'd say. He loved that name, stretched it out a long way. 'The Meesseesseepee Reever.' His dreaming made me feel empty. The week before he'd said to me, 'Maybe I'll do an MBA stateside.' I didn't know what an MBA was but I didn't admit to it. Most of Johnny's outside information came from Jaynie, his sister, who ran the Beauty Queen hair salon near the market hall. Jaynie and her colleague, Lady Jessica, whose real name was Jesiah, were the eyes and ears of Esperanza and their clientele included the ladies from higher up the hill who could afford to send their children to college in Europe or the States and still had money to fritter on manicures and hair perms.

Johnny lived with Jaynie and his father in a two-room apartment in Greenhills just behind the Espiritista chapel. They had their own tiny kitchen but shared an outside bathroom with four other families. Johnny got up every day before dawn to go to market and he'd rolled out his stall and was cooking over the butane gas stove before Jaynie was even up. He ate all his meals at the stall and when he got home he washed and slept and got up before dawn to do it all over again.

'So now *you're* Elvis?' I said, pointing at last to his hair.

'You think it suits me?'

I didn't, but I said, 'Sure.'

Johnny looked pleased for a second. Then he said, 'It's crazy about the Pope, eh?'

'What about the Pope?'

He stared at me. 'You work too hard,' he said. He thrust his chin in the direction of Primo's store, where a group of men and women had gathered at the doorway. Through the windows I could just make out the fitful, bluish light of Primo's countertop TV. As if afraid I might be lured away by it, Johnny said quickly, 'So how are the boys? Benny, Dub?' Listing them as if I might be uncertain which boys he was referring to.

'Fine.'

'Eat my dust!' Johnny had taken to this phrase, having seen it on the back of one of Dub's t-shirts. Dub was fast becoming legendary around Esperanza. 'Get the same shirt for America. She moves quick for an old lady.'

'She's a devil in an old lady's body.'

'Jessica describes herself as a woman in a man's body,' he said, which stalled the conversation as both of us tried to imagine it. I looked away again in the direction of Primo's store. 'Still going strong,' Johnny said cheerfully, waving at Abnor who sat as always at his tea-stall in front of the store. For some time now Johnny had had his eye on Abnor's pitch, which was a short distance from the Espiritistas and the Redemptorist church. Perhaps he imagined himself ready to nourish the congregations as they emerged from communing with the dead, or meditating on moderation and self-restraint, the money burning in their pockets. Abnor waved back. I raised my arm to wave too and Abnor patted the stool next to him in invitation. Johnny wasn't quite ready to let me go. 'Salon might have to close,' he said.

'Jaynie's place?' I was surprised. Like his and Abnor's stalls, it was part of the fabric of the street.

'That bastard Eddie don't want to renew the lease.'

'Isn't his wife in there every week?'

Johnny pushed his jaw forward, lowered his eyelids and, holding his arms out as if he were a politician delivering a speech, said in an exaggerated mimicry, 'Change is inevitable.' I didn't know if he was pretending to be Eddie. I stared at him blankly. 'Forget it,' he muttered.

I looked back at the Bougainvillea. 'Aunt Mary likes the gate closed by now,' I said.

Johnny picked up his ladle and pushed the *pinakbet* roughly round the pan. 'There are no tyrants where there are no slaves, man,' he said. 'Rizal.' I was pretty sure Rizal hadn't said *man* but I didn't correct him. Johnny picked up his book again and for a moment I thought he might be about to assail me with another quote, but he shrugged and sat down.

I turned to leave. Across the street, Abnor hooked a stool out with his foot and started wiping down a cup with a rag. He set the cup down firmly. I started over to him. He'd poured out a tea for me before I'd even reached his corner. Winking, he stirred in an extra spoonful of sugar and handed me the cup. I wasn't used to sweet tea anymore – Aunt Mary preferred it made without – but I took the cup without hesitation. Abnor never let me pay so I tried not to drink his tea too often, which was a shame because I enjoyed sitting here.

Abnor had roots in the same village as America and they flirted affably whenever they met. For no other reason than that, I trusted him. Abnor's tea-stall had got all of his younger siblings through school, two through college, and then married. They were long since grown and gone but still Abnor stayed put, sleeping under the wooden wings of his stall in all weathers until Primo put down a folding bed for him in his store room. Now every evening after closing up shop, the two of them sat side by side on Abnor's wooden stools, sharing tea and cigarettes and watching the street like a television.

Today, Primo's doorway was still open, the windows unshuttered. A group of men and women stood at the threshold, more sat on the floor inside the store. I heard the brusque, urgent music of a news programme. Primo leaned back against the glass of his shopfront, blowing on his tea.

'What's going on?' I said.

Abnor raised an eyebrow. 'The Pope's been shot. He's in hospital. It's been all over the news.' He crossed himself. Behind him, Primo fiddled with the cross around his neck.

I cast a glance across the street at Johnny, said apologetically, 'Aunt Mary's not so keen on TV. It's sometimes on for the guests in the evening, but we've been quiet.' I stood up and craned to see the screen. The Filipino anchorman, a fair-skinned mestizo, sounded almost American. He looked nothing like any of the people who had gathered to watch. The footage was a few months old: on a tour of the country earlier in the year, Pope John Paul II reminded the sea of people who had come to see him not to use contraception.

'It's a bad thing,' Abnor said, 'the way the world is.' He shrugged.

I sat down again, sipped my tea. I looked more closely at the people clustered in the doorway, grief painted on their faces, a grief that seemed scenic somehow, distant, because I didn't feel it. The Pope being shot, like most things, seemed like a matter for everyone else but me. Abnor watched me. I wasn't sure what to say. 'They think he'll be all right, though?'

'It's up to Him,' Abnor said. He pointed up at the sky and despite myself I looked up. 'At least he's in His good books.'

'You hear about the salon?' I said.

Abnor's voice dropped and he frowned as he intoned like a movie hero, 'A man can't ride your back unless it's *bent*.' He jabbed the air with a finger like he was conducting an orchestra, emphasising alternate syllables.

'*Man*,' said Primo quietly.

Abnor leaned in to me. 'Martin Luther King!' The two men laughed softly. I glanced guiltily across the street at Johnny. His head was back in his book of quotations. The sight of it made me smile suddenly, but only because the incline of the pages was in the same plane as his quiff. It would have made a good photograph. Abnor patted me on the shoulder.

From out back, a cockerel started up a ragged call. 'I'm going to *eat* that bird some day soon,' Abnor said. Primo kept a fighting cock in the yard behind the store. It had lived with him in his apartment until the neighbours complained about its noise. He crooned a soft pocking noise deep in his throat. The cockerel quieted. 'That bird's like having a wife,' Abnor muttered. 'Always wanting to talk.'

He took the cup from my hand, filled it again. He reached for the sugar. From inside the store, the news channel jingle came on again. The people at the doorway started to disperse and, as they passed, one of them bumped Abnor's shoulder. 'Oy,' he muttered crossly as a shower of sugar crystals scattered over the rim of the cup, bouncing off the counter of his stall like raindrops. I watched him gather them together with the side of his hand, sweep them into his palm. And I remembered then, quite unexpectedly, the only time I'd ever seen Aunt Mary angry. Over dinner at the boarding house one evening, during the Pope's visit back in February, she'd raged about the First Lady's decision to build a wall in

Manila along the route of the Papal motorcade to hide the slums. In her agitation, she'd knocked the rice spoon out of my hand as I served her. I went to fetch a dustpan and came back to find her picking the tiny grains of rice one by one from the pile of the rug with her fingertips, her other palm cupped to receive them.

'God loves the poor,' I murmured, testing the words. It was something Mulrooney often said in church. But coming out of my mouth, it sounded phoney. Abnor glanced at me curiously. He put the refilled cup in my hand. I looked down at it. I pictured the Greenhills children, sweeping the market for discarded fruit as the traders packed their stalls away, plucking snails from crevices. I lifted the cup to my mouth but didn't take a sip, instead studying the two men over its rim. Abnor's eyes were milkier than I remembered. Primo dressed like someone much younger than his years but, close up, the gap between him and Abnor diminished. It wasn't just the effect of age, I thought. They both wore a kind of contentment which, now that I considered it, might just as easily have been resignation. The thought was so abruptly dispiriting that, though the tea was still hot, I drained my cup, burning my throat.

As I stood up to leave, Abnor said, as I knew he would because he'd said it innumerable times before, 'Say *Hi* to my girlfriend.'

# *HALO-HALO* SPECIAL

When Aunt Mary returned to the Bougainvillea, she brought her mother with her. I hadn't seen Lola Lovely for three years. Twice a year, she summoned her daughter, and sometimes the boys, to Manila, rather than manage the journey to Puerto. It wasn't a long trip, but Lola Lovely liked things to be a certain way and so tended to avoid travelling. She was in her late sixties, but she barely looked her age and she flirted in a desultory fashion with the taxi driver as he hauled her luggage out of the trunk. She looked over the façade of the Bougainvillea, pursed her lips at the boarding-house sign. Behind her, Aunt Mary's demeanour was cool and I wondered if Lola Lovely had kept at her for most of the way with her demands: 'Adjust this cushion, fetch a drink, call the steward.'

Lola Lovely lived by herself in Manila. The house was hers, left to her when Judge Lopez died; most of the rest of his estate went to Aunt Mary, who was courting but not married then. The Manila house was modern and much larger than the Bougainvillea – too large really for Lola Lovely, even with her maid and the houseboy, the only staff she was unwilling to do without. It had been designed by an architect who was an old family friend, a fraternity brother of the judge. I'd never seen it but had heard about its big spaces, the skylights that cut blocks of light over marble floors, the waterfall that no longer cascaded in the lobby. Lola Lovely chose to stay there after Mary and Uncle Bobby were married. She loved *the arts*, couldn't bear to be *too far from the pulse*, she'd once said. The proper upkeep of her beloved home would have been covered by her allowance from the Lopez lands if Uncle Bobby hadn't developed a passion, if not a talent, for poker. Still, Lola Lovely clung to the house, managing as best she could with the remainder of her inheritance. But each time Aunt Mary returned from seeing her, I'd hear her listing to America the latest signs of decay.

I opened the door and took the bags into the house. Lola Lovely smiled anxiously at me. When Benny came down the stairs, she looked relieved and said 'Ah!' She had draped a shawl over one arm and made no move to give it to me. When eventually she put it aside, I saw that her arm was in plaster up to the elbow. 'My wrist,' she explained irritably to America. She was not the kind to accept without resistance the encroaching signs of frailty.

America had prepared lunch and I'd laid it out in the dining room by the time Lola Lovely had settled herself in. 'Sheets of music everywhere in one room, sketching paper everywhere in another. You boys inherited your untidiness from your father,' Lola Lovely said to Benny as she sat down at the table.

'I'm sure they'd have tidied up if they thought they were due an inspection,' Aunt Mary said.

'It's only me. Their old Lola.'

She waited for a moment and it was America who said, 'You look just as young as the last time, ma'am.'

Lola Lovely looked pleased. 'I should take you back to Manila with me,' she said. America laughed off the invitation uneasily.

Lola Lovely ate carefully with her free arm, concentrating on her plate. She picked at her main course, but when I brought the *halo-halo* out she smiled and sat forward in her chair. After a while, she said, 'So why is that boy working in a garage? Shouldn't he be off to college?'

'He's not made any set plans yet.'

'You give them too much freedom,' she waved her sundae spoon at her daughter. 'I'd have threatened to cut him off.'

'He wants to be a musician,' Benny said. 'He doesn't need college for that.'

Lola Lovely started laughing. 'He should study law like his grandfather. Make some proper money.' Lola Lovely looked at her daughter and said, 'It's fine to encourage these things when they're *young.*'

'Not everyone wants money,' Benny persisted.

'Of course everyone wants money! Even Marcos started off with ideals. But power corrupts!' Lola Lovely said this with a sudden glee; I'd forgotten how she enjoyed holding court, enjoyed proclamations. 'It's that wife of his. She's twisted him. Women shouldn't meddle with their husband's politics.' Aunt Mary's spoon hesitated on its way to her mouth. Lola Lovely continued, 'You know, your father always had an eye on the Senate. He'd have made it too, but then of course that scandal – '

'Aunt Cora said all politicians have mistresses and no one blinks,' Benny said. His mother stared at him, startled.

Lola Lovely looked stung. 'It may be gossip for her, but it was my life,' she said.

'It was her life too,' Aunt Mary interjected softly, a look on her face as if she recognised a danger. Lola Lovely looked at me warily and I turned to leave. She needn't have worried; the whole barrio knew the story. Cora Sanesteban who, along with her husband, Ignacio, ran the Coffee Shak and the Baigal Bakery two blocks down the hill from the Bougainvillea, was Aunt Mary's step-sister. Cora's mother, the mistress of Judge Lopez and a mere filing clerk at his office, had died when her daughter was six, after which Cora and her older brother – for the judge had fathered two children with this woman – came to live in the Lopez household. The judge would not, could not, have turned them away, but Lola Lovely had plenty to say about it and after a while the two kids were made to sleep in the garage, when even the servants slept in the main house. They stayed there for several years. Then the judge died and they inherited just enough to be asked to leave and make their own way in the world. Aunt Mary was a child herself, ten years old, when Cora and her brother came to live with them, and maybe if she'd been older, things might have been different.

Now at least there was a kind of peace. Aunt Mary owned the freehold on both the Coffee Shak and the Baigal Bakery, the only freeholds that Bobby Morelos hadn't gambled away, but – against the family lawyer's advice – she refused to charge the Sanestebans any rent.

As I turned to go, Aunt Mary gestured to me to wait. Perhaps she hoped my presence might deter her mother, but Lola Lovely said, accusingly, 'I kept you safe, didn't I? When the Japanese were everywhere?'

'Mom, please.' Aunt Mary set down her spoon.

'He comes back from the war, different. Acted as if I couldn't *possibly* understand. As if we hadn't been through hell as civilians too. Did that woman understand him any better than I? A filing clerk! And she could barely spell. And then, just when I think we've got our lives back, he presents me with her offspring. I had to think of the effect on you,' Aunt Mary sighed. 'They were just children then. They didn't know about any of that.'

'Everyone feels they can judge me. That's why I stayed away.'

'Mom, no one's judging you. Shall we just eat?'

But Lola Lovely was not to be placated now and she said, looking at Benny, 'Fine! You've already proved you're a better person than I am. Are you happy?' Aunt Mary gave her mother a warning look.

'Why were you looking at me?' Benny said. 'Is this about Aunt Cora?'

'*Aunt* Cora!'

'Well, what else am I supposed to call her?'

'I suppose it's accurate enough.'

'She's doing ok now. She's not a bitter person.'

'Even *you* have an opinion about it! Why, you're just a child.' Benny made as if to respond but closed his mouth again, looked at his mother. 'And your mother with her feminism and her activism,' Lola Lovely continued. 'Seeing my terrible example and determined not to make the same mistake with *you*!'

'Mother!'

Lola Lovely threw down her spoon. 'We can't even be together one day without a fight.'

'Mom?' Benny looked lost.

But she said, 'Benito, would you finish your dessert in the kitchen?'

'I haven't done anything wrong!'

'Well, she's hardly going to dismiss *me*, is she?' Lola Lovely said shrilly.

I stepped forward to take Benny's glass but he shrugged away my help. I looked at Aunt Mary. Her face was dark, lips pressed tight. I followed Benny to the kitchen but he didn't stay there. He left his half-eaten dessert on the kitchen table and went to his room, closing the door behind him.

America helped me clear the dining room and then took me out into the yard to eat. 'She's not at all like her mother, is she?' I said.

'Mrs Lovely wasn't born into money,' America said casually. I was intrigued but feigned disinterest and America, seeing through it, tossed me a few grains anyway. Lola Lovely, the daughter of a hospital porter, a girl without the benefit of a university education, had somehow managed to land a man like Jimmy Lopez and had climbed into his unfamiliar world. 'Until he gave her a ring,' America said, 'she wouldn't even let him see where she lived. She made him stop at the corner of the block so that he had to follow her in secret.'

America and I took our time eating and by the time we returned Lola Lovely had retired to the sala, where she sat at the piano fanning herself. I asked if she required a drink and she shooed me away. 'Just see if my daughter's finished yet,' she said without looking at me. The door to Benny's room was shut, and from behind it I heard the rhythm of Aunt Mary's precise, melodic sentences. I slipped quickly past the sala to avoid Lola Lovely on my way back to the kitchen.

America regarded me severely. 'You better not have been listening at the door,' she said. 'You make as much noise as a whole herd of *carabao*.'

'Is it about Benny? Is he Cora's boy?'

She started laughing. 'You'd better not start pecking at my head. You think people have nothing better to do than to explain every last thing to you?'

'You enjoy knowing things I don't.'

It was a mistake. I'd forgotten that America, too, was pricklier during Lola Lovely's rare visits. Her face soured and she said, 'Let that boy learn his own story without you crowding in on it.' And with that she barely spoke to me for the rest of the afternoon, except to tell me what to do.

# BOBBLE-HEADED JESUS

Eddie Casama sat in the sala at the Bougainvillea, in the centre of the settee, his arms stretched out in both directions along the back of it, shirt sleeves rolled up. Close up, he was younger and softer-looking than I'd imagined. He looked like the kind of man who'd let his kids ride on his back at weekends.

He'd brought another man with him: Cesar Santiago, Pastor Levi's brother. Cesar was a lawyer and, though he ran a public practice, everyone knew he worked almost exclusively for Eddie, leaving any other cases to his junior partner. Cesar at least was familiar; the Santiagos weren't rich, but their family had been in Esperanza for three generations so everyone knew them.

Cesar sat in an armchair under the window. The blinds were high and the light on his face was revealing. He smiled wanly at America when she came in to ask what the gentlemen might like to drink. America nodded back at him but, unnerved by the presence of Eddie Casama, she returned briskly to the kitchen, pulling me with her. She sent me back out quickly enough with calamansi juice, soda water and peanuts. 'Take your time,' she said.

In the sala, Aunt Mary was leaning forward in her

armchair. 'My son Benito is at the same school,' she said as I came in.

'Antonio says he's tall,' said Eddie. 'A basketball player.'

'Just one of his obsessions. And how is your wife? I believe I met her at a school concert.'

'Oh, Constanza. Eating my head about what this person or that person said to her. She thought the world of you, though.'

I looked around the room to find somewhere to put the tray, but Eddie's cigarettes and lighter were on the side table.

'On the piano will do, Joseph,' Aunt Mary said.

I balanced the tray with one hand and with the other moved the photographs of Uncle Bobby off the cutwork cloth, laid them gently aside. I set down the tray and poured out mixers of juice and soda, taking care not to let any spill onto the rich, glossy wood of the piano. I glanced at Aunt Mary but she looked pointedly at Eddie. I knew how things worked and, though I wondered about giving Cesar a drink first because he'd smiled at America, I brought the tray to Eddie, who took a glass without looking up.

'Calamansi and soda,' he said, 'freshly prepared. Nothing better.' He took a sip. 'This is probably the best I've tasted.'

'Absolutely the best,' Cesar said.

They were exaggerating of course but Aunt Mary accepted the compliment, though she was too European in her ways for imprecision and said, 'Joseph made it this morning.' Eddie looked surprised, as if he hadn't noticed me up till then.

'Excellent,' he said, appraising me without interest, looking away again quickly.

Eddie Casama had been elected barrio captain several years ago, holding office for three years before standing down. In those days, he'd been a small-time businessman running a bakery near the basilica but, even then, he was heading for a laundromat, a chain of dry goods stores, a nightclub, a cockpit, an apartment for his mistress and a 24-hour café at the passenger-ferry terminal. Things had gone well for him, and when he stood down it was to concentrate on *business*.

When anyone talked about Eddie Casama, it was with a tone that implied he was meant for big things, bigger than whatever the rest of us had in store and, what's more, that it was inevitable he would get there. It was another constant in the neighbourhood, like Abnor's tea-stall or the mischief of the jetty boys. There was a rumour that he'd been born clutching an amulet that would guarantee him success in everything he did. Back then I believed it, too, believed that our fates were already decided, that some were simply meant to succeed and others to fail. It was a way of thinking that was deeply ingrained. My mother's voice had always dropped at the mention of such things, as if even the words held power. My father, claiming greater rationality, had extolled only the power of physical work and a Catholic God, though after my mother died, he turned his back, for a while, on the latter. I wish I could have talked about these matters with Aunt Mary, for I'm sure that she would have been, with her overseas education, level-headed about it. I didn't see then how these beliefs provided an excuse for inaction, though of course the amulet rumour might also have been about not having to give a man like Edgar Casama his due.

Eddie was quiet for a moment and then, afraid perhaps that he hadn't finished with all the niceties before he got down to business, he asked after Dub and even Lola Lovely, whom he'd been told was visiting. Satisfied with the answers, he put down his glass and said, thoughtfully, 'Progress is impossible without change, don't you think?'

Aunt Mary said, 'That will be all, Joseph.'

'Anything else to eat, ma'am?' I said. Aunt Mary looked at each man in turn. Eddie Casama raised his hands to decline.

'America will need some help,' she said firmly to me. And to Eddie, 'It's one of our foreign guest's birthdays. He's asked for a Filipino feast.'

'Have you warned him he'll be eating for a week?' said Cesar. Aunt Mary smiled.

In the kitchen, America was standing in the slanted light from the window, like a woman from a painting in one of Aunt Mary's books. She'd been deseeding a pumpkin and thin orange threads quivered from her fingertips. 'So how are things in the corridors of power?' she said. I repeated what Eddie had said about progress and change. 'That crook,' she said. She cupped her hands and moved over to the sink. She rinsed her hands briskly. 'He's up to something all right. Whatever it is, his kind always land on their feet.' She uncovered a filleted milkfish that I'd left on a dish beside the sink, ran her finger lightly along its flesh, feeling for bones. I'd deboned it earlier with an old pair of tweezers and I knew she wouldn't find any. She nodded and covered it over again.

I waited for Aunt Mary to call me back into the sala but she didn't. It wasn't until Lola Lovely came in through the front door with Benny in tow, tired from a trip downtown, that I had the excuse to go back out. Benny stayed by the door as he was introduced but slipped away quickly, loping through to the kitchen to see what he might take to eat in his room. Lola Lovely stood just inside the threshold of the room and eyed the men expectantly. They rose to greet her. She appraised Cesar, her eyes narrowing, and said, 'You look familiar. Are you a doctor?' She cupped a hand under the elbow of her plaster cast.

'A lawyer, ma'am. Cesar Santiago. It's nothing serious, I hope?'

Lola Lovely waved the cast impatiently, said 'Oh, it's nothing. The Santiago brothers. The lawyer. Ah, yes.' She looked impressed.

'Mrs Lopez,' Eddie said, holding his hand out. 'I've never had the pleasure. Edgar Casama.'

Lola Lovely smiled at him. 'Mr Casama. Are you from round here?'

'Greenhills born and bred.'

'A Manila man!'

'No, ma'am,' Eddie laughed. 'Greenhills, Esperanza.'

Lola Lovely looked alarmed, 'How can that be?'

'I was born behind Colon Market.'

'But there are no proper houses there.'

'There are houses, most certainly. Not as elegant as this one.'

Lola Lovely looked perplexed as she took in Eddie, the Rolex on his wrist, his expensively cut jacket, which he had declined to let me hang up and had now discarded carelessly over the armrest of the settee. She studied him, trying to place him correctly in her world. 'You're a friend of my daughter's?' she said, and I saw Aunt Mary shift forward in her chair, ready to intervene. 'She was always interested in the other side,' Lola Lovely continued. 'A social reformer at heart.' Aunt Mary cleared her throat.

'Then of course Mary will know that the key to social change is opportunity!' Eddie beamed.

'Why, yes,' Lola Lovely looked doubtful. She never seemed entirely at home with other people's politics.

'Take me for example,' Eddie's tone was almost flirtatious. His eyes shone at her. 'Why, I didn't attend school beyond tenth grade.' I thought how he gave just enough away to seem vulnerable, certain now that Lola Lovely was no threat to him. Lola Lovely allowed herself to be charmed.

'We knew such difficulties during the war too,' she said. 'I had to live in a village with my husband's foreman and his family. Our house here was stripped by the Japanese. I took what valuables I could carry and we left in the night on an ox cart. Can you imagine it? Mary was just a little girl.'

Eddie laughed. 'You must have dazzled the entire village,' he said.

Lola Lovely threw her hands up, delighted. 'I had to learn how to milk a cow. I had to put my hands down there!'

'Madam, there is such *dignity* in working with ones hands,' Eddie exclaimed. Of course, he spoke like a politician; who could be sure what he really thought? Still, I liked the sound of it.

'Will you stay for some food?' Aunt Mary said, though she knew they would hardly have done so at such short notice, and so by asking she gave them their cue to leave. Lola Lovely looked disappointed as Eddie declined.

The men lingered in the hallway for maybe another fifteen minutes saying their goodbyes, edging towards the door with each exchange – last minute queries, mostly from

Lola Lovely, about school grades and health, which couldn't be answered briefly – until eventually Cesar, who had stood gripping the door handle for several minutes already, turned and stepped out into the late-morning sun, moving aside almost immediately to allow Eddie to precede him.

Lola Lovely followed the men out onto the verandah and looked on as they climbed into the back of Eddie's Mercedes. She waved as the car pulled out of the driveway, a tiny plastic Jesus nodding his endorsement through the back window. 'How unexpected,' she said loudly as she stepped back inside. 'A Greenhills man and quite refined.'

# TWO PRIESTS

Aunt Mary remained preoccupied for days after Eddie Casama's visit and though America claimed to have interrogated her about it, we remained unsure as to why. Then, late one afternoon, I opened the boarding-house door to find Esperanza's two priests side by side on our doorstep. Esperanza being such a populous barrio, it was unusual for the two men to make house calls together and so I was alarmed at the sight of them. The women of the household were at home, but the boys were out and, immediately, I imagined the worst. Father Mulrooney spoke hurriedly: 'No calamitous acts of God, Joseph. We just wanted to talk to Mrs Morelos. Is she in?'

Father Mulrooney was in his forties but still had a boyish handsomeness about him that made the older women of Esperanza flirt kindly with him and enquire as to whether he was eating properly. He had an air of naivety too, the kind inevitable in men who had entered the seminary at seventeen and known no other life. His hair was coarse and tousled and sandy-coloured and his skin was of the kind of paleness that was ill suited to our sun and had a perennial tinge of redness to it. He had a slightly crumpled look – the sort of man who might in another life have been well advised to marry. Mulrooney was popular in the neighbourhood and well known, for twice a day without fail he walked out from his meagre *convento*, once before breakfast while the sun was still low and again before supper when the heat was abating. I liked to imagine that these times were chosen deliberately so that the sight of his flock and their uncertain circumstances might curb his appetite, for he remained of slender build.

Pastor Levi, by comparison, enjoyed his wife's cooking. He was an earnest man, his face prone to smiling and deeply crevassed. He was younger than Mulrooney, in his late thirties. He had travelled a roundabout route through the Lutherans, the Anglicans and an agnostic period during which he had acquired a wife. He returned to Roman Catholicism, kept his wife, though he never completed any official Vatican paperwork on the matter, and carried on to father five children; Mulrooney was the youngest's godfather. Although Father Mulrooney was officially Levi's senior, the name of Pastor stuck to Levi: it had a good ring to it.

The two men settled themselves in the sala while I went to fetch Aunt Mary. Both had been to the house before but they, like many of our visitors, seemed not entirely at ease; the place was too impeccably tidy and the presence of the grand piano gave the room a kind of old-fashioned formality. Also, though Bobby Morelos had been dead for years, his presence persisted in the room; his graduation certificates were on the wall, photographs of him on the piano. I'd often admired the portrait of him in naval uniform as I dusted the piano, once I was trusted to do so, my fingers itching to press the keys but afraid of making a sound. In a certain tricky late-afternoon light that gave the present the texture of the past, it almost felt as if he might walk into the room at any moment.

Aunt Mary was upstairs at her desk. She wasn't expecting visitors and she moved quickly on hearing that both priests were here to see her. I followed her down the stairs, heading to the kitchen to fetch water and iced tea, which I knew was Father Mulrooney's favourite drink. I brought the drinks to the sala but before I could serve them Aunt Mary sent me back out again to fetch America.

'It's a terrible thing about the Pope,' said Aunt Mary, as I came back in, as if she might have been talking about the men's favourite uncle.

'Yes. Thank you,' Father Mulrooney nodded. No doubt he'd had plenty of practice by now with his responses. But he didn't dwell; there was other business at hand. 'I'm not at liberty to reveal my *sources* . . . ' he enunciated carefully and, so saying, he blushed. Aunt Mary smiled at him encouragingly. Later in the conversation, on an unrelated matter, he wouldn't be able to refrain from saying the same name aloud more than once: Jaynie. Johnny Five Course's sister who ran the Beauty Queen salon. Eddie Casama's wife was one of her regulars, though it was widely known that Eddie himself was no stranger to manicures. 'Several days ago,' Mulrooney continued, 'I learned from my *sources* that Eddie Casama has submitted a planning application.'

'As part of a consortium,' Pastor Levi said. I looked at America who, like myself, uncomfortable with the idea of taking a seat next to the others, was leaning in the doorway. She looked bewildered; the language of our world had no need for terms like *consortium*.

'He wants to build a shopping mall in Esperanza,' Mulrooney continued. 'My sources are facing eviction because their business is situated in the area earmarked for redevelopment.' He flushed again. I pictured the Beauty Queen, squeezed in among the pharmacy, the noodle joints, the market hall and any number of places that were the body of Esperanza.

'Father Mulrooney came straight to me when he heard,' Pastor Levi said.

'To speak to Cesar,' Mulrooney said to Aunt Mary.

'Cesar was cagey. But I got it out of him eventually.'

'They submitted the application months ago,' Mulrooney said, 'but it was buried. Displayed publicly all right, but in English and on some village official's door.'

'He came to discuss it with me a few days ago,' said Aunt Mary. 'Bobby and I had friends in government. Engineer Reyes and Joey Robello were part of Bobby's poker crowd. And the Robellos are related to me by marriage. I suppose those men might not normally have been in Mr Casama's circle.' She glanced at Mulrooney and added carefully, 'Of course, a man like Mr Casama hardly needs *my* support.'

'Yes, yes, Joey Robello, Engineer Reyes,' said Mulrooney darkly. I shot a complicit smile at America, but she stared back coolly. She knew I'd never met either of those men even if, like everyone else, I'd heard their names. Joey Robello, a judge like his father and grandfather before him, had his eye on a seat in the Senate and Engineer Reyes had been elected to the District Council three times, though it was unclear who exactly had voted him in. There was a story about Engineer Reyes known to everyone in Esperanza. Fresh out of university and ambitious with his father's money, he had tried to dig a basement under his father's house, planning to turn it into a games room – I remember Abnor repeating the words over and over with obvious amusement: a room just for *games*. The basement was barely excavated when it flooded and though it was drained and the work restarted, it kept on flooding. Finally, the foreman explained to him that there was an underground spring, which eventually led to the sea, running beneath the street; the same water that was tapped further along its course by the pump in the market hall. Reyes, known then simply as Frankie Reyes, was furious. Why hadn't the man thought to tell him before? The foreman explained that he'd assumed Reyes had known all along, he was, after all, an engineer. Work ceased and, after some wrangling, the men were finally paid, though less than they'd originally been promised: a mistake on Reyes' part for the whole of Esperanza quickly heard the story. From then on he was always addressed as *Engineer* Reyes, though he never practised as one.

'They're all in league with each other,' said Mulrooney. 'Busy lining each other's pockets.' I thought I heard in his voice a note of defeat, or perhaps if not defeat, then doubt, as if the odds against Esperanza were approaching some critical threshold. But Esperanza Street was used to change, I thought. Like anywhere, it had been formed in layers, each one built upon the last by the generations of people that had lived and died here, though until now the process of its changing had been like the gradual shaping of a shoreline over centuries. 'Of course he's arguing that it will bring money into the local economy,' Mulrooney said, 'implying that everyone stands to benefit.'

'Did he mention the full extent of it?' asked Pastor Levi, and he watched me closely as he listed street after street in Greenhills, including, finally, my father's. For a moment I thought it sounded too ridiculous and I couldn't believe that anyone would allow it. Then Levi added, 'Cesar said they plan to build a multi-storey car park over the north half of the cemetery.'

America grabbed my hand, squeezed it hard and I gaped back at her. If our dead, my mother among them, were not to be allowed their rest, I thought, then there was little hope for the living.

# THE BEST COFFEE
# ON THE ISLAND

The Coffee Shak was my favourite place on Esperanza; it felt like somewhere things could happen. It was also Esperanza Street's *famous* place, being listed in foreign guidebooks. I passed by it most days, but once a week, if the Bougainvillea had foreign guests, I got to go inside to pick up ground coffee. In its present form the Shak was relatively new to the street, but it had been around in other incarnations for years, starting life as an unnamed, brightly painted vendor's cart – a wooden contraption on wheels with room for a small motor underneath to run the grinder and a big steel urn bolted onto the counter. When Aunt Mary's stepsister Cora first met Ignacio Sanesteban he was running a shop selling machine parts on Esperanza Street, but he didn't have much of a head for it and was, as she often recounted, *bleeding* money. She took charge and turned his shop into the Shak, the only place for miles around where tourists and expats, tired of being served cups of lukewarm water with sachets of instant coffee, could relax with the real stuff. It was immediately popular.

Cora took to grinding the day's beans fresh in front of the first customer every morning. It was this ritual that earned her a place in the guidebooks, framed pages of which decorated the pillar nearest the door, alongside a large, framed photograph of the old cart.

Inside, the air was thick with the smell of coffee and vanilla and it was as heavy to breathe as that on the street, barely stirred by the ceiling fans that churned overhead. A sign on the door said 'air conditioned' but the cooler was always just being fixed. Cora usually kept the door wedged open instead which made no difference except that the scent of freshly brewed coffee hung in the air outside.

Ignacio Sanesteban was straightening the tables and putting out the fresh flowers that his wife insisted upon. He looked up as I walked in. Ignacio was a big man with a sleepy voice and heavy-lidded eyes that gave him an air of languor or conceit, though he possessed neither. He rose at four every morning to bake the pastries that drew regulars from as far afield as Cabugon or Pasay, including Eddie Casama, who sent his driver down at least once a week.

I looked round the Shak to see what was new. Every wall and pillar was busy with paintings, mostly Cora's own. Some were really good, as good as you might see in any gallery. A few were framed, most were stretched between bamboo canes, the canvases ragged at the edges. There was one of Abnor sitting at his tea-stall in a bleached early-morning light, the kind you'd get on a day when it might become too hot to move later. Foreigners were always trying to buy it and Cora invariably refused.

From the back of the Shak, the sound of the Eagles started up from an old Wurlitzer that stood by the kitchen door casting its colours in a fan over the wall.

Ignacio slipped back behind the counter. He smiled at

me, pushing a dish towards me across the glass. It was full of coins, tips from customers. I sifted through it, picked out a few. Ignacio started to tip beans into the grinder. I walked through to the back, towards the Wurlitzer.

In the furthest booth, next to the jukebox, sat Cora. She wasn't alone. Benny was with her, his back to me. I hadn't seen him for days. He'd stayed in his room, emerging only to eat and sometimes not even that, so that America or Aunt Mary would send me up with a tray, which he'd make me leave at the door. I hadn't been worried; he often immersed himself in his drawing, filling page after page at his desk, reappearing suddenly to raid the Frigidaire or pilfer food straight out of America's pans before gathering up garlic bulbs and bunched banana leaves for a *still life*. It seemed quite natural now that I should see him here, surrounded by so many paintings, even a few of his own. He didn't look pleased to see me. 'Joseph,' he said, with a slight formality.

On the table in front of him his sketchbook lay open, loose pages spilling out, each containing a series of frames like a komik book. The images were bold, arresting. I leaned forward to take a look but he angled the pages away from me. I moved over to the Wurlitzer. Cora said, 'Tell him I'm wise to him. He never did like the Eagles.'

I shifted the coins in my palm. 'You think I could get away with Sam Cooke today?' I said.

'Not a chance. You know him. It's got to be a girl.'

I scanned down the list, selected *Dusty in Memphis*. Cora moved aside on her bench and patted the red leatherette next to her. I sat down. The upholstery, already sticky with the heat, was warm and pliant from her body. Ignacio arrived with three Cokes and a plate of cookies. He slid them onto

the table, tapped the rim of the cookie plate with his finger-
nail. 'That's for Dusty,' he said. He returned to the counter
and carried on polishing glasses and cutlery, all the time
smiling his approval at the neat lines of pastries layered
with fruit and cream and curls of chocolate that sat chilling
under the glass. Ignacio said little as a rule. Cora, in contrast,
seemed to talk at a thousand words a minute. I thought, as
I had many times before, how unlike Aunt Mary she was:
prettier, livelier, with a deep, grating laugh. It was hard to
imagine they were related. I looked down at the sketches.
Benny started to slide them back in between the leaves of
his book but Cora placed her hand on them.

'They're good,' I said. Benny scowled at me.

'Revolutionaries!' Cora said gleefully. She held up a sheet
to look closely at it and as she did so, from underneath it,
the gloss of a photograph caught my eye. The girl under the
yellow bell tree. I was surprised; it wasn't like America or
Aunt Mary to leave anything lying around. Benny reached
out to tuck the photograph away again, but Cora had already
spotted it. She took it from him, squinted at it; a pretence,
her eyesight was sharp enough when a customer glanced
at a pastry or edged towards the door without paying. 'Girlfriend?' she said.

'No!' Benny said.

'Who then?'

'She used to work for Mom.' Benny's tone was light
enough but I looked hard at him then; his voice carried
something new. He avoided my eye.

'Pretty. Bet your father was always sniffing around her,'
Cora said. Then, a second later, 'Sorry.'

Benny shrugged.

'You know, I think I remember her. Doring or Dora or Doreen or something. She didn't last long.'

'What was she like?'

'Oh, well, I have no idea. Never really spoke to the girl. Never really spoke to any of them. The pretty ones were always gone in no time.' Benny stared fixedly at the sketches on the table.

'Did you know Pop?'

'Not as well as he'd have liked!' And then again, 'Sorry.' Cora sighed. 'You know how it is, baby. A snake only knows how to be a snake. In case you're worried, you're nothing like him. More like your mom.'

Benny's eyes jerked up at her and then, unexpectedly, he exclaimed, 'I wish you'd been my mom.'

Cora gave a high, crisp laugh. She sat back and studied him and after a minute reached out and stroked his cheek with her thumb. 'Just look at you! She did a great job. Really she did.'

'I just meant . . . ' but he didn't continue.

'I hear your Lola's in town,' Cora said. From behind the counter, the sound of the grinder stopped.

'Yeah,' Benny said reluctantly.

'Give the old lady my regards.' The sound of the grinder started up again. Ignacio started humming along to Dusty, his eyebrows arched, a faint smile on his face.

'She broke her wrist,' Benny said.

'Shucks,' said Cora. Benny's eyes flashed at her and she added remorsefully, 'Ok, ok.' She leaned across the table, planted both palms flat on it as if she were about to push herself up, but she stayed sitting. 'I know just what'll cheer you up. You want to help me paint something really *big*?'

'Sure, why not,' Benny said.

'Come at the weekend. Your mom won't mind.'

Ignacio brought a bag over to the table. The smell of freshly ground coffee puffed out of it as he set it down. 'With compliments,' he said.

I reached out and tugged gently at Benny's sleeve to uncover his watch. He looked annoyed for an instant but then he held his arm up for me to take a look, tilting it so that the clockface was the right way up. I slid towards the edge of the booth and as I did so Cora started after me, bouncing herself softly along the upholstery. Seeing her move, Benny got slowly to his feet. He looked at me ruefully.

We walked back to the Bougainvillea together. The rhythm of walking seemed to soften his mood and he started to talk about the komik he was working on, *The Black Riders*. His voice had deepened recently and he'd grown so much taller than me and I noticed now too how, like his brother, he'd started to carry himself differently as his body filled out. I felt a flush of pleasure as he talked; he'd hadn't discussed his ideas with me for a long time. He talked about the komik all the way home and it was only after he'd gone up to his room and closed the door behind him that it occurred to me that he'd left no openings in which I might have asked about the girl in the photograph.

# BAREFOOT MIDWIFE

Down at the jetty, the House-on-Wheels was preparing to move on but Lorna was nowhere to be found. 'Hard to misplace someone that big,' said Lottie irritably. They'd already stayed a couple of days longer than planned because Lorna had complained she was exhausted from moving all the time. 'Two days,' Lottie said to Jonah, holding up two fingers, her voice fast, shrill. 'Two days, getting more conspicuous by the minute, the police sniffing round, helping themselves to cigarettes, letting the kids shine their shoes for free.'

'Baby hormones,' said Subong cheerfully and he looked at my father for a response. But my father was barely listening. He stared out at the boats and the boys shifting cargo further down the beach, trying perhaps to imagine how the place would change: the jetty standing empty, the smaller cargo boats and outriggers landing further up the coast near the passenger ferry, being unloaded by a new Jonah, a new Subong, a new Dante Santos.

'Stupid cow,' said Lottie. 'She'll get us all in trouble. We should just go. Let her walk round the whole country looking for us.' But she stayed where she was, the sack and the pots and the bedding still unpacked and draped variously over the House-on-Wheels behind her.

Lando put his hand on the warm wood of the House. 'She's a good girl,' he said. 'She'll be back.' He edged his thumbnail slowly along the grain, towards his wife. Lottie watched his hand like she might have eyed a cockroach before swatting it.

'If she's not back by the evening we'll all go looking for her,' Jonah said. 'What about you, eh?' he said to me.

'Sure,' I said reluctantly. Even if Aunt Mary didn't need me, I wasn't sure I wanted to spend my evening scouring Esperanza for the girl, pregnant or not. 'I've got schoolwork,' I said, but it wasn't much of an excuse and I added guiltily, 'I guess it can wait.' It could wait, too. I'd lost interest in school lately and my grades were beginning to slide. I couldn't seem to help it. I found myself daydreaming whatever the subject; nothing held my interest. At school, everything felt dead and flat. Yet, in the evenings when my time was my own, I read everything I could find – Aunt Mary's art books, books about American or European history, novels by long-dead English authors in which the language curled round itself before blooming out and presenting an idea like a bud. I was consumed for days by unexpected images: an artist walking along a coast in pursuit of the ship that had sailed with his life's work on board, succumbing to a fever before he made the next port; the architecture of an ancient people of another continent whose blood, brought here by the Spanish, flowed in our veins too. Every day brought a new thing to light and, though I couldn't have put it into words back then, I think now that I read with the hope something would finally arrive that would illuminate everything, a single piece of knowledge that would show me how my life was meant to unfold. Back then, my life didn't feel like my own; anyone else – my father, Aunt Mary, God – might have a better plan for how I might live it than I. And so I coasted at school, though I was sure my grades wouldn't escape Aunt Mary's attention for long and I'd be reminded soon enough of the importance of accurate punctuation.

I turned to leave for the boarding house but my father gripped my arm tightly. 'Some time with my boy,' he said.

Jonah looked surprised; my father was never one to ask for slack if there was still work to be done. 'Sure, Dante.' He clapped my father on the back, gently, waved us on. I'd noticed recently how he'd started giving the younger boys the heavier loads.

My father pulled me for several paces along the sea wall before letting go of my arm and then he kept walking. I followed. Fed well by America, I'd grown quickly this year and my father seemed suddenly smaller to me, more tired, his strength diminishing as mine grew. When we were out of earshot he said, without catching my eye, 'I know where she is.' I stared at him but still he looked away.

'Where?'

'Walk with me, boy.' We cut through the market and into the curandero's alley to the *sari-sari* store. Rico and his boys weren't around which meant, no doubt, that Suelita wasn't on duty. I felt both disappointed and relieved.

Fidel was at the hatch chewing gum. He was reading a komik and started when my father rapped on the counter with his knuckles. My father opened his mouth to speak but already Fidel was ducking beneath the partitioning curtain. We heard him call out to his mother. Missy was on the stoop in an instant, a half-gutted fish in one hand, a knife in the other. When she saw my father, she raised the fish in acknowledgement. She stepped back inside and we listened as she snapped orders at her son to deposit the fish in the Frigidaire, to sluice water over her hands as she scrubbed them at the pail in the yard, to bring the rubbing alcohol from her midwife's bag, to put it back.

Missy Bukaykay might have been slight but her frailty was a deception. She had a certain kind of doggedness about her, slow-grown like a callus on skin. Inevitable perhaps for the eldest of nine, born of peasant farmers who made their way to Puerto when they lost their land: a teenager when she came for the first time to the city. Missy had never undertaken any official training to become a midwife. Still, it was said she'd never lost a baby, even in the worst of conditions, so no one paid much mind to the details of her state midwifery licence, which was displayed on the wall of the shack and was several years out of date.

She was back on the stoop within minutes, her midwife's bag in hand. She sniffed at her fingers. 'Better not arrive today. Be a shame for that to be the first thing to smell on coming into this world.' She held out her fingers for my father to sniff but he waved them away, smiling.

'Baby will either love fish for life or hate it,' he said.

'Better be love because we're no distance at all from the sea.'

She walked ahead of us through the alley towards the basilica, turning off into the street of my father's apartment. She didn't hesitate as she entered his building and climbed the stairs to the room where my mother had lived and died.

Inside, the room was dark, the curtains drawn. A small fan hummed on the dining table. As we walked in, my father called out 'Lorna – ' but the rest of his words died on his lips. In the corner of the room Lorna squatted, legs apart, dress pulled up around her breasts, naked from the waist down, one arm gripping the table, her eyes like cornered prey. She was moaning. Around her feet, the floor was wet and between her legs I could see something, a dome with soft black hairs and beside it what looked like a tiny hand.

My father and I froze. Missy snapped into action, barking at us for towels, cloths, clean water. We obeyed, fumbling through each task. She lay Lorna down on the floor and I watched, nauseous now, as she pinched and pushed the baby's fingers until the hand withdrew inside Lorna's body. Missy's hand seemed to follow it and I looked away. The smell filled me, something raw and pungent, like ammonia. The room was full of noise: Lorna's moans and Missy's commands to breathe, push, fetch this thing or that, the sound of my own heartbeat shaking my body. The child emerged slowly at first and then in a rush, and when it was out and in its mother's arms my father sank into a chair and put his head in his hands.

Missy beckoned me over and together we moved mother and baby to the bed away from the blood and the mess and the smell. I gathered the dirty towels and sheets into a ball and went to fetch a pail and some phenol with which to scrub the floor.

As I passed my father's chair, I saw that he was trembling and, my senses still overwhelmed, numbed by everything that had just occurred, I registered as I would register the heat, the rain, the presence of a fly, that he was crying.

# MOTHER AND CHILD

My father spoke quickly, anxious to explain. He'd gone that morning to the cemetery to visit my mother, as he had every morning since hearing about Eddie Casama's *consortium*. He fell silent now thinking about it, and Lorna, without lifting her eyes from the baby, started up in his stead. She'd seen him there, she said, and followed him without his knowledge. She'd watched from behind the larger crypts as he wept quietly, privately, without display. She looked up at me. 'I went to the priest first, after I left the jetty. The one with the yellow hair. He told me they could help me find a home for my baby but I don't want to give her away.' She lowered her head gradually as she spoke so that these last words were murmured into the baby's scalp.

The apartment was clean now and smelled of disinfectant. Missy had left, but she'd promised to return later after Lorna had had time to rest. But Lorna, eager that I should first understand that my father was not at fault, pushed herself upright in the bed so that she would not succumb to sleep, and continued. 'For two nights I lay down between the crypts, in the shadows where the sun hardly touches the grass and where there's moss so the ground is soft. It was cold. I didn't sleep at all. Every sound woke me: the men drinking nearby, the dogs sniffing around. I was afraid of the living, not the dead. I don't know why I followed your father this morning. What else was there for me to do? When he went to the church to pray and he cried again, I decided right then that I wasn't going to spend another night in the cemetery.' When he got up to go to work, she'd approached him, seizing the fabric of his shirt as she asked for his help. She offered to cook and clean for him, to wash his clothes. She even offered herself – at which my father shook his arm free in fury and she had to run after him into the churchyard and almost halfway down the street, begging him to listen, before he stopped again. He agreed, finally, to take her home, though he wouldn't promise that she could stay. He left her there, after making sure she ate something, to go to work. He was late at the jetty for the first time since my mother had died, and he looked so tired, so preoccupied, that Jonah didn't persist with his questions.

Before leaving her, my father had told Lorna that when he returned he'd bring her parents with him, but she'd begged him not to and eventually they'd compromised on Missy, the midwife, for the baby's sake. My father was relieved at that, the weight of such a secret sitting rather heavily with him. Missy was more forceful with the girl than my father would have dared to be and Lorna, worn out from the labour, agreed quickly that her parents ought to know of her whereabouts. Besides, by then my father had acceded that, if Lottie and Lando agreed, she could stay. 'Perhaps it's a good thing to bring life into this place again,' he said. He went through my mother's things, the few that remained, and took out a dress that, till now, he'd been unable to part with. He gave it to Lorna while Missy was still around to help her get into it, so that she would look clean and rested when her parents came, her own dress being stained beyond remedy.

I wanted to leave, to return to the comfort of the boarding house's routine, but my father wouldn't let me go. He didn't want to be alone with her, was afraid of how it might seem. So I stayed, but it was a long while before Missy returned.

Lorna slept for much of that time; the baby slept too, bound in cloth against its mother's chest. Intermittently she woke to its cries and lifted its head to her breast to try and feed it. From watching her mother raise four more after her without the privacy of walls and doors, Lorna, at fourteen, seemed already to know what to do. In contrast, I saw on my father's face a look of utter helplessness.

My father and I took it in turns to watch over them through the open door, averting our eyes when the baby fed. He didn't want Lorna there, I was sure of it. He wanted no complications in his life, but I also knew that he wouldn't ask her to leave.

When Missy returned, she brought with her not just Lottie and Lando but also Jonah. The House children were left to play in the yard, listening out for when their mother might call them up.

The sun was low now behind the apartment blocks and the sky overhead was streaked like the throat of an orchid. Lottie sat on the bed, stroking the baby's foot as Lorna repeated her story. Lorna told my father's part entirely now for he stayed silent. When she had finished, Lottie let go of her granddaughter's foot and, growing agitated, turned to my father and said, '*They* came. The Police. They took our House apart, found the number trays. They'd heard *rumours*, they said.' And she mimicked their speech as she repeated it, '"Rumours of an unlicensed gambling operation." That's what they called it. They talked to me slowly, as if I was an idiot. They said that not paying a license "deprived the correct authorities of money". *Deprived the correct authorities of money!'* She turned to Lorna. 'They almost arrested your father, handcuffed him, gave him a few blows to his legs and head and back to show what they were capable of, what they might have to do if we didn't cooperate. You think they teach them at police school how to speak like that?' she said bitterly. 'Like TV cops.' Lottie had parted with three days worth of takings. '"A *reasonable* fine," the officer said.' She pulled a face. 'They took the big tin. Sure, they didn't find the small one. That was buried in the rice sack and they didn't waste time going through that. Still, it didn't have all that much in it.' It was over in minutes, their money gone, the gaming tables broken and Lando covered in cuts and bruises, the blood around his mouth already drying. 'A few minutes is all it took.' Lottie jabbed a finger at her daughter. 'And *you* disappeared without a word for two days.'

But Lorna was drunk now with the sight and smell of her baby. When she spoke her voice was soft, placatory. 'I'm sorry,' she said. 'I didn't want her to be born on the street.'

'Street was good enough for me,' said Lottie.

'You knew but you didn't say anything,' said Lando to my father. 'Were you planning to tell us some time?'

'I asked him not to,' said Lorna. 'It's not his fault.'

'Is it your baby?' said Lando suddenly to my father, his voice rising.

My father stepped forward, his fists clenched. 'You think that I – '

'It's all right, Dante,' Jonah broke in, and to Lando: 'He's all right.'

'Why can't you just ask *me* if it's his baby?' said Lorna sullenly. 'Anyway, it's not.'

'We can't stay in Esperanza now,' said Lottie. 'You'll have to pack up today. Where's your dress? Whose dress is that?'

'It was Carmela's,' my father said quietly.

'Jesus,' said Lando.

'Mine got covered in blood,' said Lorna. 'He's never touched me.'

'My father's a good man,' I said loudly. I'd said nothing till now and the sound of my voice breaking into the room surprised even me. Lottie and Lando's eyes flickered in my direction but my father didn't even turn to look at me. 'He's a good man,' I said again more quietly.

'I want to stay,' Lorna said stubbornly. She looked at my father but his face gave nothing away. It was his apartment but I could see he didn't believe it was his decision to make.

'I don't know,' said Lottie.

'Will it be safe?' asked Lando, but he said it to Jonah and I was angry with him at that. I stepped forward, but now my father stirred and put his hand on my arm.

'She'll be safe,' said Jonah. 'Dante's all right.'

Missy, who up till now hadn't offered an opinion, said gruffly, 'You could look for years and still not find a better man than Dante Santos.' After that little else was said on the matter. Lottie called the children up to see their sister and her new baby and then they left the apartment to make up their bedding for the night in the safety of the yard, in readiness to leave early the following morning. They weren't going far. 'Maybe only the next town, to repair the House and do some quiet business before we come back, to check,' Lottie said, glancing at my father.

The sun had long set when I reached the boarding house. Aunt Mary came downstairs on hearing the door. She was still in her day clothes, though ordinarily she'd have bathed and changed for bed by now. She looked tired and she was frowning as she met my eye. I wondered if she'd waited up for me. I wished I'd been able to go to her rather than have her come to me, if only to demonstrate that I hadn't forgotten my obligations to her. I started to apologise but she shook her head. 'Missy Bukaykay sent Fidel with a message,' she said. 'Have you eaten anything since morning?'

I hadn't expected the question. 'No, ma'am,' I said slowly, struggling to remember. She sent me straight to the kitchen where America, in her nightclothes, had already started warming food for me. And it was now, at Aunt Mary's generosity, at the sight of the food America laid out wordlessly on the table, that I finally yielded. I cried as I ate, and America, wise enough to know when to ask and when not, left me to do so in peace.

# PORTRAITS

News of the birth spread quickly through Esperanza and most mornings my father opened his door to find dry food, an old dress, a vest for the baby with a note from one neighbour or another. Johnny Five Course, whom I'd never thought of as a sentimental man, brought dinner for my father and Lorna every night for two weeks. Jonah brought a rattle for the child and a bottle of rum for my father, which he helped make a start on one night after work.

Missy visited most days to check on the baby and brought guava or castor-bean leaves from Uncle Bee to make decoctions for Lorna to wash her wound with or poultices for her breast to encourage her milk. She berated Lorna each time for not resting, for Lorna – afraid perhaps that her luck might end and though she was tired and sore – kept the apartment cleaner than it had been in a long time.

At the boarding house, Aunt Mary and America unpacked the boxes they'd stored away when the boys were small and found blankets and sheets and a small crib that Aunt Mary and I took to my father in a taxi. We reassembled it in his apartment, pushing the dining table up against the wall to make room. My father was now sleeping in the kitchen while Lorna and her baby, whom she was yet to name, had the main room to themselves.

America set to making batches of food full of iron or calcium or protein, whatever she'd decided a new mother needed most that particular day. Fried sardines, chickpea curry, soybeans or rice cakes heavy with anise to help Lorna make milk. If Aunt Mary knew of the few extra groceries that were diverted in this way, she never complained. I wondered at the time why they would want to do all of this for Lorna, or even for my father. Now I understand that at least a little of it was for me.

I helped America silently at first but found my voice again soon enough; America's cooking had a rhythm to it that felt right and it pulled me out of myself. When she decided I didn't need to be handled gently any more, she stopped her cooking and supervised me making a fig and black molasses cake, partly for Lorna but enough for the rest of us too, snapping her instructions like a colonel, her voice losing the softness of the preceding few days. 'Mix that like you mean business,' she said as I turned the flour and eggs together. 'It's not made of diamonds.'

'Diamonds are the hardest thing in the world. Nothing like mixing a sponge,' I said, testing her.

'Don't get clever with me. Your reading better get you further than this kitchen if you're going to feel free to talk to me like that.' She picked up the tin of molasses and put it down again roughly. Not so roughly that I'd figure she was really cross, just roughly enough that I'd think twice about contradicting her again. I smiled to myself.

'Haven't seen much of Benny lately,' I said.

I'd said it just to make conversation, but now America

glared at me. 'Stop fishing,' she said curtly. I looked at her, surprised, noticing as I did so how weary she looked this morning, her rash bright across her cheeks. My attention had been inward these last few days and I felt ashamed of it all of a sudden. For now that I thought about it, America had seemed really distracted this last week too, and it occurred to me that perhaps she'd cooked such a lot as a kind of solace. I recalled that I'd come into the kitchen the day after the birth to see her and Benny sitting together at the table as if they'd been *talking*. They'd fallen quiet as soon as I walked in. America had got up sharply and sent me off to fetch shrimp paste, though I was sure there was an open jar in the Frigidaire. When I got back, Benny had gone. America left the jar I brought on the kitchen table for a couple of hours before putting it back on the pantry shelf.

She watched me now, warily. I turned the cake mixture more firmly, as if doing so might appease her. 'You think the sun moves around you?' she said.

'The sun, the moon, the stars,' I said lightly and pushed the mixture round so fast that some spattered onto the table.

'Watch it! That cake's got to fill eight people.' I stirred more carefully. 'Why don't you just ask him?' she said suddenly.

I stopped stirring. 'You think I could?'

'He'll tell you if he wants to. It's his own business. Jesus, Joseph, you're such a baby. You don't need my permission to talk to him.'

I stared at her. 'You get mad at me if I do anything without checking with you first.' I expected her to respond to this with a crack about how men needed to be told how to wipe their own noses.

Instead, she said softly, 'You'll do just fine.' She didn't give me a chance to ask her what I'd do just fine with, but opened the molasses tin, thrust it at me and said, haughtily, 'You may pour.'

When the sponge was ready, she cut a big slice for me to take up to Benny.

He didn't answer straight away when I knocked, though I knew he was in because I could hear music. Then he said, 'Door's open, Joe.' I wondered stupidly how he knew it was me, even though I knew the difference too between his footsteps and anyone else's.

He was sitting cross-legged on his bed, his sketchbook across his knees, a packet of Marlboro by his feet. I took in the cigarettes, glancing up at him, surprised. He stared back and I looked away. I stayed just inside the door.

Benny's room was at the front of the house. It was broad and often filled with sun and so gave the impression that the doors and windows were wide open even when they were not. It opened onto a wooden balcony that overlooked a corner of the garden in which, in the old days, a poultry house had stood. The walls of his room were papered with his own work. Sketches of Esperanza: Johnny Five Course's stall; Cora grinding coffee, her eyes glinting over her glasses at the artist; Ignacio decorating pastry, looking like he was humming while he worked; Dub's motorbike and on the same sheet of paper the wolf's head on the back of his jacket. On the wall above Benny's desk, taped over what might have been pictures of the jetty, were several portraits of the girl under the yellow bell tree. I moved forward to take a closer look. In a couple of them she seemed different; she was smiling. I turned back to him. He'd been watching me and now I saw his face darken like a monsoon sky. 'Get lost,' he said, coldly.

As I left, the door was bolted behind me. I looked down. I was still holding the plate, the dark wedge of sponge upon it still warm and fragrant. I turned back and though I knocked more than once, he didn't reply. The music grew louder, something angry, reminiscent of Dub's *punk*. I looked again at the plate in my hand. I heard something shift inside the room and the door shuddered as if someone had sat down suddenly against it. I left the plate on the hall table, setting it down noisily so that he might know it was there, though it didn't seem likely he'd hear it.

When I first arrived at the Bougainvillea, I slept on a mat next to America in the kitchen as the previous houseboy had done. But after a while Aunt Mary set me the task of clearing out the old pantry at the back of the house so that America might have some privacy. However, America, used to the open nipa huts of her village, refused to sleep in it, preferring the broader space of the kitchen, and so the room came to me.

My room could only be reached through the kitchen. It had a window, but it fell under the shade of trees and so remained dark and cool most of the day. It was small: if I sat on my bedding with my back against the wall and my legs stretched out, the span of them took up more than half of its width. Nonetheless it was mine. Apart from my bedding, I had a small bookcase and a chair and table where I read whatever I found. I did my schoolwork at the kitchen table or in the dining room after the household had eaten and the boys were in their rooms but, when I read for myself, I preferred the quiet of my room where I could create a world entirely in my head without the intrusion of America's singing or the carriage clock's rigid division of the evening.

Above the table, I'd taped to the wall a photograph of me as a boy of perhaps two or three with my mother. In it, my mother squinted under a bright sun while I reached forward from her arms, towards the camera. The picture was taken by my brother, on a camera he bought at a pawnshop, much to the disapproval of my father who chided him about his spendthrift nature till the day he left home. I still remember the day he took it, but only vaguely, like a texture rather than an image. I remember the bright light, the sensation of being held higher than the ground, of being smaller than everything.

I'd tried once to sketch a portrait of my mother as I remembered her, to display on my wall, but I was no artist and soon gave up. Instead, I put up pictures from magazines that Aunt Mary was throwing out. And so, flanking the photograph of me with my mother were the exotic spires of the Sagrada Familia and a man in a cigarette advertisement. The man had thick black hair (though not as long as Dub's), a long, straight nose and European features, except for his eyes, which were narrow like my own. He sat casually on the edge of an office desk, one foot on the floor, the hand holding his cigarette resting on his thigh. In the doorway behind him stood a woman, her image blurred so that her features couldn't really be made out, though it was clear that she was watching him. She had blond hair. I liked these two pictures and they had stayed up the longest, so long in fact that the rectangles of wall beneath them were brighter than that surrounding.

In the evening after dinner, Benny came to my room. I heard his footsteps along the corridor but I didn't quite believe them until I saw him in the doorway. He hadn't been to my room in years and he looked around now, inspecting it. 'Smaller than I remember,' he said softly. He reached up, tried unsuccessfully to touch the ceiling, laughed. He looked at the magazine pages I'd pasted up, at the photograph of me as a child in my mother's arms; he gazed at that for a long time. He'd seen it before, but he looked at it now as if it were new to him. He pointed at one of his own sketches, a portrait of me, and smiled. He'd made me pose for it, sitting at the table with my hands folded in front of me, my face framed by towers of jars filled with America's homemade pickles, pyramids of vegetables. He'd taken a long time to arrange each object, explaining his composition as he went. He'd leaned back to check everything when he was done and told me to look serious but I'd struggled not to laugh as he drew me, and he'd captured in his sketch the tightness of my mouth as I held it in. It was the same expression my mother had when she was trying to stay angry at my father while he clowned around to distract her.

Benny sat down against the wall facing my bed. He crossed his legs, laid his sketchbook across his lap and started, silently, to work. I knew better than to try and make conversation. I picked up the book I'd been reading, one of BabyLu's, about a village girl in England whose fate lay not in her own hands but in the hands of two men. I struggled to imagine the damp, green valleys that filled the book, the encircling silences; they were like nothing I'd ever known. I tried to read again now, but had made no progress at all when, several minutes later, Benny pulled out a photograph from his sketchbook and, leaning forward, placed it on the bed next to me. I picked it up slowly and looked at it, at the girl, her eyes narrowed against the sun, her image flashing under the bleak electric light in my room. I looked at the photograph on the wall over my table, where my mother creased her eyes on a sunny day. 'Who is she?' I said at last and wished for a moment that I hadn't, for the question seemed to break into the stillness of the room, crashing over the walls like surf.

'She was my mom,' he said. I looked again at the girl in the photograph, her small neat features, the long fingers on narrow hands. Her hands, her eyes, her mouth were Benny's. I stared at him, not knowing what to say. I opened my mouth but he shook his head and I was relieved; I was sure that nothing I might have said then would have been right. He worked at the sketchbook for a while longer and then he gathered his things together and, placing the book flat on the floor, tore the page out and handed it to me. I looked down at it and he left. I closed my eyes to listen to him moving away over the stone flags of the passage and the kitchen beyond.

When I could no longer hear him I opened my eyes again and looked at his sketch. In the centre of it I lay on my bedding, a book by my side, open but discarded, and instead in my hand was a photograph, the girl under the yellow bell tree recognisable even from the few lines that gave her substance. Behind me, the walls of the room crumbled away to reveal a rich landscape, not the concrete and colour of Esperanza Street but a jungle thick with palms and creepers, prehistoric. Over the shattered walls vines crept in, reclaiming the room, the house, and in the centre of it all I lay without fear, a look in my eyes of certainty, of belonging.

I went to the kitchen to find something to fasten the picture to the wall. America was lying on her mat, her arm over her face and her eyes closed, but she wasn't asleep. As I came in, she rolled away from me. I searched through the drawers, wary of making too much noise. 'What are you looking for?' she said crossly but I'd already found where she kept the tape in a tin box with scissors, strips of paper and a pen; America liked to label everything. 'You put that back when you're done,' she said without opening her eyes.

Back in my room, I held Benny's sketch up next to the photograph of my mother and taped it over the man in the cigarette ad.

When I returned to the kitchen America was sitting at the table. I sat down opposite her. 'He's told you,' she said and she sounded relieved. 'I'll tell you the rest if it'll stop you pestering me, but you'd better not breathe a word.' She leaned in to me, trying perhaps to be menacing, but all I saw was how exhausted she looked. She'd have been asleep at this time on any other day.

'It's *Benny*,' I said, softly.

She took a slow, deep breath, nodded. I guess she was trying to build up some suspense but I wasn't impatient, I knew she wanted to tell me. It must have been a lot to carry all these years. I smiled at her and she frowned. Maybe she'd imagined the moment of telling someone differently. 'The girl was called Dorothy. She was Mary's housemaid, one of many when *he* was still around. Of course he took a liking to her. Careless, selfish man. It was bound to happen. She tried to hide it for as long as she could until *I* spotted it.' America tapped her temple. 'You know, the way she stood, the way she walked, even before it really showed. It was Captain Bobby that told her she had to go, the day he left for Manila on business. He threw some money onto the piano and strolled out the door. More money than the poor girl might have seen in a year. He expected Mary to banish her there and then, expected to return to an orderly house. Well, that man never appreciated the kind of stuff his wife was made from. She took us all to her country estate – me, Dominic and the girl – leaving the houseboy in charge here. She saw the girl through her pregnancy and promised her the baby would be cherished. I remember her saying it. *Cherished*. She had to explain to the girl what it meant. Afterwards, she told Dorothy to disappear without a fuss and she did. She never came back, though she did send letters. A *lot* of letters. The first ones were addressed to Mary, then after that to Benny. He never got any of them. As far as I know, Mary never answered any either, so Lord knows what the girl was thinking. Most of them she burned without even opening them. I thought about suggesting she kept one or two for him when he grew into a man. But she was young. Who can blame her?' America paused for a moment, tracing a square on the tabletop with a finger, watching me coolly. 'I hid the photograph or she'd have burned that too. I thought he'd find out some day and have a pile of questions. There wasn't really anywhere else I could put it,' she glanced over at her mat on the floor. 'Maybe I hoped it would fall out one day.' I stared at her. 'Anyway, I'd forgotten about it.' She frowned at me again. 'That man would have come back from Manila to find an empty house. Well, *good*. You know she left a message with the houseboy that her husband wasn't to follow us and that if he did he wouldn't be let in at the gate. He never showed his face.' Even after so long, she looked disgusted. 'Sure, he *phoned*. Once or twice. Anyway, a few months later, we came back, Mary carrying a new baby that she'd called Benito, after her grandfather.' America sighed heavily. As she got up she said, 'You know, that man never even asked about the girl.'

# PEARLS

Lola Lovely looked round the dining room with the mournful expression of someone visiting a landscape after a long time to find the places of her youth obliterated. 'There were only ever friends and family in the house when I was here,' she said. 'Strangers don't respect a place in the same way.' She ran a finger over the side table, looked disappointed to find it clean. She rubbed her fingertips together anyway but didn't inspect further. 'We'd have the priest round for dinner regularly in those days. Ah, but it was Father Lucien then, a handsome Frenchman. Everyone asked *him* to dine.' She stopped at the window, gazed out, perhaps seeing the garden as it might once have been. 'Always in the sun, *chut*, that child!' I peered past her but the garden was empty. Lola Lovely ran her hand over her cheek and I imagined her suddenly leaning out of the window calling down to where Mary Morelos, the schoolchild, sat alone playing jacks. *America! Tell that child to play in the shade at least. I don't want her getting dark.*

She glanced round the room once more, at the bowl of glass fruit, the cutwork place mats, the glossy surface of the table. She frowned as she looked in my direction and I moved aside, so that she could complete her inspection.

'Things have got a little *tired* over time,' she said, 'but do what you can. And put out the best china, Joseph.' And with that she left, pulling her *pañuelo* round her shoulders as if she was cold and the thin silk might provide any warmth.

I polished the dining table again and checked that everything was straight and lined up. Lola Lovely wasn't in the room – she'd gone to check on America – but the sensation of her scrutiny persisted. When I'd finished, the room looked no different so I was glad she'd seen me get to work, for she nodded, pleased, when she came in again. I doubted either Father Mulrooney or Pastor Levi would take in the state of the room; the dinner invitation was hardly a social one anyway, more to discuss what could be done to halt Eddie Casama's scheme.

Lola Lovely, assured that all preparations would be carried out to her satisfaction, went to take her siesta and I found myself in the sala with Aunt Mary, who had managed to avoid her mother most of the morning. We sat together, in silence, Aunt Mary on the piano stool, me on the rug polishing the boys' shoes. I liked these moments; there were fewer of them now. More often these days, Aunt Mary left me to maintain the house without her direction, closing the door of her study softly behind her.

The blinds had been lowered part-way and the windows of the sala thrown open. Through them came the fragrance of the jasmine that was in full flower, mingled with the scent of the hot street and, somewhere, faintly, an open gutter. The noise of the street felt close and intrusive but it was too hot to close the windows again.

Aunt Mary sat with her back to the keyboard, a pile of sheet music on her lap. The piano lid was open, but Aunt

Mary hadn't been playing. She frowned as she ran her hand over each sheet, as if the texture of the paper or the music it described might ignite some lost memory. The sheet music had been ordered and reordered countless times: alphabetically by composer, or categorised by style, genre, era. It was a kind of meditation for her. I'd never heard her play. I watched her out of the corner of my eye, saw her hands pause over the pile and then, without warning, she exclaimed, 'Damn it, Joseph.' Startled, I jumped to my feet, uncertain what I'd done wrong. She waved me down again, apologising. Then she marched into the hallway straight to the telephone. I heard her exclaim, 'Constanza! Mary Morelos here. Oh! Connie, then. I was wondering if you and Edgar are free this evening. I know it's very last minute.'

Dub and Benny, called by their mother, came down just as the doorbell rang at seven. They kidded around with each other as they walked down the stairs. They were uncomfortable to be dressed smartly, in shirts chosen by their mother that I'd pressed for them that afternoon. They stood awkwardly side by side in the sala, like acquaintances waiting to be introduced at a wedding.

Father Mulrooney and Pastor Levi were punctual. I was conscious of the slightest throb of disappointment as I opened the door to them, but only because I'd steeled myself for the arrival of Eddie Casama. Aunt Mary stood behind me as I opened the door, to direct the men into the sala. Father Mulrooney, less crumpled than usual, was wearing a shirt and slacks. I'd expected him to come in his robes. Perhaps Lola Lovely had too, for she said as he entered, 'How fashions change, Padre.' He smiled at her and she held her hand out as if expecting him to kiss it. He hesitated and then took her hand in his, bending his face only slightly towards it, an abbreviated but polite gesture. Lola Lovely held her hand out to Pastor Levi and said, 'I'm sure I remember you as a boy. Why, nothing really changes.'

Mulrooney smiled again and Pastor Levi said, 'I was born in Esperanza, ma'am.'

'Of course you were,' Lola Lovely said. 'I probably knew your mother.'

Pastor Levi introduced his wife. Eveline didn't possess the kind of effortless beauty that BabyLu had, or that Lola Lovely had once exulted in, but she'd taken some trouble for the evening. Her dress, long and plain in cut and the colour of an afternoon sky, flattered her. She'd applied a little colour to her face and, though it seemed obvious, inexpert somehow, the effect was agreeable, like a high-school teacher chaperoning at a prom. Lola Lovely's eyes sparkled as she took her in and, beaming, she reached out and squeezed Eveline's hand, pulling her gently towards the piano, where earlier I'd laid out a selection of drinks.

The priests turned to speak to Aunt Mary but only for a moment, for now Lola Lovely drew away the shawl that she'd draped over her cast so that Eveline exclaimed and the men turned to look. Mulrooney said, as Cesar had several days before, 'I hope it's nothing serious.'

Lola Lovely's cast drew a nonchalant arc. 'An inconvenience,' she said serenely. I started towards the piano but she waved me away. She lifted a bottle of Johnny Walker Black Label, her cast dismissing Mulrooney's mild objections without even turning to look at him. She poured the priests a tumbler each. Neither man's protest was sustained. Lola

Lovely poured slightly more modest glasses for herself and Eveline and then raised her eyebrows at her daughter. 'Fizzy drink?' she said.

Dub stepped forward, smiled disarmingly at his grandmother. 'I'll get ours,' he said. Lola Lovely moved to the settee and sat down. She looked for a moment as if she might commandeer the centre of it, leaving the men with too few seats, doomed to stand, but then she sat on one side and patted the seat next to her for Benny to join her. He shot me a look as he sat down. Lola Lovely arranged herself with more than her usual care, her feet neatly turned like a dancer. I saw Benny glance down at her feet and wondered if he too saw the artificiality of it. I knew from America that Lola Lovely had never been a dancer, though after she started courting she took to affecting a certain gait and poise when walking or sitting. She was always pleased, America said, when later, in *those* circles, people often asked if she was, though she never quite confessed, admitting only to *loving the ballet*. I imagined Lola Lovely's disappointment when her daughter, despite being sent to the most expensive dance academies, showed neither aptitude nor interest.

Aunt Mary left for the kitchen and it was while she was out of the room that the doorbell rang again. I expected her to come out into the hall as I opened the door to Eddie Casama and his wife but she did not. I showed them both into the sala. My eyes were drawn to Dub as I followed them in. Dub had got home late and, kept occupied by America in the kitchen as she doubled up on ingredients and grumbled good-naturedly about stretching the chicken, I hadn't had a chance to warn him. I saw now how his easy manner wavered when Eddie's eyes levelled with his and appraised him for longer than they might have. If the older man was troubled in his turn by Dub's height, his beauty, he showed no sign.

By the time Aunt Mary returned, Connie had seated herself and I'd served both her and Eddie their drinks. I was surprised, knowing how old-fashioned Aunt Mary was about certain things, preferring to welcome invited guests herself. 'I'm so glad you could make it,' she said easily as she came in. She was unreadable as she shook first Eddie's hand and then pressed her cheek to Connie's.

'Eddie rearranged a few things,' Connie said.

'I hope I haven't caused you any trouble,' Aunt Mary's voice sounded sufficiently concerned but not apologetic.

'We hardly see you,' said Eddie, 'or your boys,' he smiled at Dub. 'Joey Robello was saying only the other day how you hide yourself away.' Aunt Mary showed no outward tremor at Eddie's casual mention of Judge Robello.

Beside Eddie, his wife fiddled with her necklace. Connie Casama's face was somewhat heavy-set with age, but she was nonetheless a handsome woman. She looked eagerly at Lola Lovely, at her cast, her face twitching into sudden concern as she said, 'Does it hurt still?'

'What beautiful pearls,' Lola Lovely said emphatically. 'Quite symmetrical.'

'Eddie bought them for our anniversary last year,' Connie cupped the beads in her palm, displaying them. 'In Singapore.'

'Of course, *old* pearls have an incomparable lustre,' said Lola Lovely. She looked Connie over, smiling. 'Would I know your mother?' she added.

They sat down to dinner late, for Lola Lovely insisted on more drinks all round and made no move to get up from the settee. When they finally moved to the dining room, all eyes were on the platters steaming at the centre of the table. Pastor Levi patted his belly. 'America's a real artist,' said Eveline, at the sight of the food. America had excelled herself, for she knew instinctively that her skill in the kitchen was her only weapon and, moreover, that it was only through Aunt Mary that she might get to wield it. As a result, the conversation foundered as people started to eat.

After a while Eddie said, 'This was my favourite as a boy. But you couldn't have known.'

Aunt Mary looked pleased. 'America decided on the menu. I rarely need to instruct her.'

'She's been with our family for years,' Lola Lovely said. 'I remember the day I employed her. Skinny thing she was then.'

'Fresh from the fields to the market to the kitchen,' Mulrooney said, through a mouthful. 'Not packaged in plastic in some mall.'

'Progress has its price,' Eddie said.

'Progress is an interesting concept.' Mulrooney leaned forward. 'We only measure our progress in relation to our fellows.'

Eddie smiled down at his plate. 'You're a revolutionary through and through, Father. Surely even *your* ideals must at times be checked by pragmatism?'

'That sounds so completely reasonable. You're a politician, Eddie, more than a businessman.' Levi said cheerfully, spearing a piece of fried fish.

'I'm not an evil man,' chuckled Eddie. I wondered if he enjoyed his reputation.

'How handsome you've both grown,' Connie said looking at Dub and Benny. 'You might even be courting now, Dominic.' Dub blushed lightly.

'You must have your pick of the local girls,' Eddie said and I saw how Dub struggled to look at him. 'No one special?' Dub opened his mouth to speak and then stopped, glanced at his mother, then up at me. I felt helpless. Aunt Mary looked puzzled and her gaze lingered over her son, before considering me briefly.

Connie laid her hand over her husband's. 'Filipino men are famous for playing the field, I guess. But there comes a time when a man has to *choose*,' she said. Her husband smiled evenly and let his hand rest under hers, putting his fork down to pick up his glass.

Once again, Dub started to speak and faltered. I saw Benny look at his brother, assessing him with his artist's eyes. For a moment, Aunt Mary looked alarmed and then her gaze swept the table and she turned to me and said briskly, 'More rice, Joseph,' though the bowl was still half full. And to Pastor Levi and Eveline, 'I don't believe you've tried the pork yet.'

I didn't return straight away. America needed my help to turn a sponge while she iced it. I wasn't gone for long, but when I returned the air seemed charged and Eddie was flushed. A space had been cleared on the table and Pastor Levi was drawing an imaginary Esperanza with his finger. 'But that area must have at least a thousand households.'

'At least,' said Eveline. 'Why, there are several storeys all along the river.'

'You can't just break up a community that's been there for generations and expect there to be no consequences,' said Pastor Levi.

'There's no place in business for sentimentality,' said Eddie.

'You can't dismiss it as sentiment,' Mulrooney said angrily. 'These are real lives.'

'We've considered a number of alternatives.'

'What will be *your* sacrifice?' Benny said suddenly. 'You said everyone would stand to lose something. What will you lose?' The room fell silent. Aunt Mary put her fork down carefully. 'Boys,' she started.

'Am I answering to teenagers now?' Eddie smiled. 'Antonio wouldn't dream of interrogating his elders.'

'Nevertheless, it's an interesting question,' said Pastor Levi.

'I'd certainly like to hear the answer,' said Mulrooney.

'I grew up in Greenhills,' said Eddie quietly to Benny. 'There's no point clinging to a history. We can move with the times or be left behind. It's a choice.'

'Not for everyone,' said Aunt Mary firmly. 'Not everyone has a choice.' She looked at Benny, a fleeting pride in her face.

'This should be a discussion for adults,' said Eddie, catching her expression, 'For those who will actually be footing the bill.'

'It depends on what you mean by footing the bill,' said Eveline hotly. Pastor Levi reached out and squeezed her hand. I saw Mulrooney look at their hands on the table. I wondered if he ever thought about getting married himself. I imagined Jaynie next to him, their hands side by side, almost touching, looks exchanged as they leaned together during the conversation.

'Let's not ruin such magnificent food with an ideological debate,' laughed Eddie.

'It's a worthy discussion for a good meal,' said Mulrooney.

'It's not as if I'm on my own,' said Eddie, 'as if I'm the only interested party. The scheme will go ahead with or without me. I'm simply making the best of an opportunity.' I'd never imagined Eddie as a small fish and I wasn't quite ready to believe it, but the table fell silent again after he said it.

'Wasn't it your idea?' said Aunt Mary, eventually.

'Well, ideas can't be owned,' said Eddie, sitting back, his hands spread out, like a picture of Jesus at the last supper. 'They take on a life of their own in no time.'

'Nothing can really be owned,' I said softly.

Startled, Eddie looked round at me and then started laughing. Lola Lovely straightened up in her chair and said, 'Perhaps you're needed in the kitchen, Joseph.'

'What a household you have, Mary,' Eddie said. 'Full of youthful romanticism.' He stared at Dub. Dub met his eye but looked away again quickly and then, suddenly, pushed himself back from the table and stalked out of the room. Immediately, Aunt Mary excused herself; as she followed him I moved forward to start clearing the empty platters away, my body blocking the view of the hallway. When I came out with the plates, I heard her say, 'Don't you dare leave. I want to talk to you.'

'Sure,' said Dub unhappily.

She gave him a long look. 'This evening is important to me,' she said. 'If you can't behave graciously, you may have your dessert in the kitchen, if America has room for you.'

Dub didn't return to the table but slipped up to his room and closed the door. He didn't answer when I took a plate of America's sponge up to him and I brought it down with me again. A little later, I heard the front door close and the sound of a motorbike engine, but the voices in the dining room continued without pause and Aunt Mary didn't emerge.

I was kept busy in the kitchen, brewing coffee and clearing up with America. Every now and then America and I paused in our work and glanced at each other when we heard the voices rise to a crescendo, but we couldn't make out what was being said.

Eddie Casama and Connie left early. I read the disappointment in Aunt Mary's face and understood that nothing had been resolved. She walked upstairs to Dub's room and pushed the door open and when she came downstairs her mouth was a thin line. 'Did he say where he might be heading?' she asked me. I shook my head. And then she asked me what I knew, whether her son was seeing a woman, whether there was some connection with Edgar Casama. And, for the first time, I lied to her and knew that she saw it. She looked at me, through me, and then without another word she left the kitchen and retired to her study.

# VIEW FROM THE HEADLAND

Two days after Eddie Casama ate at our table, Dub came to see me in my room. He stooped a little as he stepped through the door. He'd never set foot in it before and I saw his surprise as he looked about him. 'Not much of a window,' he said. 'I'd go crazy. It's like a . . . ' He glanced at me, reddened.

'I don't spend so much time in here,' I lied.

He threw a book onto the bed next to me. 'She said you *had* to read this one.' I glanced at the upside-down cover, recognised a detail from Picasso's *Guernica*, a painting that Benny had marked in one of his mother's art books. I touched the book lightly. If Dub hadn't been there, I might have raised it to my face, sniffed it. *The Age of Reason*. It looked like a serious book and I was flattered. I'd read everything she'd sent me, even rehearsed opinions on them in case she ever asked, though of course she never did.

Dub moved further into the room and I was conscious of an urge to shrink back against the wall to accommodate him. He sat down against the wall, in the same spot Benny had occupied, and stretched his legs out, pushing his feet into my bedding. I'd been reading when he came in and he smiled at the book already in my hand. Dub had little interest in books. He was too alive, too connected to the world to need to evade it. 'Good?' he asked, looking away again before I answered.

'Sure,' I shrugged, though I was only a few pages into it and, my thoughts still in thrall to the last book I'd read, I was disinclined to enter a new world just yet. I thought how if he'd been Benny I'd have said as much.

'One of hers?' Dub's voice softened. I'd noticed before that he never referred to BabyLu by name when he spoke about her with me; she was our only common ground.

'One of your mom's actually.' He frowned up at the doorway at the mention of his mother. He didn't say anything for a while. I listened for any sounds coming down the passageway. I'd left America in the kitchen but I couldn't swear she was asleep; it was too quiet.

'You want to go for a spin?' Dub said suddenly.

'Now?'

'Sure, why not. America's sleeping out there. Mom's in her study.'

'I don't know.'

'What don't you know? How to have fun?'

I stared at him, surprised. Then I stood up.

America opened her eyes as we came out of the passageway and watched us, silently, as we crossed the kitchen, her eyes slitted like a cat's. I pretended not to notice. She'd looked fed up all evening, banishing me to my room a little earlier than usual, but I wondered now if she'd wait up just so she could grill me when I got back. I didn't care; I'd never been on a motorbike before.

Dub wheeled the bike out onto Esperanza before starting the engine. I locked the gate behind us. He held out a helmet, the same one he'd given to BabyLu. It still smelled of her. It was tight as I pulled it on and I struggled for a while with the straps, as she had done. Dub, already astride the bike, glanced back at me, his foot tapping lightly against the gear lever. I gave up and climbed on behind him, the straps hanging loose under my chin.

We cruised down Esperanza and took the coast road out towards Little Laguna. Out here, the street lights fell away and the night swamped in towards us, submerging us. The road became coy, revealing itself only by degrees in the headlight. The wind tugged at us and I clung to Dub as BabyLu must have done. He slowed down. I took a long, deep breath. The smell of the sea was sharp and clean. I felt fully awake, exhilarated.

Ahead of us a signboard floated in the darkness, marking the way to Little Laguna Beach, but Dub sped up as we neared it. I wasn't disappointed; I didn't want to stop at all. A minute later he slowed again and turned onto a short track that pointed towards the headland. The track was uneven and the bike crawled along, the wheels crunching over sand and shingle. Soon enough we stopped and Dub turned off the engine. He looked over his shoulder at me, waited as I dismounted first. I was still in my shorts, my legs stiff with cold, and I moved slowly, clumsily, back from the bike. Around us the blackness seemed almost solid, as if I might reach out and at any instant encounter its surface. I could barely make out my feet.

Dub left the bike's headlight on and we followed the path it cut, our shadows sliding ahead of us over the rocks. We climbed a short way over the boulders and, as the light thinned, we stopped, settling ourselves side by side to look out over the sweep of the bay. Down below, the lights of

Little Laguna were strung like beads in the darkness and overhead the sky was crammed with stars. It was nothing like the stretch of coast at Esperanza, punctuated by the jetty and lined with shacks.

The wind was playful, capricious. It smoothed Dub's hair down over his face, gusted it away again. He started talking, raising his voice to be heard over the sounds of wind and sea. He talked about Little Laguna, about the bars, the sunsets, about women in bikinis or in diving suits, about fights he'd seen, about freshly caught fish still struggling in buckets sold to foreigners on the beach at sundown. As he talked, I watched the lights down below. Little Laguna Beach was no more than five kilometres out of town along the coast road, a fifteen-minute ride in a jeepney from the jetty. I'd never been.

He fell silent and stared into the distance, and I knew that he'd brought her here too. 'She sat right there,' he said, 'where you are now. The night I took her for a ride. We were gone maybe three hours. He was supposed to be away on business but when we came back his car was in the street. You know, when she saw it she wanted me to ride on but I wasn't afraid of him so I pulled up. The car was empty. He was already upstairs. Well, he owns the place, I guess. His driver was on the sidewalk, leaning against the bonnet like John Wayne, rolling his sleeves up like he was getting ready to get his hands dirty. I wanted to go up with her but she wouldn't let me. When she handed back the helmet, she pushed it into me so hard I almost fell off the sidewalk.' His hand came to his chest, rubbing it lightly at the remembered sensation. He sat up a little straighter. 'His driver looked me up and down but he didn't come over.'

I studied Dub's profile and I wondered if there was anyone in the neighbourhood who wouldn't have recognised Aunt Mary's eldest boy.

'She didn't even kiss me goodnight,' he said.

He had stayed for a while in the street, his bike engine idling. After a few minutes, he heard the sound of arguing from upstairs, but he couldn't make out what was being said. It must have been loud to filter down into the street, to be audible over the sounds of Prosperidad even at that hour. He turned off the engine and made to get off the bike but the chauffeur pushed himself up slowly from the bonnet and took a step forward. They stayed like that only briefly, for soon enough the raised voices stopped and soft music started up. The chauffeur looked down at his watch and then pointedly at Dub, who started his engine and rode away into the night.

Dub fell quiet. Eventually he said, 'I need your help, Jo-Jo.' *Jo-Jo.* It sounded wrong when he said it. My eyes ran along the line of lights in the distance to where the last of them was swallowed up by blackness. I waited. I hadn't been so enthralled by the ride to forget that he must have had a reason for bringing me here. 'She won't say if it's mine or his.' He picked up a pebble and flung it into the darkness. I listened to it clatter away over the boulders. When the sound of it had been lost altogether, Dub said, 'You know the curandero? He's a friend of yours, right?' And I thought, *Uncle Bee? What does he have to do with anything?*

'Sure I know him.'

'If it's his, she'll never leave him. And if it's mine . . . Joseph, I'm only nineteen.' I leaned forward to pick at my sandals. I didn't want him to say another word. When eventually he spoke again, his voice was uncharacteristically shrill, the timbre taut and unpleasant, like a blade ringing against a stone. 'You could get me some herbs or something, right?'

I felt a knot form in my chest. I sat up straight and the abruptness of the movement made him turn to look at me. When I didn't return his gaze he looked away again. He picked up another pebble and lobbed it into the night. I waited for the first strike, the second, the third, and as I listened, I thought how the sound of each impact lessened in strength even as it remained unchanged in character. The thought seemed so perfectly fitting at that moment that I smiled into the darkness and consequently sounded almost cheerful when I said, 'But your mom . . . '

'What about my Mom?' he said testily.

'I don't know. What I meant was – '

'I've thought a lot about it. I've thought about nothing else.'

'What does *she* want?'

'My *mom*?'

'BabyLu.' The wind pulled her name away from me as I spoke it.

'I don't know. She doesn't know, I guess. It's not like I get a lot of chances to talk to her.' I shut my mouth hard at this and waited, relieved when he spoke again. 'It's such a mess, Joe.' His voice in the darkness was desolate.

*Your mess,* I wanted to say.

'You'll help me won't you?' I felt the knot in my chest tighten. I didn't answer, and after a moment he turned to look at me. 'You *have* to help me.'

Still I hesitated, aware of his gaze. 'Sure,' I said at last.

He gripped my forearm gently, squeezed it before letting go. 'I *knew* you would.'

Dub pushed his hands into his pockets, withdrew them again. He lit a cigarette, cupping his hands round the end of it for a long while until it caught. He smoked silently and when he'd finished it, he pushed the stub into a crevice in the rocks and lit another one straight away. His hands were trembling and, seeing it, I felt sorry for him. The knot in my chest felt heavy, like a stone. 'Dub . . . ' I started to say.

'Sorry, Joe. I didn't think.' He held his cigarette packet out to me. I shook my head. He looked puzzled and put it away again, pushing himself up from the ground in the same movement. He was walking towards the bike before I'd even got to my feet. He started the engine as I reached him and waited, staring into the distance while I climbed on. My head was loud with thoughts and, later, I scarcely recalled the ride home, though I remember that we looped down to the beach and he pointed out a floating bar, its lights bobbing in the blackness.

America was asleep as I slipped across the kitchen. She stirred and turned over and I quickened my step till I was safe in my room. I sat on my bed, my back against the wall, and closed my eyes.

'*JeenPaulSarter*. Aren't you clever?' I opened my eyes to find America leaning in the doorway, her finger poised at the centre of *Guernica*. 'You want to tell me where you've just been?'

'For a ride.'

'I know that. Why?'

I looked blankly at her. Her eyes were lined and red. 'Just for a ride.'

'Just nothing. What trouble have you found now?' I fought the urge to pull my blanket over my head and shut out the sight of her. She sat down at the table, looked around distastefully at the walls, the tiny, shaded window. She shifted round in the chair to keep the passageway in view. 'Anyone else brings you trouble and it'll be *you* that has to carry it. You understand what I mean?' I closed my eyes again. 'I'm just saying,' she carried on. 'Course you think you're a man now.'

I slid down the wall till I was flat on my bed, studied the ceiling. I waited. America sniffed forcefully. She got up, making more noise, I thought, than seemed necessary. I watched from under my lashes as she pushed hard against the chair to stand, her other hand already reaching for the doorframe. She hesitated at the threshold and I thought she might have more to say but she cast a weary, ill-tempered eye over me and walked out.

I got to my feet. Usually my door remained open, my room being too small and claustrophobic a space to be shut inside. But now I closed it and as I did so, I heard America's footsteps pause in the passageway at the sound before continuing into the kitchen.

# A BADLY PLACED URN

The hatch of the *sari-sari* store framed Missy Bukaykay's face. A face which bore echoes of her daughter in the lines and angles that she'd handed down to her, but none of the beauty. Missy's face had long since lost its plumpness, lost any trace of softness, if indeed it had ever possessed it. Her teeth were stained red with betel and in generally poor shape. Because she didn't see me often and because she'd been so fond of my mother, she always smiled when we met and I, unable to pull my eyes away, bewitched by the inevitability of it, always looked straight at her mouth. She looked up now as I approached and grinned. I smiled back at her but I was disappointed that it should be her in the store hatch; I'd hoped for Uncle Bee, whose eyes were certainly less astute than his wife's. 'Shouldn't you be in school?' Missy's gaze levelled with mine.

'Had to run an errand.' My voice came out husky, thick.

'Mary Morelos asks you to skip school for errands?'

It was disconcerting to hear Aunt Mary's name just then. 'You won't tell her?' I said.

'Sure I will. Next time I'm at the country club.'

I thrust my hands into my pockets and looked up and down the alley.

'Ah!' Missy leaned forward over the counter. 'You can talk in the street or you want to come inside, Meester Bond?' She rocked back on her stool, twitching a finger in the direction of the stoop.

I went round to the front of the shack. The door was open and the partitioning curtain had been drawn back to let the listless afternoon air circulate and provide Missy with a clear view of the front door. She watched me as I came in, raising an eyebrow as I closed the door behind me. Under her shrewd eyes, I moved awkwardly across the room to the stool she'd pulled out for me. I sat down heavily. Missy looked amused. She waited, her eyes on me as I gazed about at the shelves of jars, the vine-like strips of detergent sachets, the polished scales and brass weights. I studied her framed midwifery certificate, her delivery bag by the door. 'You've come to borrow it for a movie premiere?' she said.

Now that I was actually inside, the opportunities for backing out seemed to evaporate in an instant and the necessity to speak, to act, grew suddenly pressing. I took a deep breath. 'I know a girl,' I said.

Missy's smile vanished. '*You've* got a girl in trouble?'

I looked up, startled. 'Not me.'

She nodded. 'I wouldn't have figured *you'd* get into a mess like that.'

I wasn't sure how to take this. Sure, I wasn't exactly handsome. I sat up straighter, tried to meet her gaze squarely, looked away again too fast. 'What if she can't keep it?' I said. My voice sounded weak, childish.

'Wait a minute! Is this about one of the Morelos boys?' she cried suddenly.

I felt the heat shoot up to my face. I looked down at

Missy's feet. She wriggled her toes, like someone might drum their fingers on a table. 'No,' I said. I heard her snort.

'What are you lying to me for? You think I can't tell?' she said peevishly. 'Well, I can guess which one. Anyway, what does the girl want?'

I spoke quickly. 'I was just asking. You know, I thought, if it's early and if there are some herbs. I mean, they're just herbs, they wouldn't make her really sick, right?'

'They put you up to this?'

'I'm not a kid.'

Missy glared at me. The room felt hot, closed in, and I fought the urge to dash to the door and wrench it open. The sound of a coin rapping on the counter of the *sari-sari* store broke into the room. Missy got up. She jabbed a finger at my stool, anchoring me to it. She slipped behind the partitioning curtain, pulling it closed behind her. I heard her greet someone loudly, cheerfully, and shortly the sound of boxes scraping, things being shoved aside. I looked around at the shelves again, at the herbs and pastes in relabelled jam and coffee jars. Uncle Bee had catalogued their contents for me once. I tried to replay his voice. He had intoned as if he were reciting a poem, or perhaps that was just how I remembered it. *Kataka-taka, angelica, for toothache, boils and burns; Niyog-niyogan, Burmese creeper, for intestinal worms.* Nuts and seeds and roots, for body odour, dandruff, hair loss; for pains in the head, teeth, eyes and joints; for piles and for snake-bite. Remedies for a broken heart or to make a person fall in love with you. Or for girls in trouble to get rid of their trouble before anyone could ever guess, before the trajectory of their lives changed forever. But though I could almost feel again the grain of that morning, the details remained hazy, unreliable. I reached out and ran my fingers along a line of jars, up and down, my fingertips marking out the level of their contents. How easy it would have been to take what I needed had I even known what it was. My hand dropped to my side again.

Missy swept back through the curtain and sighed throatily at the sight of me, as if my presence brought to mind some tedious chore momentarily forgotten. She stared at me, her eyes unexpectedly soft, ignoring the jars behind me. It wouldn't even have occurred to her that I might have tried to steal what I'd come for and, at the thought, a feeling of gratitude almost like a physical weakness washed over me. Missy walked through into the kitchen, returning quickly with a glass of water. She held it out to me. 'Drink,' she said. 'It's a hot day. You don't look so good.' The glass was beaded with condensation, the water chilled from the Frigidaire. It felt good in my hand. I took a sip. My mouth was dry and the water had a pleasant sourness to it. 'All of it,' Missy said. 'Or you're waiting for a little umbrella and a straw?' I gulped some down. 'You want to help anyone, you help yourself,' she continued. 'You don't have to fix other people's troubles for them. I said the same to your father.' I reddened at the mention of my father. I looked up at Missy but her face had an obstinate set to it.

The sound of another customer came from the store hatch but Missy, calling out to them, stood over me as I finished drinking, her arms crossed, brows stitched into a frown. I made a show of draining the last drops noisily, holding the glass up for her to inspect. She smiled, her mouth closed.

'You have any more errands or it's back to class now.' She said it flatly, a statement not a question. I started to get up, then sat down again lightly, perched on the edge of the stool. I'd been too easily dissuaded, I thought. I looked up at her. 'No,' she said firmly, as she turned away. 'You care about that girl at all, you tell her to come talk to me. Now, you get straight back to school and I might forget I saw you.'

She seated herself again at her store hatch, looking out over the alley. In the slanting yellow light that filtered into the dark interior, the back of her head had a stubborn solidity.

I hurried away along the alley, eager now to be out of sight. On reaching the corner I glanced back and caught the slightest movement within the lean ellipse of Missy's face. She'd stuck out her tongue at me. She leaned forward over the counter and waved before settling back to be obscured at last by a fan of Mr Chips packets.

I made as if to walk uphill in the direction of the school. But a few steps on from the corner, hidden by Primo's store, I stopped and turned again seawards to where, in the distance, the afternoon sun picked out the whitewashed planes and roof thatch of Jonah's office. Idly I imagined chancing upon Uncle Bee as he stepped out of a jeepney or browsed for herbs under the eaves of the market hall. Beyond the jetty, the fine blue cloth of the sea was studded with boats, white lines of surf trailing from them like pulled threads. Dotted about in the shallows, the jetty boys were at work. Involuntarily, I found my eyes searching for my father and, though from this distance I couldn't have been certain that the dot I recognised was really him, just the knowledge that he was among them disheartened me, as if he might, even from so far away, fathom what I was up to and disapprove. I turned once again to face uphill but I was far from resolute.

I cast a final look into the mouth of the Espiritista alley and at that moment I saw the figure of Missy Bukaykay step off her stoop and manoeuvre around a deep rut in the track before heading off briskly in the direction of Colon, midwife's bag in hand. I stood and watched till she was out of sight. I almost wished I hadn't seen her leave. When she was gone I walked back to the Bukaykay shack, uncertain, even as I neared it, of what I was going to do.

The store hatch was closed and the front door shut. I sat down on the stoop. There were people about as always but I kept my eyes down, inspected the blistered turquoise rectangle of the step framed by the dry brown skin of my feet. The sun was hard and the texture of my skin was as clear as wood grain. In contrast, my thoughts were like fragments of conversation heard through water. I stood up and tried the door. It was locked, and the relief that coursed through me left the crown of my head prickling. The act of standing and the warm metal of the door handle seemed to bring me back to the surface of things. The noise of Esperanza boomed again. I felt sick. My hands were sweating. I rubbed them on the legs of my shorts and sat back down. I looked up at the door. It was hardly sturdy enough to withstand me for long if I was determined, I thought. The shack, like most of the neighbourhood, depended as much on the proximity of other dwellings, on being overlooked, on the renown of its inhabitants, as it did on locks and bolts for its security and I suppose it was so rarely left empty. I'd have time enough to look through the shelves, read labels, find something, anything, that might trigger a memory – or take a handful from each jar, work out what I needed later on. I tried to imagine doing it, but the Joseph in the image seemed flimsy, like a sketch or a cartoon. I wondered why, when I had no trouble imagining a more substantial Joseph driving Suelita around in a red American convertible of the kind I'd seen in one of Aunt Mary's photographs. *Niagara!* I stayed on the stoop. People passed in front of my eyes first one way and then the other, a few glancing incuriously at me and, though there was probably no suspicion in those glances, their eyes made me feel ashamed. Yet I was also a little excited. I'd never stolen anything in my life and for now I indulged myself with the possibility of it as I sat, cradling my head in my hands, palms over my eyes as if preparing for the moment I might act without hesitation.

'Jeez-*us*. Are you praying?' Suelita's voice was disdainful. I looked up to see her in front of me in her school uniform, her weight thrown onto one leg, school bag propped on her opposite hip, like a woman might carry a child. I hadn't even heard her approach. She regarded me coolly, the same eyes as her mother's. 'You want to wait inside, or you'd prefer to sit out here like a badly placed urn?' Her arm swept a glamorous curve through the air like a movie actress flaunting a cigarette holder, and she fluttered her eyelids, smiling as if she'd said something smart. I stared at her. The gesture was ill-suited to her. If she'd been BabyLu, I thought, or even Lola Lovely, it would have been convincing.

For a few seconds she held her posture, her hand poised in its arc like a hovering gull, awaiting a response which was slow in coming. Until, discomfited by my silence, her smile grew stiff. Seeing it, I snatched at something to say. 'Where exactly would a well-placed urn sit?' I cast my eyes about the stoop for show. I'd intended to put her at ease, perhaps by providing her with another clear shot at me, but I'd miscalculated, for when I looked up again, her expression was combative. She rearranged herself, throwing her weight onto the other leg. The action snagged her skirt and drew it up by a fraction on one side. It took some effort not to look at the extra centimetre of skin. She smiled again, and the icy bow of her mouth suddenly made me want to grip her wrist and pull her roughly to me. I'd never allowed myself such a thought in her presence before. What might she have said, I wondered, if she'd known that only a moment ago I'd been thinking about breaking into her home and stealing from her parents? I stood up, a feeling like electricity in my fingertips. Her smile widened. She had dimples. I'd forgotten how good they looked. My hands dropped to my sides. She stepped forward to climb the stairs of the stoop, brushing past me, the cloth of her sleeve rasping against my shoulder as she passed.

She waited in the open doorway, her eyes shadowed now by the eaves. 'Why are you here, anyway?' she said. For the shortest instant I imagined asking for her help. She waited. 'Did an owl peck your tongue out?' she said at last.

'Everyone knows you're smart. So what?'

Neither of us had expected my response. Suelita's cheeks pinked and she pursed her mouth. She considered for a moment before she said, 'I skipped history. I waited on the other side of Esperanza till I saw her leave.' Her eyes were on me as I took this in. 'If you'd been Rico, you wouldn't have waited before you tried the door and then you wouldn't have sat down again.'

I felt hot suddenly, the sun ruthless on my head. 'He's a hero,' I muttered.

'He's a jerk.' But she looked about as she said it. I felt a brief flare of pleasure.

Suelita shook her head and the movement seemed to leave a void that I spoke quickly to fill. 'First time in a long while I haven't seen him here. He's almost worn the bench thin.'

'So?'

'I guess he hasn't got what he's hoping for yet.'

She pouted at me. 'If guys were trains, he'd be the one heading for the broken bridge.' She leaned back against the doorframe and looked out across the alley. I turned to follow the line of her gaze, took in the dismal alley with the traffic of Esperanza flowing across its mouth. She'd have been greeted by this same vista every day of her life. 'You're all the same.' She sounded bored again. 'I listen out for long enough and eventually I hear the dud note. With him at least it was straight away.' She looked directly at me as she said this. I had a sense of things dropping away from me.

We stood for a long moment without speaking. We might only have been a couple of inches apart. 'Why is it,' she said at last, softly, 'that Fidel never had to learn to cook but I did?' The question felt almost too prosaic for the moment, though of course she was right to ask it.

'If I was a train . . . ' My mouth refused to form the rest of the sentence.

Suelita started to laugh, her teeth flashing, mouth open, the moist rose of her tongue as fascinating and remote as a sunset. 'You want to come in anyway?' she said. I wished she hadn't said *anyway*.

I thought about it long enough that when I finally gave my answer her eyes were intent on me. 'No,' I said.

'Suit yourself.' But she sounded surprised.

I was smiling as I walked away but with neither pleasure nor amusement. I had cut short with a single word the only time we might ever be alone together. I imagined her eyes on my back as I moved through the alley, but when I looked back from the brink of Esperanza, the door of the shack was closed and she was gone.

# SEA BLUE, BLOOD RED

My father leaned forward, his forearms resting on the pew in front. He stared up at the life-sized wooden Jesus on his cross. Jesus' paint was peeling and his robes, which had once been a blue the colour of the sea out over the reefs, had faded to early-morning sky or, in places, chipped away altogether to reveal the grain beneath. It had been a while since my father had brought me here and I hadn't rushed to remind him. He'd been quiet all the way from the jetty but, looking at him, I was sure he had something to say. There was no one else here now. He'd waited for the last person to leave and still he glanced anxiously at the door, fingering the bamboo pendant about his neck – another cross with a minuscule Jesus on it, which I remembered playing with as a kid, hopping it up a mountain of peas that my mother had asked me to shell.

'Missy says you asked about . . . some girl.' He said the last two words delicately. I felt my skin bristle. I should have realised she'd go to him. He waited and when I didn't say anything he added, 'You don't have to fix anyone else's mistakes, Joseph.'

He watched me as he said this and though I knew I shouldn't have, I said, 'Why is everyone so sure it's not *my* mistake?' The question rang out louder than I'd intended in the close air of the chapel. My father's face grew livid. His grip tightened on the wood of the pew till the skin over his knuckles was stretched and pale. He looked up at Jesus, his eyes apologising for his son.

'You think it's a joke?'

I slumped back in the pew like a child. 'You took in Lorna. That wasn't *your* mistake,' I said quietly.

'What has this to do with her? I'm older than you. You're at the beginning of your life.' In fact, I felt at that moment as if I were at the end of it, as if everything was worn out. I looked about me at the shabby chapel. I could imagine a hundred places I would rather have been with my father and yet I'd obligingly followed him here. I waited for him to say something else but he closed his eyes and bent his head to pray. I sat without moving, my hands balled in my lap until he'd finished. When he was done, he stared up at Jesus again, at the hands and feet bleeding red paint, and said with an air of finality, 'Missy won't help you. Neither will Bee. You stay out of other people's trouble.' And he started to his feet before he'd even closed his mouth again, afraid perhaps of allowing me any chance to respond. I thought to myself that he might just as well have stayed seated, for his words alone left no room for mine. He inched round into the aisle, his knees still bent, for the pews were placed too close together in order to allow Jesus a little more leg-room. My father's shuffling movement seemed suddenly comical and I looked away quickly. He straightened up and moved down the aisle to where Jesus' arms seemed to embrace the candle stand and the donation box beside it. My father plucked out the stub of the taper he'd placed in the stand earlier. The candles were cheap and, having sagged almost immediately in the heat, had spilled their wax over the side of the stand onto the floor, exhausting themselves too quickly. He tossed the stub into a nearby pan. When the pan was full, the wax would be melted down, the wicks picked out, the candles refashioned so that they could bleed their gritty whiteness over the floor again in a day or two. He rubbed his fingers together and, seeing him do it, I rubbed mine too, imagining the greasy feel of the cooling wax as it clouded and flaked off his fingertips. He lit another taper and pushed it into place, throwing me a look. *This one*, his eyes said, *is for you.*

Dub took his supper at the boarding house that evening, the first time in a long while that he'd done so, and ordinarily Aunt Mary would have been delighted by his presence at the table. Her manner was certainly light, almost cheerful, through the meal, but there was a tautness to her voice and she watched me more closely than usual. America had said something to her, I thought. As I served him, Dub looked up at me and smiled. I looked away, glancing automatically at his mother. Had she been looking our way just then, she might have read something in my eyes that disquieted her, might have seen the shade of complicity between her houseboy and her son. Afraid of what I would give away, I retreated to the kitchen as soon as I could.

Usually the first to leave, Dub lingered at the dining table as I cleared the dishes. When I started back with the last of them, he excused himself to his mother and, smiling at her as he slid his chair neatly back under the table, followed me to the kitchen. He didn't look at America but said to me, 'Can you bring me up some coffee?' He slipped away again quickly. He was usually happy to fetch his own coffee and America glared at me as I prepared it, but she didn't pass any remark.

When I reached his room, Dub was waiting by the door. He closed it behind me. He ignored the coffee in my hand and said, 'Did you get them?' I looked down at the cup for a minute, puzzled. 'The *herbs*, Joseph.' I held out my free hand, palm up, spread the fingers. He stared at it for several seconds, as if on closer inspection, it might not have proved to be empty. He pushed both hands through his hair and turned away. 'She hasn't told him yet.'

'They won't give them to me.'

'Can you take them?' he said quietly. I pictured the rutted turquoise of the Bukaykay stoop, the smooth brown of Suelita's thigh. The cup grew suddenly hot in my hand. I looked for somewhere to put it down. I remembered my father's face in the chapel, his hand on the wooden pew, candle grease on his fingers but not on mine. I looked away. Dub threw himself onto the bed. 'She'll have to tell him soon,' he said softly. 'You have to think of something. I don't know who else to ask. Can I trust you?' He pushed himself up on his elbows and looked at me for a long moment. The closed door seemed to hulk behind me and I felt myself rounding my shoulders against it. I nodded. He lay back again, staring up at the ceiling.

'Where do you want me to put your coffee?' I said.

He waved a hand without looking at me. 'I don't feel like it now,' he said dolefully. I walked out, closing the door behind me. I paused on the landing and looked at the cup in my hand. It didn't feel like the same coffee I'd carried in and I held it at arm's length as I moved down the stairs.

America looked at it sourly as I came through the door. I emptied the cup into the sink.

'He doesn't want it?' America said. I stared at her aghast for a moment. She waited for me to say something and when I didn't she said, caustically, 'You think I want to ask you your important business? You're such a big man.' I imagined pulling a face at her. Maybe she guessed because she added, furiously, 'You think I even *care*?' I'd long since learned when it was best to keep quiet, and soon enough America subsided, though she watched me for a while as I busied myself at the sink.

Dub didn't come down for another coffee or for any other drink that evening, staying in his room all night and leaving for the garage before I could see him the next morning.

# A LIGHTED WINDOW

From Earl's forecourt, I watched the light from BabyLu's apartment shift over the dusky terrain of her balcony as someone moved about inside. The balcony doors were open to the evening and the light washed out, gilding the leaves of her potted palms, the fronds of her bougainvillea. I couldn't hear any music coming from inside, though it would have been hard to tell; Prosperidad was busy. I looked up and down the street. There was no sign of Eddie's car. Still, I stayed where I was in the shadows around the forecourt, rehearsing what I might say. I imagined myself, just for a moment, as a character in one of Aunt Mary's books: an elderly man, staring up at a lighted window from a Parisian square, the edges around him softened by the evening, waiting to see the beloved face that he hadn't set eyes on in decades. The thought made me feel a little ridiculous and I laughed at myself softly, becoming conscious as I did so of the attention of people coming home from work or bringing in their washing from the nearest balconies of Prosperidad; I'd been standing there with no discernible purpose for a while. And so, though I scarcely felt ready, I crossed the road and climbed the stairs to her apartment and, on reaching it, still hesitated at the door. But she must have been waiting after seeing me loitering below for, the very moment I knocked, the door flew open. She looked at me, her eyes grave. It occurred to me that I should have thought to bring one of her books; it would have been a better reason for being there.

I sat down at the dining table. I hadn't been in her apartment since I'd eaten there with Dub. She'd been animated that evening, a light in her eyes that wasn't in them now. I thought about the baby she was carrying, how in other circumstances, the knowledge of it might have made her eyes even brighter.

'How have you been, Joseph?' she said, and I felt abashed. I should have asked her first.

'Ok,' I said. 'He told me.'

'No foreplay then?' she said tersely. I flushed deeply. Looking remorseful, she said, more kindly, 'You want a drink?'

'Sure,' I said but she stayed in her seat.

'Did he tell you the first thing he said was *shit*?' She exaggerated the word, pulling her mouth into an ugly shape as she said it. I opened my mouth and closed it again. I felt ashamed for Dub. 'Not quite how I pictured it,' she laughed, her voice throaty, rich. She'd been crying.

'What do *you* want?' I said.

She leaned towards me, her eyes moist, beseeching. 'You know *he* never asked me that?' I wasn't sure which *he* she meant, or perhaps I just didn't want to think it might be Dub. Maybe she realised that because she said, 'I haven't told Eddie yet, but I'm going to. Tonight.'

I didn't feel like defending Dub just then, but I said, 'He hasn't been able to think about anything else.' It was the truth at least.

'Really?' she said, more brightly.

'Sure,' I nodded.

'I do know what I want, Jo-Jo,' she almost whispered. Her eyes glistened. Her face was soft, her lips slightly parted. Even with reddened eyes and fatigue seaming her face, she looked exquisite. Of course, I knew then what she wanted and wondered that Dub could have missed it. I should have asked but instead, seeing my opportunity on the brink of collapse, I said, 'I know a woman. There are herbs. I can take you to her. She can sort things out.' The words stumbled out of me and lay scattered and dreadful between us. I watched BabyLu's face change.

Her breathing became shallow, controlled, and she was pale as she said, 'Did he send you to say that?' I felt sick. I wanted to gather everything back up and start again. She stood up. 'You tell him not to come round here again.'

'BabyLu . . .'

'I thought you might understand, but you're just his flunkey. You do as you're told, whether you think it's right or not,' she cried, her voice brittle, the words like fragments of glass. 'Or maybe you just don't think at all.' She jabbed at her temple with her finger furiously, her nails long and scarlet. I wanted to fold her hand softly, safely, into mine but I didn't. I leaned forward, my palms out, wanting to apologise. Her eyes flared and she groped around on the table for something to pick up, but, finding nothing, she crossed her arms again. 'Go away,' she said petulantly, like a child. She looked small, her very daintiness an accusation.

It felt almost unbearable to leave everything poised at that point and yet I was grateful to have been dismissed. As

I reached the door I turned to look at her and, seeing me turn, she clenched her jaw, raised her chin; she would hold everything in until I was gone.

I ran down the stairs and out into the night and set off down Prosperidad, away from Esperanza Street and the Bougainvillea, a dull, hard feeling in my chest.

The apartment blocks here were at least four storeys tall with jutting balconies overlooking the street. In soft globes of lamplight, people ate together, talked over the sound of TV sets, rolled out bedding. It was a street where neighbours hung over railings and called to each other in the darkness, the red tips of cigarettes looping through the air as they talked. I tried to imagine what it might feel like to once again belong somewhere like this, perhaps even with someone, by choice rather than happenstance. But I couldn't quite capture the sense of it, as if there had grown over the years some barrier as light as gauze, floating between me and everything else. BabyLu was right, I thought. It didn't matter whether I knew wrong from right when all I did was whatever I was told, without questioning the role that had been written for me by everyone but myself. And when it was required of me to break through the gauze, when it really mattered, I could not.

I walked about aimlessly for some time before I realised I was crying. I wiped my face with my arm, grateful for the darkness, and then I started running. I tore back through Prosperidad, heedless of the surprised faces around me. As I neared her building, I looked up at her balcony, the room beyond it still full of light. I ran up the stairs. I might not have been so hasty had I recognised the Mercedes, half in shadow, rolling softly away onto Esperanza.

I hammered on the door and when she opened it she looked frightened. I hadn't meant to alarm her and I started explaining all at once as I blundered into the room, still out of breath, imploring her forgiveness.

'Joseph,' she began.

'You were right. I am his flunkey.' I clutched at her hand. 'But what does it matter that I can think or act for myself when nobody requires it of me?'

Behind her, Eddie Casama stood up from the chair I'd occupied only a short while ago, his jacket slung across the back of it, a tumbler in his hand. His tie was loose, his collar buttons undone, a man returning home after a long day at work, hoping for tranquillity. He looked at his watch. He seemed amused and I wondered if this might be a good sign. BabyLu shook her head at me.

'If you had the time,' Eddie said, 'I'd ask you to make up some of your delicious calamansi juice, but you seem in such a hurry.'

BabyLu pushed me gently towards the door and out onto the landing. I let her steer me as I stumbled backwards, offering no resistance. She held my gaze as she closed the door, her eyes the last thing I saw as the sliver of light between the edge of the door and the frame narrowed to nothing and I was left standing in the darkness.

# SOIL AND SAND

This last encounter with BabyLu was so unsettling that it seemed only fitting when, shortly after it, a sorcerer visited the market hall. When he came, America and I were at the boarding house making *leche* flan and, though she didn't mention anything at the time, she later claimed a stab of dread at the precise moment the sugar melted in the pan.

The sorcerer was first seen walking along the coast road from the direction of the passenger jetty. His shirt and trousers were worn thin but, according to Jonah, he walked like a prince. He smelled bad and later, when Jonah retold the story, he said that the smell had preceded the man by quite some distance, so that when he eventually came into view there was little doubt that his presence meant something evil. He was clean-shaven and young, unremarkable except for his eyes, which were penetrating, like a bird of prey's. Over his shoulder he carried a bamboo vessel strung on a cord, and it was this that first gave him away; this and the fact that he made no attempt to disguise it, though of course everyone was already certain what it must contain. He walked unhurriedly, and those he encountered crossed the road to avoid him. When he arrived at the jetty, he paused as if getting his bearings before turning in towards the market hall. The market was quiet when he arrived; most of the day's business had already been completed and the sun was beginning to edge towards the horizon. At the end furthest from the jetty the market hall housed a water pump, at the site of an old well that had long been boarded up. This tap and the well before it supplied all of the surrounding households. The sorcerer took a good look about him and sat for some time on the wall of the old well. He knew of course that no one would ask him to move on. So he lingered, washing his feet under the tap, rinsing his mouth, head and face.

When he left, no one saw in which direction he walked, for it was dark by then. Later still, it was conjectured that he'd made himself invisible, transformed himself into a creature or simply disappeared. At any rate, it was a while before anyone approached the tap, and when they did, what they saw sent them straight to the curandero. When Uncle Bee arrived, he found what he'd feared he might. On the wall of the well was a dead insect, seven legged, with a hair tied around its middle, and next to it a skull, perhaps that of a dog, under which was a small pile of soil and another of sand. Uncle Bee, a healer trained to cure people's ailments with botanics and Latin prayer, was at a loss. Word spread quickly, and soon everyone had shut their children and pregnant women indoors and the elders of the households stood together, some distance from the well, to discuss what these things might mean.

By now the sorcerer was long gone, although, as everyone knew, he had the power to change his shape at will and so, for the next few days, any strange dogs or cats were chased away, a relentless task in a market that sold meat and poultry.

It was decided the proper solution was to bring in the help of another sorcerer to negate the spells of the first. And so a woman who lived some distance away, on the very edge of Greenhills, was cautiously approached and came to assess the situation. She was, Jonah reported, quite perturbed by what she saw but was persuaded, at some risk to herself, to attempt to offset whatever forces of ill had been called into play. Her task accomplished, she too was given a wide berth on her way home and, for some time afterwards, received a kind of wary gratitude from the barrio. However, only the following morning a beetle was found in a bed in a household opposite the market hall and, that same afternoon, a child passed a worm in a neighbouring alley and once again, panic set in.

Uncle Bee did his best to allay his neighbours' fears. Kids, he insisted, passed worms all the time, and who hadn't found a bug in their bed at some point? But these otherwise simple events acquired a magnitude in the light of the sorcerer's visit that they would not have possessed on their own, and the neighbourhood's anxiety grew. Father Mulrooney was approached and eventually, reluctantly, agreed to bless the well and the market hall publicly, an event which, he wryly noted, had a better turn-out than his twice-weekly mass.

The timing of all this was unfortunate, for only the day before the sorcerer's visit a date had been fixed for a rally to protest the impending redevelopment of the area. The rally was to start with public speeches in the market hall, followed by a march through Greenhills and along Esperanza to the town hall on the other side of Salinas. As I'd have expected, Cora, Father Mulrooney and Pastor Levi had been central in organising the event, but so, I learned, had Jonah and – most surprisingly of all – Dante Santos, my father. The group hadn't been secretive about it; Cora's windows were filled with posters, and more decorated the jetty office and the noticeboards of every church in the barrio. The pictures were striking, a vibrant red and black, catching my eye every time I passed by the Coffee Shak. I saw, as well as Cora's style, Benny's hand in them. I determined to ask Cora if she'd save one for me after the rally was over.

With the date fast approaching, Aunt Mary sent me to the jetty as often as she could spare me. And so, a couple of days too late to see him, I stood by the sea wall, glancing along the road now and again in the direction the sorcerer might have walked. A line of boats was in and I watched my father in action; he and Subong carried long bundles of sugar cane between them, like they were carrying a bier. He saw me and smiled. Although I supposed that even my father might sometimes be pleased to see me, seeing him smile was still something of a rarity. I guessed I had Lorna and her baby to thank for his rejuvenation. As they came closer, I heard that he was singing: 'Everybody loves to cha-cha-cha.' But he'd scarcely come into earshot when he cleared his throat and started singing, 'God of mercy, God of grace, show the brightness of thy face,' but only a few lines of it and in the style of Elvis and to the tune of 'Love Me Tender'. I heard a chuckle behind me and turned to see Father Mulrooney.

'Dante's regained his old humour then.' He stopped next to me, and we watched my father and Subong deposit the cane on a waiting cart and head back for another load. When they were done unloading the cane, they came over and greeted the priest. My father clapped me on the shoulder twice but didn't say anything to me. 'You boys ready for the big day?' Mulrooney said.

'Sorcerers don't scare me.' Subong clicked his tongue disdainfully.

My father smiled at him slyly. 'Can't be sure till the day what kind of turn-out we'll get,' he said to Mulrooney. 'People are saying Casama sent him. It's a clever move if he did.' The rest of the jetty boys, always keen to discuss the supernatural, drifted over to join us. In front of Mulrooney they were dismissive of the neighbourhood's reaction. Later, with Pastor Levi, their voices would be softer, less certain, as if they might confess a secret fear to him that he, being a local man, would understand.

'You sure it'll be all right?' Subong said to Mulrooney. 'I mean, you being a man of God and all.'

'It'll be fine, son,' Mulrooney said, but he sounded cross. 'He was just sent to frighten people. It's a trick.'

I listened to their talk. The atmosphere of excitement, of defiance, had been subdued somewhat by the sorcerer's visit but was now starting to resurface. Preparations had resumed. There was to be music and street food to accompany the speeches and already Esperanza was blossoming as it did during a fiesta. Bunting was being hung on the beams of the market hall and soon enough every railing, pole and handle along Esperanza and throughout Greenhills would bob with yellow balloons. The door of Jonah's office stood open, the room beyond a jungle of placards and banners. In the market hall, lengths of bamboo scaffolding were being hoisted into place ready to house a set of public-address speakers that had been borrowed from a nearby school.

There was a flavour of anticipation in the air. The street kids, only dimly aware of the purpose of the rally, were excitable and, gathering to watch the preparations, dared each other into harmless stunts.

I too felt hypnotised by the atmosphere and stayed longer than I meant to, unwilling to return just yet to preparing the Bougainvillea for dinner.

I left my father and wandered over to the market hall where earlier I'd glimpsed Suelita clinging to the top of a ladder. She was there now, one end of a strip of bunting held up to the eaves of the hall, the other end trailing in knotted loops to the ground. I wished she hadn't been wearing a skirt. 'Need any help?' I said, keeping my eyes on the length of bunting between her hands.

She let a few seconds pass before she answered. 'Sure, if you want to grab the other end and help me untangle it.' Her tone was cool. She slipped down to stand next to me and we worked for a while in silence. 'How's the baby?' she said after a while, her voice a little warmer, her eyes flickering in the direction of the sea wall where my father worked with the other jetty boys. The way she said it made it sound almost like she thought it was *my* baby.

I shrugged. 'Fine, I guess.' I watched her coil the unknotted bunting slowly between elbow and thumb. She seemed almost relaxed as she worked. I imagined asking her if she wanted to go for a walk sometime. Or maybe for a movie, not at the proper movie house in town, which I couldn't afford, but a video played on the TV that Caylo ran off a car battery in his front yard. *If guys were trains*, I thought. I waited for her to speak again but she didn't. Her silence made me talkative. 'You know, in America they're going to build a telescope to launch into space. We'll be able to see further into the universe than ever before.'

She laughed then. '*We?*' she said.

I flushed, misunderstanding, and said tersely, 'Can you imagine this place gone?' I suppose I'd hoped to upset her, but she watched me impassively as she smoothed out the bunting, her closed smile settling back on her face.

'All the time,' she said.

I wasn't surprised. 'You think of escaping a lot?'

'Sure. Don't you?'

'Don't know where I'd go.' She looked at me with what I suspected was pity and I said, 'You think you'll actually make it out of here, then?' I was sorry straight away that I'd said it. She jerked the last length of bunting out of my hand and turned away.

'Joseph!' I looked in the direction of my father's voice. Ever mindful of my responsibilities, he was pointing at his watch. I turned back to Suelita but she'd moved away and I saw, from the other side of the market hall, through the lengthening shadows, her mother approaching. I waved at Missy and moved off quickly in the direction of Esperanza Street while she was still out of earshot.

# BARKADA

The shadows were long and deep as I walked up Esperanza Street. I was brooding over what had passed between me and Suelita, replaying everything I'd said, imagining any number of ways I might have said things differently and, preoccupied in this way, I paid little attention to what was going on around me. I was almost past the mouth of the Espiritista alley when the sound of my name being called interrupted my thoughts. I stopped, perplexed for just an instant before I heard it again. I looked back into the alley.

Rico sat on the bench outside the Bukaykay's store. Behind him the hatch was closed, the windows dark. 'Psst,' he beckoned me over, his palm downwards, fingers scurrying in the air like he was scratching an invisible dog. I hadn't seen him for a few days. It didn't surprise me to see him on the store bench now, even though the house was empty. I so rarely saw him anywhere else that it almost seemed the bench was where he belonged. I wondered anxiously for a moment whether he'd seen me alone with Suelita and even as I did so I chastised myself; Rico could hardly claim her as his property. *He's a jerk*, I thought.

I walked over to him. 'You take your head out of your books only to put it straight in the clouds? I was calling and calling,' he reproached me, but his tone was genial, over-familiar. I heard noises behind me and saw that the rest of the Barracudas were there too, in the shadows, one on the corner of Esperanza as if he'd been behind me the whole time.

Rico rose, slipped his arm around my shoulders and said softly, 'Let's walk, Joe,' as if he didn't want to wake anyone, though there were still people about and noise and light leaching out into the evening from behind shutters and doors.

I became conscious now of how late it was. 'I should be back already,' I said, 'but I can come tomorrow.'

He laughed. 'You act so serious all the time, Joe, but actually you're quite funny.' I hesitated, but he pulled me forward with him, his arm heavy across my shoulders. 'It won't take long,' he said.

We walked together through the back alleys into the depths of Greenhills, until the shacks dwindled into coarse grass and litter-strewn streams and long shadowy stretches in which little could be made out. Here, there were few people about. It seemed just the sort of place for the kind of shady business I imagined Rico to be involved in. We stopped under a tree and he turned to me, his eyes meeting mine then looking away again. He laughed again, softly. Somewhere in the darkness I could hear a pig straining at its tether and underneath that, the sound of a radio or perhaps a TV. 'Your pop,' Rico said, 'he's been hard at work on this rally, eh?'

'It affects everyone,' I said. 'You too.'

'I know *my* place.' If I hadn't known him better I might have thought he sounded sad. 'And your boy. He thinks he's a real rock star, huh?'

*Who?* I thought. I heard the *barkada* boys move in closer.

'Can you carry a message for us, Joe?'

'Sure.' I wondered at the theatricality of bringing me through the back of the shanties to this place, if all he wanted of me was that I carried a message.

Rico lowered himself slowly onto an empty oil drum that lay on its side under a tree. Someone had beaten a hollow into the top of the drum to make it into a seat. It would be a good, cool spot even at the height of day. He leaned back against the trunk. 'Sorry, Joe,' he said. He started to hum, a tune I didn't recognise at first, and then, softly, to sing. I heard the words *kung-fu fighting*. I was surprised. His voice was good: melodic and smooth. He might have been a choirboy. The *barkada* boys closed in. They started to beat me, carefully, neatly, with a restraint that I didn't understand at the time. I found myself wondering if Rico only knew the same two lines of the song, for now they seemed to repeat over and over. After what might have been seconds or minutes, the blows stopped and the boys stepped back. Rico's face frowned down at me. 'You'll make sure the message gets through, won't you, Joe?' he said. 'I don't want to do this again.' In the darkness, his eyes looked wounded. His face retreated again and the boys moved back in. I focused on a point somewhere deep inside my body, away from the surface, away from my skin, from every sensation and, after a while, through the gauze, behind the dull tumult, I became aware of thoughts arising and breaking up, distantly, like surf. Down at the jetty, under the market-hall roof, everyone was still working to prepare Esperanza for the rally. None of them even knew I was here. I'd have liked to be with them. I thought about Aunt Mary and almost immediately I pictured Dub. The rock star. I pictured a guitar, the exact model: a

second-hand Stratocaster, a real beauty. A motorbike bought
with his dead father's money. Either object worth far more
than a few stolen herbs. I felt a thin, sharp line of rage that
brightened and dissipated. And then another thought, clear
and unperturbed, about how practised Rico and his boys
were, how professional. I smiled.

# GIRLS WITH JASMINE BRAIDS

The *barkada* boys ebbed away again, leaving me on the ground. Rico knelt down, put his hand on my shoulder, watched me. I was still smiling. 'Joseph?' He sounded puzzled. I looked up at him, wondering what might come next. 'You'll be all right getting home?'

I laughed, wincing as I did so for my chest hurt with even the smallest movement. He laughed quietly too then. And, his hand resting on my shoulder, he patted me once or twice, before leaning into me to push himself up to standing. I closed my mouth hard to stop myself making a sound. 'Got another job to get to,' he said, but he stayed where he was, looking down at me. I kept quiet and still, my eyes open, staring straight ahead at the dark tussocks of grass, the forest of legs. After a moment Rico turned away. 'See you, Joe,' he said as he moved off, his boys falling in behind him.

I listened as their footsteps receded. I let a few more minutes pass, absorbing distant noises: the hum of a truck, a cockerel whose call, raised in pitch at the end, sounded like a question. I took a slow, ragged breath. The smell of earth and leaves filled me, became suddenly nauseating. I rose stiffly, carefully, to my feet.

I sat down on the oil drum from which Rico had directed his boys and stared at the spot where I'd lain, but in the darkness it divulged nothing. I ran a hand slowly over my face and body. My other hand ached. My left eye was starting to swell and from above it a sticky crust of blood or dirt came away under my fingers.

I cleared my throat and said out loud, 'Where to?' The sound of my voice surprised me; it sounded as it always did. I thought about the Bougainvillea. The boarding house was full for the weekend and the guests would still be awake at this hour. The Bukaykays would likely still be down at the jetty with my father, Jonah and the boys, and even if they were not, I didn't want Suelita to see me like this. There was only one other place to go and so I set off for my father's apartment, knowing that Lorna at least would be in, and if not, then perhaps Elisa and Aunt Bina next door. It seemed to take a long time to get there; Rico and his boys had spared my legs but, even so, every step jarred.

The courtyard of my father's building seemed to gather around me as I entered it. It was quiet for that time of evening. A few of the windows were dark and the light from the others settled in mid air in a milky haze, leaving the ground in shadow. I lowered myself onto the bottom step of the stairwell and leaned back gratefully for a moment against the cool concrete wall. Overhead, my father's windows were open and through them the sound of Elvis Presley curled out into the evening. Elvis sounded far too cheerful.

I got to my feet again and climbed the stairs. At the top, I glanced at Bina and Elisa's door, but even if Elisa was in, her mother might have answered first and Aunt Bina would certainly have pressed me for details.

I knocked softly on my father's door. Elvis quietened and I knocked again. After a moment, the door opened. Lorna must have been expecting my father, for she opened the door smiling but when she saw me she screamed. I hadn't anticipated that and said rather stupidly, my hands protesting in the air in front of me, 'It's only me. It's Joseph.' My hands were filthy, bloodstained, puffy. She stared at them, appalled, and then up at my face. Behind me, Bina's door flew open and Elisa peered out, her eyes bright with alarm. When she saw me she clapped a hand over her mouth, but she quickly regained herself, for she called inside to her mother, 'It's ok, Mom. Lorna just saw a rat.' She shrugged at me, apologetically.

I heard Bina say, 'That good-for-nothing landlord. I tell him we have rats and what does he do about it? Nothing.'

Elisa closed the door quietly behind her and came out into the passageway. The two girls half pulled, half pushed me inside my father's apartment and into a chair. Elisa took charge. She peered at me closely, at my face, my eye – which had almost completely closed up – at my hands and chest. She had a mournful expression, one that seemed suddenly adult, and I considered dully where I'd seen it before. I felt shaken when I remembered; Aunt Bina had worn the same look at my mother's vigil. 'What happened, Joseph?' Elisa said, and pursed her lips at me when I shook my head, another of her mother's expressions. I kept quiet and was grateful when she didn't persist. 'Does Dante keep iodine and bandages?' she said to Lorna. I was startled to hear her utter my father's name without the prefix *Uncle*. Lorna shrugged helplessly. She went into the kitchen to look but came back empty-handed. My arrival had disturbed the baby and now it started to whimper and then to cry. Lorna picked it up, rocked it. After a minute the baby hushed but she continued to rock it, staying at the other end of the room.

Elisa stood up. 'We have iodine,' she said. She walked to the door, her movements brisk, officious, though her slightness gave the impression of a child playing at adulthood. She left the door ajar. Lorna came closer and sat down on one of the dining chairs and watched me. She held the baby tightly, its head facing her breast, away from the sight of me, and rocked it rhythmically, rapidly. I wondered if she was trying to comfort herself or the child.

Elisa returned, a small bottle pressed to her lips like a finger. She closed the door carefully, making barely a sound. Shaking the bottle gently, she knelt down in front of me. Her face grew stern. She worked without speaking, only hissing occasionally if a crust of blood came away and started to bleed afresh, or a cut looked deeper than expected. I was aware of the smell of her scalp and of the jasmine the girls had braided through their hair. She bathed the flesh around my eye and dabbed it with iodine, moved on to my hand and to every other cut and scrape. She glared at me now and then as she worked. All the while, Lorna rocked in the chair with the baby.

When Elisa was done, we sat quietly for a while. My eye had completely closed over now and my face ached. Lorna kept the baby turned away from me until it was asleep and then took it back to its crib. She went into the kitchen and started to prepare rice and boil some water for a drink. My father would be home soon.

Elisa sat back on her haunches, her arms crossed over her knees, and studied me. The hardened jut of her mouth reminded me of Missy Bukaykay. 'Want me to stay till he comes?' she said. I'd have liked to say yes but I didn't. Elisa repeated her question. I shrugged. I was exhausted. 'I'd better go then,' she said reluctantly, 'or Mom will come knocking and then you'd have some explaining to do.'

After she left, Lorna, uncertain what else to do but feed me, put a plate of rice and beans in front of me. She stayed in the kitchen doorway, hugging herself like a child, her eyes still fearful. 'You heard from your family?' I said thickly, for my lip was swollen and my jaw stiff. I had to say it several times before she understood me.

She shook her head. 'Eat.' Her voice was scarcely more than a whisper.

I turned my attention to the food, more for her sake than my own; I wasn't hungry and eating was slow going, every mouthful painful and laborious. I'd hardly made any progress when we heard my father at the door. Lorna stepped forward, her body blocking his view of me. She was silent as he came through the door, yet he said, straight away, 'What is it?' He looked past her to me, taking a few seconds to understand. He threw his cap onto the table and rubbed his hand over his hair. 'Who?' he said. I stared at him. He sat down next to me and surveyed my injuries. He nodded at the iodine stains. 'Bina?' he said.

'Elisa.'

'I'll take you to Bukaykay.' I shook my head. 'You need a *doctor*?' he looked worried as he said it. I shook my head again.

Lorna brought out a plate for him but he pushed it away. It was me that pushed it back towards him but it wasn't until I bent once again to my own plate that he started to eat, slowly and without relish. He finished before I did and waited. When I'd had as much as I could manage, he took my plate and we moved to the sink together to wash our hands. Lorna took his place at the table and started to eat a little now. 'I tell her we should eat together, or she should eat first if I'm late, but she waits on me anyway,' he said.

There was nothing more to do now and my father walked back to the boarding house with me. The night air was cool. The ground had all but given up the last of the day's warmth. 'I didn't want to ask in front of her,' he said as we turned onto Esperanza. I knew what was coming. 'Was it anything to do with what you asked Missy? About this girl and her trouble?' His eyes scanned the street as he spoke, his last word a murmur. His delicacy infuriated me suddenly. I didn't reply and he didn't ask again. I wondered if he might tell Aunt Mary but he would be concerned about how it might look to her, I thought scornfully, how it might reflect on him. We walked on in silence, my father slowing his step frequently for me to catch up.

When we arrived at the boarding house, I wanted to go in through the kitchen door, slip straight to my room, but my father strode right up to the front door and hammered on it. America must have been waiting for me because she opened it almost immediately, her mouth pinched with the effort of holding in whatever lecture she'd prepared for my return. But as soon as she saw me, the words deserted her. I still hadn't seen myself in a mirror and didn't know how dreadful I looked. I stared back at her miserably.

She ushered us into the kitchen and left us there. I rose from the table hissing at her to come back. I didn't want her to tell Aunt Mary what state I'd returned in. America, if she heard me, didn't even slow down and when she returned it was with Aunt Mary in tow. The two women looked over my injuries, America with a look of dread, Aunt Mary with the same kind of contained anger that Elisa had worn earlier, that showed only in the precise line of her lips. Her voice when she spoke was business-like. She asked my father what had happened before she asked me. 'He won't tell me,' my father said.

I stayed silent and closed my eyes. All I wanted now was to sleep but Aunt Mary and America examined in turn my arms, my hands, my face and chest. Finally, satisfied that nothing was broken, America moved to the Frigidaire and took out some milk to heat for me. 'No,' I said softly. She replaced the milk and poured out a glass of chilled water instead and I sat turning it in my hands as they talked.

'The rally is just days away,' Aunt Mary said, and I knew what she was thinking, how obvious a target that made me when both she and my father were involved.

Lola Lovely came down the stairs and into the kitchen, her *pañuelo* wrapped tightly about her, over her nightgown. 'I heard the door,' she said. Then, on seeing me: 'Oh!' She crossed herself. I stood up but Aunt Mary pressed me gently back into my seat. Lola Lovely said, 'Has he been fighting?'

'Ma'am,' my father started to explain.

But Aunt Mary said, 'This isn't Joseph's fault. He was set upon.'

Lola Lovely glared at her daughter, ignoring my father. 'This is what your politics bring into the house!' she said. 'Look at the boy!' I folded my arms on the table and sank my head onto them. I didn't want to hear any more. The shock and anger that had propelled me home had by now quite evaporated and I was spent. America shook me gently.

She pulled me to my feet and, picking up my glass, started towards the passageway that led to my room. I followed her mutely.

The room was just as I'd left it. Its familiarity, like the sound of my own voice in the darkness earlier, was almost absurd. I lay down on my mat, pulled my blanket over me and listened to my father's voice for what seemed like a long time but may only have been minutes, for his words blended into my dreams, and when I woke again it was morning.

# FILIPINO DELICACIES

When Uncle Bobby was still alive, Aunt Mary's house was rarely empty. Back then, of course, it wasn't a boarding house taking in strangers. The guests were friends from the rich families of Puerto or weekending from Manila: the women, perfumed, wore dresses from Paris; the men came in suits made by their family tailors. I imagined sometimes how it might have been and, in my head, the men all looked like the model in the cigarette ad on my wall, beautiful and silent, and the women like Vilma Santos, their laughter breaking out in the dark rooms like sunlight through cloud. There were photographs from that time, taken on Uncle Bobby's camera, the guests posing stiffly around the settee, glasses raised, or captured without warning, heads thrown back, teeth and throats exposed, arms blurred by movement. It was hard to imagine Aunt Mary in such a gathering, besieged by glamour and chatter. It seemed to me that she and her house were meant for stillness. But she was unfailingly hospitable and I imagined her watching for empty glasses or foundering conversation while Uncle Bobby shone at the centre of things, his voice slowing, his gestures becoming more expansive as he drank, blind to anyone's needs but his own.

America's cooking even then was the talk of dining rooms across the island, or so she said, and the guests tried to poach her for their own households many times over, each wage offered bigger than the last. But she stayed, loyal to Aunt Mary, and when I asked her why, she said that Aunt Mary had a way of talking to her that made her not mind being a servant. I knew exactly what she meant.

When Uncle Bobby died, the house fell into silence, though whether this was because of grief or Aunt Mary's innate need for solitude, I never knew.

Before that week, in all the time I'd been at the Bougainvillea, Aunt Mary had never thrown a dinner party. Though close friends and relatives came to stay on occasion and America cooked for them, these were informal evenings, without display. It was unexpected, then, when she announced, in the run up to the rally, that we would be entertaining for a second time. 'Well, good,' said Lola Lovely. 'This place can get like a morgue sometimes.'

'Do you remember the Robellos, Mom? Joey and Alice?'

'*Alice!*' Lola Lovely pinched her brow as if she was thinking hard before she added, 'Well a man will make one or two bad choices in his life. It can't be helped.'

Aunt Mary continued without a flicker. 'I'll invite Frankie Reyes and his wife too. It's been a long time since they'll have seen you; they won't refuse.'

'Perhaps America could serve. We could give Joseph the evening off,' Lola Lovely looked anxiously at my bruises.

'Do you not feel up to it, Joseph?' Aunt Mary said.

'I'm ok, ma'am.'

'But how will it *look*,' cried Lola Lovely. 'As if our houseboy indulges in street brawls.'

'He has nothing to hide, Mother. If they ask, I shall tell them.'

'If they have any breeding, they'll be too polite to ask. So there goes your plan.' Aunt Mary seemed not to hear this.

It was painful to move around and I knew there would be a lot of extra work involved but I was grateful for the distraction and found myself looking forward to it. I leafed through the recipe books in the sala and wondered what Aunt Mary might suggest America cook. Something French, I thought, the food arranged on the plate like a portrait. And so I was surprised yet again when Aunt Mary asked America to fetch a pork leg in time to prepare crispy *pata*, which she said was one of Judge Robello's favourites.

Judge Robello looked like he had many favourites. He kept his eye on every tray I brought round and tried everything that America sent out without it seeming to shrink his appetite for dinner. He was a large man, which made him look older than he must have been.

'Still the same woman?' he said, through a mouthful.

'Yes, America is still with me,' Aunt Mary said.

'It's easy enough to find a woman who can cook,' said Alice Robello, 'but to find a woman who can follow instructions and keep a clean kitchen, too, is nearly impossible.'

Alice Robello, several years younger than Aunt Mary and years younger again than her husband, had once been a beauty queen: Miss Puerto. She went on to compete in a national pageant but wasn't placed, becoming instantly one of the group of girls who fell into shadow as the crown was lifted onto another's head, left to look on, smile graciously. But by then she'd been proposed to by Joey Robello and married quickly into money. She appeared younger than her years and spoke and moved as if an invisible camera were always on her, turning her best side towards the most attractive man in the room – not always, as America noted wryly in the kitchen, towards her husband. Though she was now mother to three children, she was still slim, and when she came in, she flashed a critical eye at Aunt Mary's figure, hiding her triumph quickly. Wherever she moved, she left behind her a trail of vanilla.

'We've had a succession of cooks and servants,' the judge said. 'No one does it quite the way Alice wants. Low fat! Where's the pleasure in that anyway?'

'Not easy to find someone who cooks like *this*,' Joni Reyes, wife of Frankie Reyes, cut in.

'*I* found her,' said Lola Lovely, coming in late. She was wearing a short-sleeved dress the colour of amber and she cradled one arm carefully with the other. I saw that her cast had been removed. Alice Robello and Joni Reyes stood up to greet her. 'Of course, before that we had a succession of girls,' Lola Lovely continued, 'but the pretty ones, you know, they don't think they need to learn how to keep a house properly. Our America was quite plain.' Alice Robello exclaimed her pleasure loudly at seeing Lola Lovely again after so long. Lola Lovely smiled beatifically. 'Yes, I'm still alive. Manila hasn't killed me yet.'

'How's your beautiful house?' Alice Robello said.

'Joni,' Lola Lovely said, 'I'm sure America would be happy to give her recipes to your cook.'

'We don't have one at the moment. The girl got herself pregnant. Frankie had to fire her,' Joni Reyes said. Lola Lovely's eyes glittered. 'Anyway,' Joni continued, 'we like eating out.' She wore a look of mild discontent, perhaps disappointment, which didn't leave her all evening. According to America, Joni Reyes had met her husband at university, where she'd studied briefly before dropping out to get married. They'd had their only child, a son perhaps Benny's age, not long afterwards, at a private hospital in Puerto. I'd never seen her husband, Engineer Reyes, before, and when he arrived he already looked drunk.

'Nice to see the old guy again,' he said, lifting his glass to the pictures of Uncle Bobby on the piano. 'We used to have some good games. He was lousy at poker though.' Joni glanced at Aunt Mary but if Aunt Mary was thinking about the freeholds her dead husband had lost to Frankie Reyes she showed no sign. Lola Lovely tapped her fingers irritably on her glass.

'Change is inevitable. Isn't that what our friend Mr Casama always says?' said Aunt Mary.

'Please don't get the men started on *that*!' Alice Robello said, fanning her hand in mock exhaustion.

'Mr Casama came to see me recently,' Aunt Mary continued, smiling at her. 'I hadn't had the opportunity to really meet him properly before. Do you know him well, Judge?'

'In passing,' the judge said. 'You've been out of circulation for some time.' Judge Robello's eyes wandered over the pictures on the piano, the flowers on the card table. 'You've kept that marvellous cook to yourself for too long.'

'Joseph, would you see how America is doing please?' Aunt Mary said.

'Over some gal?' Frankie Reyes jerked his glass in my direction, his little finger pointing out my bruises.

'Joseph's father is one of the organisers of tomorrow's rally,' Aunt Mary said, and she put a hand lightly on my arm to keep me there for a moment. I kept my eyes on the tray I was holding while everyone looked at me. The women turned away quickly. Lola Lovely raised her glass to her daughter.

'I boxed at university,' the judge said. 'It won't spoil your looks.' I glanced up at him but he didn't meet my eye.

'What do you know of Mr Casama's plans for Esperanza?' Aunt Mary said to no one in particular.

'Oh, come, it's been far too long since we saw you, Mary, let's not talk business,' the judge said.

'I've been out of circulation but not earshot,' Aunt Mary said.

'I just love this old, solid furniture,' Joni Reyes said, running her hand over the coffee table. 'Frankie likes all the smoked glass and chrome stuff. He'd prefer to live at the office, I think.' As I turned to leave, I caught the flicker of annoyance in Aunt Mary's face.

Back in the kitchen, America had laid out the serving dishes on the table and was sprinkling coriander leaves on mounds of hot chicken and stuffed squid, wiping away errant spots of gravy. She talked to herself as she worked. Her eyes glinted happily at me as I walked in. 'They might know about *consortiums*, but no one knows about food like I do,' she said. It smelled so good I had to swallow several times.

When I got back to the sala, their voices seemed faster, more heated, as if a hard truth had been unearthed. I stood in the doorway, waiting for an opportunity to announce dinner. Judge Robello was saying, 'He was born right in Colon Market. His mother was a *balut* vendor. And *he's* not sentimental about the place.'

'He's a real businessman,' Frankie Reyes said appreciatively. 'He understands profit.'

'He said he didn't even wear shoes till he was a grown man,' said Alice Robello. 'They couldn't afford them. Said if he took his shoes off we'd see the feet of a beggar! Can you imagine?'

'Pisses higher than anyone now,' Frankie Reyes said.

'Frankie!' His wife feigned embarrassment.

'Sorry, ma'am,' Reyes twirled his glass in Lola Lovely's direction. 'Seriously though, might be worth thinking about investing in his scheme. You'd get ten-, even twentyfold back on your money.'

'I'm not really interested in investing. I'm more concerned about the effect on our community.' Aunt Mary frowned.

'Of course there'll be losers,' Judge Robello said, a little impatiently, I thought. 'But there'll always be people who win and people who lose. It's our duty, for the sake of our families to make sure we stay on top, don't you think? I mean, people depend on us. And not just our own children. They all come to us – *I need money for my son's wedding, Uncle, for my daughter's school books, Uncle* – for this, for that. Everyone from the gardener to the chauffeur. Hands in their pockets or hands held out for something.'

Frankie Reyes laughed in agreement. 'Yes, a quiet redistribution of wealth,' he said.

'Some of these families have been here as long as our own,' Aunt Mary said. 'This is their home and they'll be made to leave it.'

'They don't own the land,' said Frankie Reyes.

Aunt Mary studied him gravely. 'Is there no alternative to simply sweeping them aside?' she said. The men were quiet, amused even.

'Looks Italian,' Lola Lovely said, leaning forward to finger the lapel of Alice Robello's suit.

'Milan. Joey and I were there last year on vacation.'

Aunt Mary sat back in her chair. 'America is ready,' I said from the door. They looked up at me, surprised. They hadn't noticed my return.

'Perfect timing, eh?' said Frankie Reyes. Then, apologetically to Aunt Mary, 'I'd just been wondering what your Monica had made for dinner.'

As they settled themselves at the dining table, Alice Robello said, 'Rome, Florence, Bologna, Milan, Venice, Rome.'

'So much *art*,' said Joni Reyes.

'Did you get to the Brera gallery in Milan?' said Aunt Mary. 'There's a very moving painting there of a march by agricultural workers. *Fiumana*. It puts me in mind of tomorrow.'

'We saw a lot of paintings.'

'Everyone does the gallery thing,' said Joni Reyes, 'but after a while, the paintings all start to look the same, don't you find?'

'This particular one – ' Aunt Mary said.

'And Leonardo Da Vinci!' said Alice Robello. 'I said to Joey, wouldn't that David look great in our lobby?' Everyone laughed. Even Aunt Mary smiled.

'Will you be at the rally, Mrs Lopez?' Judge Robello asked.

'Oh, I'm not one for crowds, Joey,' Lola Lovely said.

I stood in the corner of the room, watching for cues from Aunt Mary. I'd learned so much from her about generosity. Her eyes flickered over the serving dishes, noting what was left, what might need refilling. I knew she took in her guests' plates too, noticed who had eyed an out-of-reach dish more than once. When she looked up at me, I stepped forward quickly, trying to anticipate each request. I knew the painting Aunt Mary had mentioned. I'd seen it in one of her books and would have liked to tell her that I'd been moved by it too, by the way the figures emerged from the canvas like ghosts, like stories waiting to be told. Of course I didn't, though later I decided that she'd have liked to hear it, even if it was only from me.

After dinner, the guests returned to the sala and I brought the coffee through. I thought I'd tell Cora who her coffee had been served to the next time I saw her. I imagined her eyes full of mischief and fury.

Aunt Mary tried again as everyone settled back in their seats, Frankie Reyes leaning against the piano. 'We really must talk about what is going to happen to these people if we don't *do* something.'

'Why?' said Judge Robello. 'You're not even one of them, Mary.'

'Exactly!' said Lola Lovely, her voice triumphant. I looked at Aunt Mary, her dismay, and I thought that, after all, the judge was right. She, like the rest of them, would endure the storm to come; it would be the likes of America and I that would be washed away.

After that, no more was said about it. They talked instead about their children and their plans for university, about the coming year's vacations, about the scent of oleander, the feel of good silk. When they left, Aunt Mary shut herself in her study and was still there when I retired to my room for the night.

# ACRYLIC ON RICE SACKS

The small square of my window was still dark when America woke me the next morning. 'Quit grumbling,' she said. 'I left you as long as I could,' though I hadn't said a word. I followed her to the kitchen where I was met by rows of cooling bread rolls and sponge cakes already sliced into rectangles in their trays. Aunt Mary was up too, dressed for the day in a blouse and skirt, her hair neatly pinned even at this hour. She smiled at me as I came in and though my entire body ached for sleep I smiled too, for the kitchen, rinsed by a blue-grey light from the yard and filled with the round, dark smell of baking, felt welcoming. Aunt Mary had prepared coffee and she poured out a cup for me, stirring in a spoonful of sugar without my having to ask. She tapped the spoon on the cup's rim to shake off the drops, frowned as the sound rang out in the thin early-morning light. She looked pale and I wondered if she'd slept at all. She placed the cup carefully, almost noiselessly, on the table in front of me.

America sat down beside me and started to slice tomatoes and cucumber, humming softly to herself as she worked. Aunt Mary moved about in silence, an absorbed look on her face. She fetched a tray of rolls from the counter and placed it on the table. I put down my cup and picked up a roll, split and buttered it, sprinkling sugar inside before closing it up again. Aunt Mary sat down opposite me and started to layer sandwiches. 'Not quite so much sugar perhaps,' she said. 'I doubt many of the Greenhills children bother to clean their teeth properly.' She emphasised the last word. I hadn't thought to ask who the food was for. I buttered the next roll more heavily and Aunt Mary, watching my hands, smiled at me again. 'I thought,' she continued, her tone almost apologetic, 'that the symbolism might not escape Eddie Casama and his consortium.' I liked the way she said *symbolism*: easily, without pause, as if certain I'd understand her.

Around us, the boarding house lay still and we worked without interruption; Benny had left for Cora's before even America was up and Dub was still in bed. When, eventually, I heard Dub on the stairs, I pushed myself back from the table and started to assemble his breakfast. I examined my face in the polished surface of his breakfast tray as I placed his food on it. If anything, I looked worse. The swelling had subsided but the bruising had risen and spread and was livid to look at. My arms were no better but I had worn a long-sleeved shirt with my shorts, resisting the urge to roll up the cuffs when they got in the way.

I took the food through to the dining room and arranged it before Dub on the table without raising my eyes. I started to pour out a coffee. Dub smiled up at me but, on seeing my face, looked away again unhappily as he had done several times over the preceding days. He picked listlessly at his plate, and though he opened his mouth as if he might say something, he seemed each time to reconsider. I withdrew to the kitchen to let him eat in peace.

A little later he came through into the kitchen. He looked about at the trays of rolls still on the counters, the skyscrapers of newspaper-wrapped cake on the table. America leaned forward, ready to swat his hand, but Dub thrust his hands into his jeans pockets and bent down to speak to his mother. America nudged me. I got up from the table and walked through to the dining room to retrieve Dub's breakfast tray. He'd hardly touched his food. I covered his plate before I returned to the kitchen, kept my back to America as I scraped the remains into the waste bin. Her eyes were on me as I turned back.

A strong yellow light washed the kitchen now, accentuating the lines around America's mouth and cutting shadows under the carton flaps as she packed up the food. As she filled each box I carried it through to the hallway and, when the last of them was done, Dub and I loaded everything into a taxi under Aunt Mary's direction. His eyes swept over the dark stains on my hands and face as we worked.

The back seat full, Aunt Mary climbed into the front of the cab. The driver waited, his brown arm languid out of the open window, fingers gently drumming the warming metal as Dub moved over to his bike and kicked it off its stand. Together, they pulled out of the drive for the short ride to the jetty where Dub was to help his mother unload, before doubling back to Prosperidad and Earl's garage.

Back in the kitchen I skulked about, finding small tasks and avoiding America's gaze. 'You plan to sneak about here all day?' she said eventually. I buffed the spoon I'd just washed, studied my upside-down reflection. 'I might not know all the details,' she said, 'but I'll bet you're the last person who should be shamed by how you look.'

*

Esperanza Street teemed under a cloudless sky. People moved in drifts downhill towards the market hall, while overhead banners snapped like sails between lamp posts and balloons tugged against their tethers at door handles and railings. In the distance, the public-address system was being tested: Jonah's voice. The air smelled different, lighter. It smelled of the ocean and of warm asphalt. Gone was the scent of fried pork and hot oil, for Johnny Five Course had wheeled his cart down to the jetty the evening before to be certain of a pitch, a roll of bedding strapped across his counter. On the other side of the street, Abnor's tea-stall was still in its usual spot, but it was closed up and padlocked and, behind it, Primo's windows were shuttered.

Halfway down the hill, the stretch of sidewalk outside the Coffee Shak was empty except for Ignacio Sanesteban, who was working away at something on the Shak's frontage, his movements uncharacteristically quick and jerky. Behind him, still stacked indoors beside the pastry counter, the white plastic sidewalk chairs formed a bright column. Ignacio straightened up as we approached, placed down the wooden board he had just pulled away from the window frame. He stepped towards us, his hands out like a policeman stopping cars. He crunched as he moved and, in the same instant that I recognised the sound, I made out the mound of broken glass behind him on the doorstep, sunlight scattering from its innumerable edges. From it, a trail of dust and shards tracked back into the interior like the tail of a comet. I gaped at the empty frame of the Coffee Shak window, a few glass teeth still protruding in places from the wood, mouthing its belated protest. Ignacio shrugged. He looked me over, his hands on his hips. 'You gave the other guy a good hiding too, I hope,' he said.

'Looks like a bomb,' America eyed the broom that leaned up against the doorframe.

I remembered Rico's voice in the darkness: *got another job to get to.* 'You see who did it?' I said.

'I got my suspicions. Still, it's just a window.' He looked down at my hands. I pushed them into my pockets. 'Your pop's been working hard on the rally too, eh? Cowardly way to do it though – get at a man through his kid.'

'No-names-mentioned wouldn't be where he is if he did things straight like the rest of us,' America muttered. Ignacio cast his eyes about the street and, seeing him do it, America added testily, 'At my age what have I got to be afraid of?' She threw me a dark look.

'Want some help?' I said to Ignacio, hopefully.

'*You* don't need to be near anything sharp right now.' He turned a piece of glass over with the edge of his sneaker.

'You better take it easy today, Joseph Santos,' America glowered at me. She managed to make it sound like a threat. I was disappointed. I'd have liked to stay at the Shak, hear a little Dusty, keep out of sight.

Ignacio moved back to the window. He pulled a cloth out of his back pocket and bent down to study one of the remaining fragments that clung to the frame. It was peaked like the fin of a milkfish. He wrapped the cloth around its point and, gripping it gingerly between forefingers and thumbs, started tugging it back and forth, loosening it. 'I'm ready to believe,' he said softly, drawing out the word like an evangelist, as he got to his feet and held the freed shard up to the light, 'that it doesn't pay to be honest in this world.'

'Amen,' said America loudly.

At the seaward end of Esperanza Street, where it broadened to run alongside the market hall before merging with the coast road to become the jetty, a sizeable crowd had gathered. The air was rich with the smell of food. Stalls lined every alleyway, the vendors talkative behind mounds of fruit or meat, pyramids of cans and bottles.

The market hall had been cleared out and under its canopy, on the Greenhills side, a stage had been built with speakers on either side of it. Towards the back of the stage, a row of red plastic garden chairs waited. A microphone lay in the well of the centre chair, its lead coiled under the seat like a snake.

In front of the stage, Cora and Benny were busy with something on the ground. The Greenhills children, clustered about the nearby pillars, watched them at work. Every now and then Cora looked up overhead and around her, as if considering some invisible structure, and when she did, the kids looked up too, scanning the roof for clues.

I stopped when I saw Benny and made as if to go to him but America had spotted my father standing with Jonah near the sea wall. She started towards them and, after a moment's hesitation, I trailed after her. When the men saw me, they came to meet us. 'Looks bad,' Jonah said as they drew close. 'Dante says you won't tell him who did it.'

'Only one candidate,' America said.

'I remember him when he was starting out,' Jonah said. 'Not so obvious then what kind of a man he'd turn out to be.'

'You sleeping any better?' my father asked me. I was still aching too much to sleep through a whole night.

'Like the dead,' I lied, without thinking, and I saw how it startled him.

Subong came over and looked me up and down. He whistled through his teeth. 'They spared your legs, huh?' he said. He looked at my father. My father ignored him.

The men eyed me curiously for a minute or two. I looked away, back towards the stage. 'What's left to do?' I said.

'Sit for a minute. One of the boys can fetch you a drink,' Jonah said.

'There are enough hands about today.' My father placed his hand on my shoulder, carefully.

Jonah looked over to where a group of jetty boys loitered near his office. He put his fingers in his mouth and whistled. One of the boys broke away from the group and jogged over to us. It was Dil, one of Rico's Barracudas. For a moment, I couldn't remember whether Dil had been there that night, but then I saw him again in the shadows under the tree, near the oil drum, the distant sounds without origin in the darkness, the smell of earth and sweat and blood. My stomach lurched and I felt a chill break over my skin and subside again. My father's hand tightened momentarily on my shoulder. Dil raised an enquiring eyebrow at Jonah, then turned to regard me blankly. I glared back but he held my eyes. I looked away first. 'You look rough, Joe,' he said easily.

'Get him a Pepsi,' Jonah said. 'Cold. On my tab.'

'Sure, Boss.' Dil smiled at me and walked to the *sari-sari* store near the corner. I watched him move away, his step casual, blameless. He returned just as leisurely, winked as he held the bottle out to me. I didn't want it but I took it and as I did so my finger brushed his. Involuntarily, I flinched. It was scarcely perceptible, but I was sure he noticed. He smiled at me again. 'See you around, Joe,' he said, and walked back to Jonah's office. I felt a surge of fury, as much at my own response as at him.

I held the Pepsi, forgotten for a moment until Jonah said, 'Better cold, eh?' Still feeling sick, I sipped slowly, barely tasting it. My father studied me as I drank. America's eyes remained on Dil for several minutes and quickly enough the Barracuda busied himself, keeping his back to her.

There was plenty still to be done but no one would accept my help, their eyes first asking my father's permission only to be refused. I felt fraudulent standing idle while around me everyone worked and at last I excused myself to go in search of something to do.

The chatter in the market hall formed a steady low note pierced every now and then by the bright, clear counterpoint of Cora's voice. I followed the sound to its source, to where she stood with Benny, her hands moulding the air between them as she talked. Benny, bending to hear, hefted a hand drill from one palm to the other and back again. On the ground in front of them nine large panels lay face down on plastic sheets. Cora stopped talking and started to circle the panels, swooping now and again to chalk red marks onto each frame. She looked up as I approached, staring at me for several seconds before she uttered a cry of comprehension and then, throwing down her chalk, she marched over to me. She lifted my chin, her fingers red with chalk dust, moved my head this way and that, inspecting my face. 'Benny told me,' she said. 'Your father said you won't say who.' I looked past her to Benny. He glanced guiltily down at the panels, his hands still, the empty palm open, waiting. Cora brushed red dust from my chin with the heel of her hand. I tilted my face like a child to let her finish. 'Any part of you still a normal colour?' She looked me over. I wriggled my toes. She smiled down at them.

'I saw Ignacio,' I said.

'He was wearing gloves like I told him?'

'Sure, I think.' I dropped my eyes.

'You think, eh?'

'So where's this famous mural?'

'You're looking right at it,' Cora pointed to the nearest panel with her foot.

'Magnificent,' I said.

'That's the back of it.'

'I know.'

She smiled crookedly, made as if to jab a finger into my chest, stopping just short of me even as I recoiled. 'Only bad jokes till it stops hurting, huh?'

'What still needs doing?'

'Oh no,' Cora pulled a face, her hands waving a vigorous protest. Benny started shaking his head. But I was insistent; to do something physical was a kind of defiance. Cora's eyes gleamed at me.

Under her direction, I steadied each panel as Benny drilled holes in the frame. We bolted the panels together, screwed in a line of hooks along the top edge, threaded through a rope. The mural was to be hauled upright and suspended from the rafters just above the stage. I was keen to get a look at it. I ran a finger along the frame, over the line of staples that secured the rolled edge of the canvas, rubbed the tip of my thumb gently against a familiar mark on the fabric. 'Gold Cup,' said Benny. I peered closely at the mark. The panels were constructed from rice sacks stitched together and stretched over wooden pallets, the Gold Cup brand on the cloth just visible in places between the slats or emerging through the paint at the very edges.

When we were done I got to my feet slowly, like an old man, conscious of Cora and Benny's eyes on me. Cora wagged a finger at me first, then at Benny. 'Stay put,' she said. She stalked away, glancing back over her shoulder more than once.

Benny relaxed back against the stage. He pulled out a peso and started playing with it, doing sleight-of-hand tricks. I smiled as I watched him; he wasn't very good, fumbling the peso several times. The circle of kids watching him drew in closer, their eyes on the coin. After a minute or two of bending to retrieve it, Benny stopped and, studying the gathered children, handed the coin to the smallest before turning his back decisively. The kids didn't pester him. They moved away to try their hand at palming it just as he had done and with little more success. Benny, here without his sketchbook, watched them for a while.

He turned back to me and, smiling, started to roll his shirt-sleeve down, shaking the cuff over his hand. There were paint stains on his sleeve, a crust of colour on the stiff edge of the cuff. He bunched the fabric in his fist and, reaching up, wiped my cheek carefully. I blinked at him, surprised. He didn't say a word but carried on and when he was done, he rolled his sleeve up again, thumbing the red chalky smudge into the cloth before he folded it. I eyed his sleeve and wondered how easily I might get the paint and the chalk dust out of the fabric when it came to laundering it.

Benny took out a Marlboro and lit it. I stared at him. The whole of Esperanza might be about, any number of people who knew his mother, but he relaxed back against the stage, smoking. I pictured the man in the cigarette ad, the blond woman's eyes on him. Aware of my gaze, Benny turned to me, puzzled, and opening the packet again, slid a cigarette towards me with his thumb. I looked at it, thought about Rico on the bench outside the Bukaykays' store, a cigarette sloping in his fist, waiting for the day Suelita might board his train. I shook my head.

I glanced about the market hall. In every corner, some-one was working away. From the direction of the jetty, I saw Missy Bukaykay coming towards us. I sank down to the floor of the market hall, the cement cool against my legs, as if the change in level might render me invisible.

'Oh boy,' said Missy. Even though I was expecting it, her voice made me jump. From behind her mother, Suelita looked down at me, both hands pressed to her mouth.

I got to my feet as lightly as I could. Missy snorted. I glanced at Suelita. 'Joe,' she murmured.

'Come back to our place. Bee can find you something for those bruises,' Missy said.

'I'm ok.'

'Ok? Stones are softer than your head. Just like your father. I don't suppose you're going to tell me who did it? And why?' She studied Benny as she said this. I looked at Suelita. 'Why are you looking at her when I'm talking to you? You know something about this?' Missy narrowed her eyes at her daughter.

I knew from the set of her mouth that Missy would have persisted then had the sound of Cora's voice not cut through the surrounding noise as she swept back towards us, a line of jetty boys trailing in her wake. Cora broke into our circle and rearranged us, making me stand aside as the boys tightened the bolts and looped the guide ropes over the rafters. The promise of the mural distracted Missy and she stood quietly beside me as the boys hoisted it up and secured it in place.

We stepped back to take a look. Cora's hand could be seen readily enough in the composition, the smaller images of Greenhills and its people around a central image of a man, woman and child: *the poor*. The woman seemed familiar. I stepped forward to inspect her more closely. It was the girl under the yellow bell tree. I shot a look at Benny but he avoided my eye. I turned back to the mural. On another panel, a man in a suit stood beside a Mercedes. Next to him a child begged while he looked the other way. There was no mistaking the figure; Cora had painted Eddie, though she'd made him look fatter than he really was.

Suelita stepped forward now too, and I felt the warm skin of her arm brush mine as she turned to Benny. 'I hear you painted half of it,' she said. He moved to stand beside her and they fell easily into conversation, their voices soft as though for privacy while they discussed brushstrokes, chiaroscuro. His long fingers played in the air as he pointed out one figure or another. Suelita, watching his hands, smiled to herself. I cleared my throat heavily. They paused and she turned to me, frowning as she took in my injuries afresh, laying, though only briefly, a hand on my arm as she turned back to Benny. As they started talking again, her hand fell away. 'Young love,' Cora whispered, and she winked at me.

'You're really *good*,' I heard Suelita murmur. Benny reddened and dug his hands into his pockets.

Missy beamed at Cora, spoke loudly. 'Suelita writes poems,' she said, and I was astonished because I hadn't known this. 'She's a good cook too. Smart. Strong.' I felt hot suddenly. Missy laughed like she was joking but her shrewd eyes appraised the back of Benny's head.

I stepped away from the group. My eyes scoured the mural, hoping to find fault with his work, and of course found none. Desperately, I appraised the whole composition until at last I decided, with a cold satisfaction, how like Cora it was, how *obvious*. And, for several moments, I didn't care if Esperanza was to be lost or not.

# YELLOW BALLOONS, BLUE SKY

The rally, scheduled to start mid morning, finally got under way just after midday, so that by the time the speakers stepped onto the stage to take their seats the crowd spilled out along Esperanza as far as the Espiritista alley, and stretched along the coast road for half a kilometre in both directions. Within the market hall, Cora moved around greeting people, like a hostess at a party. On the stage, his hand cupped over the microphone in front of him, Uncle Bee leaned forward in his chair to speak to Jonah and Pastor Levi. My father hung back, well away from the stage, with the rest of the jetty boys. I would have preferred to stand with him out in the sun but Dil was there and, once, I looked round to see the Barracuda nudge my father cheerfully as he addressed him, saw my father laugh in response. I stayed close to Benny. Aunt Mary and America, having taken a hasty *merienda* at the Bougainvillea, would be about by now and searching for us.

Coming to the front of the stage, Jonah held his hands up to hush the crowd. Pastor Levi said, 'Let's start things off right,' and he led the crowd in the Lord's Prayer. All around caps came off, heads lowered and eyes closed, voices swelled with the familiar words, so familiar that I uttered them while look-ing about me to see who'd come, to sneak glances at Suelita, who stood beside her mother near the front, her hands dug into the back pockets of her jeans, her chest pushed out like a seabird's. I watched her mouth the words tiredly.

When the prayer finished, Pastor Levi said a few words to introduce each speaker. One by one they came forward, their gestures eager, animated, passing the microphone on but lingering still at the front as the next speech started. Jonah urged my father to come up onto the stage and have his say too, but my father crossed his arms tightly, his eyes searching out mine as he turned away.

Jaynie, Johnny Five Course's sister, climbed onto the stage and took the microphone. I'd expected her to speak but instead she started to sing 'A Change Is Gonna Come'. Her voice, distorted slightly by the PA system, was fine and light. It filled the covered hall and the crowd started to clap along, laughing when the whine of feedback on the high notes set a pack of street dogs howling an accompaniment from beyond the market hall. Jaynie held the last note for a long time. When at last she fell silent, the air, already swollen with the heat of the breathless afternoon and the assembled bodies, continued to buzz. There was an extended round of applause and calls for an encore, but Jonah put his hands up again for quiet.

I turned to see that my father had been joined by America and Aunt Mary. Benny and I pushed our way through to them. Aunt Mary seemed startled momentarily at the sight of me, of my bruises. We carried the cartons of food that I'd helped to prepare that morning from Jonah's office to the side of the stage, where we stacked them, ready to give out. A space had been cleared for us there, the children already being herded into a line.

Cora stepped out now at Jonah's behest to take applause for the mural. 'Of course I had help,' she said. I glanced at Benny. He was watching Suelita and she was smiling back at him. She slipped over to where we stood. I felt my face grow hot. 'Some of these panels are the work of Benny Morelos, a very talented young artist,' Cora continued, beckoning to him. 'Can you give him a big hand, please.' I thought how like a TV talk-show host she sounded, how unoriginal. *Young love*. Suelita put a hand on Benny's shoulder and pushed him forward gently. I looked away. She was never so familiar with me.

Aunt Mary's voice was low and clipped in my ear, 'When she's finished showing him off, fetch him back to help us, Joseph.'

Electrified by the excitement of the crowd, Jonah called down to Aunt Mary to come and speak. Aunt Mary stared back at him severely. I thought for a moment that he might persist; he was enjoying himself, wanting to stretch out the occasion. But America raised her finger and wagged it at him and he abated.

A commotion arose towards the back of the crowd. I heard my father and the jetty boys whistle a signal as they sometimes did to an incoming boat, or to each other while working. I craned to look but, over everyone's heads, I couldn't see anything. Aunt Mary touched my shoulder lightly and we started to hand out the food. 'Let him through,' Jonah said from the stage. 'Let's hear him out. Though of course, Mr Casama hasn't made it in time to hear what *we* think.' At which there was a low rumble of discontent.

Eddie Casama had no need to push; people moved aside for him. He came forward with Cesar in his wake and, while Eddie seemed almost to saunter, Cesar moved stiffly, gazed straight ahead. As Eddie neared the stage, he spotted Aunt Mary and cried, 'Mary! What a pleasure to see you and your son again so soon.' Aunt Mary nodded at him coolly. He beamed at America. 'The rumours were certainly true about your cooking,' he said. America reddened. Eddie looked in my direction but didn't seem to register either my presence or my appearance.

On the stage Eddie was relaxed, a natural at addressing crowds. He looked like anybody's uncle at a wedding. 'You see,' he said calmly into the microphone, 'change is inevitable.'

Aunt Mary placed the last of the food in America's hands and pushed the empty boxes under the stage. She straightened up, studied the crowd. Eddie said, 'I'm not doing this for *me*. Eventually this project will bring prosperity to the whole town.' Aunt Mary turned back to the stage, frowning. Eddie continued. 'It's a short-term sacrifice that's asked of you. I assure you, no one will be left homeless, but you *will* be relocated. It's a generous offer. Remember, this is *not* your land. Officially, this settlement is illegal.' I thought of Uncle Bee building his house with his own hands, of the Espiritista chapel built by an entire congregation, of the Spanish who, centuries ago, cleared the land for themselves by force of arms, giving it away again only to those who served their purpose. There had been a time, long ago, when our people had spread across the islands, settling and building and growing their food in a simpler relationship with the soil. I thought about Aunt Mary and her family, for whom the mere fact of birth had been so fortuitous. Once established, the lines of entitlement preserved themselves. I felt cold suddenly, distant. I closed my eyes and imagined myself alone, staring out at an unfamiliar sea.

When I opened my eyes again Aunt Mary was climbing the steps to the stage. She looked calm as she accepted the microphone from Eddie and turned to face the crowd. I was sure she couldn't have been enjoying the scrutiny. Yet, her voice when she spoke didn't waver, 'Mr Casama is right about one thing,' she said. 'The sacrifice will be yours. Not his.' She handed the microphone back to Eddie.

From the back of the crowd, someone yelled, 'Not yours either.' There was a murmur of agreement, though muted, perhaps in deference to the regard in which she was held. She nodded, for she knew it too. I turned to America, caught the smile that moved across her face like the shadow of a cloud. Eddie shook the microphone good-naturedly in the direction of the heckler, his expression mildly reproachful. Despite myself, the gesture made me smile; he looked as if he was sprinkling holy water. He cleared his throat. Aunt Mary moved to the edge of the stage but instead of stepping down, she stopped now to examine the mural. Behind her, Eddie started to speak again. Aunt Mary studied each panel in turn. When she came to the centre one she seemed, just for a heartbeat, to hesitate. She continued her inspection for several more seconds, her profile impassive, and then moved smoothly down the steps to rejoin us. She didn't look at Benny at all. She set off without a backward glance. Benny flashed me a look as he fell into step behind his mother. The crowd parted to let her through and we followed in a line.

As we broke through the skin of the crowd we saw Eddie's Mercedes. It was parked abreast of the hall on the other side of Esperanza Street. His driver sat behind the wheel, tapping an unlit cigarette against the dashboard, frowning out of the window at the crowd. Behind him a figure took up much of the back seat and for a moment I hoped it might be BabyLu. Then the back window slid down and a man's suited arm came out and waved at Aunt Mary. 'Judge Robello,' Aunt Mary smiled, 'how unexpected.'

'Mary,' the judge replied, pleasantly enough, 'you must come to ours for dinner soon.' I wondered if he looked a little embarrassed. 'You really must. If Alice were here she wouldn't let you escape without setting a date.'

'Thank you, Joey,' Aunt Mary said, graciously.

We joined my father. There was no sign of Dil and I was grateful for that. Aunt Mary looked about, her eyes combing the crowd. People were already coalescing now into smaller groups, in readiness for the march. America put her hands on her hips. 'So anyway, where's your brother?' she said to Benny. Benny looked about then too. Like me, he'd been too distracted to notice Dub's absence. 'He could have shown his face for his mother's sake at least,' America said.

When the march left, we walked together near the rear of the crowd. As we neared the Bougainvillea's gate, Aunt Mary squeezed my arm gently. 'Find him,' she said softly. I would have preferred to march on, adding my voice to the day, rather than trail after Dub, but she patted my arm again more briskly and I slipped out of the mass and into the cool tranquillity of the boarding-house garden. I stayed at the gate for a while, watching the marchers walk up the hill, and waited until the urgency in my breast had subsided and been all but obliterated by a dry sense of duty. When I'd lost sight of them, when even the sounds of the march had faded, I glanced up at a locked and empty Bougainvillea before starting back down the hill towards Prosperidad.

# KNOTS

The doors to Earl's garage were bolted and padlocked. I leaned back against them and gazed up at BabyLu's balcony. The balcony doors were closed too and, in front of them, framed by the lines of door and railing, the leaves of her potted plants were as bright and still as in a painting. The sight was pleasing and I stayed on the forecourt for some time, the skin of my back growing slippery under my shirt against the hot wood.

I closed my eyes and thought about the cool interior of her apartment, the fan on her coffee table, her books. My mind fixed on these, I straightened up and set off across the street and then up the stairs to her door. I knocked, softly at first. There was no answer. From inside, I heard a sound like hands sweeping over cloth. I knocked again, more firmly. 'BabyLu, please. It's Jo-Jo.' I felt foolish saying it so pleadingly, like a child. I knocked and called several times. And then, finally, the door was flung open.

BabyLu was in disarray, her hair wild, her robe sagging about her. I wondered if she'd been in bed. She gasped when she saw me and stared at me, not inviting me in. 'Good,' she said at last, shrilly. I was astonished and gazed back at her, bewildered. She chewed her lip. 'I'm *glad*,' she added.

'You heard me right.' But now she looked away as she said it. Still, I didn't speak, and after a minute she said miserably, 'It was *your* idea. The herbs. He told me.'

'Who?' I found my voice at last.

'Dub.'

'Dub,' I repeated hoarsely.

'You thought he wouldn't find out?'

'Where is he?' I said, my voice rising, peering behind her into the flat.

She drew in her breath, remembering. 'Eddie's men came. They took him.' Her eyes swept over my hands and face now, taking in my injuries. 'You *have* to find him.' Her eyes were bright with fear. I stared back at her dismayed. I thought of Aunt Mary, squeezing my arm, then patting it again.

'Where?' I said. I imagined Dub sitting on a settee, drink in hand, Eddie standing over him, smiling affably, sprinkling holy water.

'I don't know,' BabyLu cried. I was ashamed at how relieved I felt at that. She crossed her arms and looked at me coldly, but now her eyes avoided the worst of my bruises.

I considered telling her the truth but her eyes started to brim over again and I felt the heat go out of me. I looked down at her belly where no sign showed yet. I felt an emptiness then, so engulfing that I stepped backwards. *Let her believe whatever suits her*, I thought. 'Jo-Jo,' she said softly, but I turned away and started down the steps two at a time.

I dropped to the kerb at the corner of Prosperidad and Esperanza and sat, my head in my hands, waiting for my heart to stop its pounding. Esperanza was quiet, and without its usual layers of noise I could hear the soft crash of the sea.

Everyone would be at the town hall by now, sharing in the camaraderie of a day from which I'd found myself excluded. It wasn't far; I could still join them. I closed my eyes, pressing the lids tightly together. I forced myself to breathe slowly, the air humid and heavy, comfortless. The street smelled of hot dust. And after all, I thought, I had no idea where he might have been taken. Really, I shouldn't even have known that he *had* been taken. I might comb the entire town and never find him. And it was hardly anything to do with me. I sat quietly. *Good*, she'd said, *I'm glad*. I got slowly to my feet and walked back to the Bougainvillea.

# STREET BARBERS

America and I waited in the dining room for much of the morning, the house quiet around us. We'd laid breakfast out, covered it over again, eaten our own meal at the kitchen table and cleared our dishes away, until at last all that was left for us to do was sit, listening for footsteps, for the sound of doors opening, water running.

They came down one by one. Dub was the last. I hadn't seen him since before the rally. He'd returned to the boarding house long after the evening meal had finished and stayed in his room, not touching the tray that America took up. She'd been tetchy when she came back down with it and straight away dispatched me to my room for the night.

I stared at him as he came into the dining room. His hair was short and ragged, as if he'd cut it himself in front of the mirror. He stared down at his plate as I stepped forward to serve him. I looked him over stealthily as I spooned out his eggs. His skin was its usual unblemished coffee-cream, his loose-limbed deportment apparently unchanged. He sat comfortably enough though he barely ate. He was quiet. All morning he stayed on the edge of things, not commanding the room as he usually did. Later, he went out with his mother and when he came back his hair was different again – sharply cut. It suited him, but I didn't feel like telling him so. Even if I'd wanted to, I had little opportunity to speak to him for the next few days, for he always seemed to be flanked by his mother or by Lola Lovely, and they were quick to send me away.

America, unsettled by the change in mood at the Bougainvillea, announced that she was going to visit her village to spend a few days with her grandchildren. Sufficiently recovered, I found myself running the household and out on errands more often in her stead and it was on one of these early one afternoon that I happened to pass by the Beauty Queen parlour.

The Beauty Queen had opened on Esperanza Street the same year that I came to Aunt Mary's and the sight of it, of Jaynie and even of Lady Jessica, whom otherwise I found intimidating, was always significant for me, like a lucky charm. And so I was alarmed now to see it in such disorder. Manicure tables, chairs, hairdryers were lined up on the sidewalk while, nearby, Cesar Santiago and another man stood next to an idling sedan, one of Eddie's, watching the salon being emptied. As I approached I heard Cesar say, with his sorrowful voice and lawyer's smile, his hands open as if offering a gift, 'So, you see, some disruption is inevitable.'

Lady Jessica was squashing a bundle of towels into a bag on one of the chairs. She nodded sulkily at me. 'You guys redecorating?' I said, shooting a look at Cesar, who stood with his face creased in apology, hands back in his trouser pockets.

'Seven years,' said Lady Jessica, her voice, naturally a quick-fire staccato, faster than usual. 'Seven years. And his boss is no stranger to a manicure. Or his wife. This was like her second home. More time here than at her own mother's.' She looked me over critically as she spoke; the bruises on my face and arms were starting to yellow at the edges. 'You need something to cover those?'

I looked at her painted face, the make-up heavier over her jaw-line and cheeks. 'No thanks,' I said.

Jaynie emerged from the salon holding a box full of creams and lotions. 'That's the last of it,' she said. Her face was greyish, dull; she hadn't slept. She looked for somewhere to put the box down but the tables were already full. Cesar lurched forward as if to help but she turned her back to him. I started to clear a space and, on seeing me, she tried a smile. 'How are you today, Joseph?' she said softly. Jaynie's voice always softened when she addressed me. I thought I would always feel like a child in her presence. I knew little about her in return; just that she'd married young to an American seaman but the marriage hadn't lasted. She had a kindness about her, of the sort that in a certain kind of person might grow, instead of bitterness, out of pain.

'What's happening?' I said, certain now that they were not redecorating.

'I'm out of business,' she said.

'We, darling. *We* are out of business,' Lady Jessica said.

Jaynie sank into one of the salon chairs and rested her head back. 'At the rally,' she said. She turned to look at me. 'That's when he served us notice. At the rally.'

'It took all the fun out of protesting,' Lady Jessica said.

Jaynie reached out and patted my arm. 'You gonna tell Mary Morelos about this?' she said. I nodded. It was news. 'You make sure you tell her *Jaynie knows*.'

'Knows what?' I had to shout over the sudden roar of the engine as Eddie's driver fired up the sedan.

'I know she tried,' Jaynie shouted back.

'Tried what?'

'She talked to Eddie. It's not her fault his balls were in his ears.' She said the word *balls* emphatically, glaring in Cesar's direction. But Cesar was already in the sedan, leaning forward from the back seat to talk to the driver.

The car pulled slowly away from the kerb. We watched it go, waited for it to return so that Cesar could reassure himself that the dryers and the manicure tables and the mirrors weren't going to find their way back inside. Lady Jessica saluted Cesar on the car's second pass. Cesar affected not to notice.

When he'd gone, Jaynie slid down in the chair and closed her eyes. Lady Jessica stood behind her, her hands on her friend's shoulders. She plucked out Jaynie's hair grips, placed them in her lap. Then she gathered Jaynie's hair together and flipped it over the back of the chair, smoothing it down so that it fell like a curtain. 'You look like you're waiting for a shampoo and set,' she said. 'I could style you right now, baby, just to cheer you up.' Her voice sounded high, forced, determined not to succumb. She pulled a hairbrush out of a box. But Jaynie sat forward, looked at the salon equipment all about her. It took up the full breadth of the sidewalk and already passers-by were stepping round it, looking on with curiosity. Jaynie was quiet for a minute. She looked up at the overhead electric cables that ran from the municipal pylons to each shop and house on Esperanza Street. Lady Jessica watched her, her eyes narrowing as she broke slowly into a smile. 'Wicked girl,' she said. I left to return to the boarding house as Lady Jessica fell into feverish discussion about circuits and insulators and voltages.

I went straight to Aunt Mary. I told her about Eddie Casama with his balls in his ears. She smiled mischievously at me. She marched over to the telephone, picked up the receiver. I heard her greet Connie Casama. 'Is Edgar back yet from Manila? No? An emergency? No, not really, Well, perhaps. Did you know the Beauty Queen salon is in trouble? I see. Yes, he plays basketball. Is there any chance that Edgar might . . . Yes, and a keen swimmer too. Yes, he still paints. Yes, yes. Well then, I mustn't keep you.' When she hung up, her face was dark with anger.

Almost immediately, Aunt Mary sent me back to the beauty salon. By the time I returned, the municipal cable had already been breached and, soon enough, a compact version of the Beauty Queen parlour offering a select range of its usual services was up and running on the sidewalk. I helped Jaynie push the unused equipment to one side to be wheeled away later a piece at a time. 'If we'd tapped it *after* the electric meter,' said Lady Jessica peevishly, 'Eddie would've had to pay for the juice.'

The rains were still intermittent and the electrics were a worry. Jaynie and Lady Jessica rigged up a tarpaulin to keep the wiring dry, but after a while Jaynie unplugged the big dryers, clipping a single hand-held dryer onto the waistband of her jeans like a gunslinger.

Like food vendors they touted for custom, but people stepped past and the salon chairs remained empty. Finally, to demonstrate that the parlour was still in business, Jaynie offered to cut Rosaline's hair for free. Rosaline, the owner of the noodle joint next door, usually had her hair cut by her sister at home over the sink with dress-making scissors.

As I stood watching Jaynie at work, imagining Dub in the seat under her expert hands and wondering what it might feel like to have one's hair blow-dried, a moped swung into the kerb. The policeman cast his eyes over the scene before dismounting. He beckoned to Jaynie but, her hands still engaged with Rosaline's hair, she twitched her brow at the empty chair next to her, inviting him to sit. The cop stayed where he was. 'I didn't come for a haircut, miss,' he said, jovially enough. Over the course of the afternoon, Jaynie's mood had steadily hardened and now she wore a look on her face that made the man hesitate before he moved in closer. 'You have a permit for street-trading?' he said, carefully.

'That's my salon,' Jaynie pointed with her scissors.

'Not what I heard, ma'am,' but the cop had caught the coolness in her voice and was aware, no doubt, of how many people were about, while he was there alone. Jaynie and Jessica were popular in the street and the extrusion of the salon onto the sidewalk had displaced to either side the barbecue vendors and lottery and cigarette stalls that usually thronged it and now, in this tight-packed space, the cop's conversation with Jaynie was the focus of everyone's attention. The cop looked about him, his eyes narrowing as he caught sight of me, lingering over my bruises.

'How about a free cut, officer?' Lady Jessica purred the last word. She stepped forward, her broad frame between me and the cop. I saw the forested dome of his head move behind her as he tried to see past her but she shifted her weight from heel to heel and soon enough he gave up. 'I can see it's been a while, officer. No ring on your finger. And so trim in that uniform!' She pulled a chair out for him, patted the seat. The cop appeared to consider, then he sat down. When he did, the tension in the street seemed to abate. The other vendors went back to their business, glancing back at him curiously now and again as he sat, quietly, a salon apron across his breast marked with the words *Beauty Queen*.

The cop's hair had been cut and he was part-way through being manicured when Father Mulrooney arrived. I wasn't surprised to see him; his walks often took him past the salon. He looked dismayed now, as I had been at the sight of the salon furniture out on the street. He looked at Lady Jessica, at me; he nodded gently at the healing bruises, glanced at the dryers and the chairs, at the boxes of combs and brushes and curlers and then, finally, delicately, at Jaynie. She was watching him, waiting to look him straight in the eye and when she did he flushed deeply and broke his eyes away. 'Come on, Father,' she said softly, her hand resting on the back of a chair, 'be my first paying customer.' Mulrooney looked at the cop, frowning slightly. The cop raised his free hand in greeting and smiled up at the priest. 'Afternoon, Father,' he said cheerfully.

Mulrooney sat down. He arranged his robes self-consciously as Jaynie floated an apron, a plain one, down over him and fixed it about his neck. She ran her hands through his hair. He closed his eyes for an instant. I wondered if she'd ever touched him before. She watched him in the mirror as she asked what he might want her to do with his hair, all the while her hands playing through the thick sandy curls. She cut his hair slowly, carefully and, unlike Lady Jessica, who besieged the cop with conversation, remained silent as she worked. It seemed there was something private that enveloped the two of them then, surrounded as they were by the noise of the traffic, the calls of hawkers, the gulls circling up from the jetty. It was a public place and yet I felt it was an intrusion to watch them, but I did nonetheless, with everybody else; when she'd finished cutting his hair and run her hands through it for the last time to watch it fall properly into place, I was sorry for both of them that she was done. Jaynie removed the apron, untying the strings of it carefully from behind the priest's neck. Mulrooney got up to pay, pressed some notes into her hand, refused to take them back, refused any change. She smiled at him – sadly, I thought.

The cop stood up now too, held out a hand, fingers splayed, nodding in acknowledgement of Lady Jessica's fine work. He'd had his free haircut and manicure and now, he knew, it was time for him to withdraw. He looked about him at the street vendors, at me leaning against the doorpost of the salon. His eyes remained on me for a while. He looked at Father Mulrooney, whose haircut had accentuated the angles of his cheekbones, his high brow, and brought out the handsomeness still alive in his face. The cop dug into his pocket and dropped a few coins into Lady Jessica's palm as a tip. 'Don't be here tomorrow,' he said, as he turned to leave. On the way back to his moped, he paused to tap on the lid of the cigarette vendor's tray. The man held up a cigarette, a Champion, and the cop took it, tucked it behind his ear and mounted his moped without paying for it. He gunned the engine and waited while the exhaust fumes drifted up through the crowd, casting a last look round without catching anyone's eye. His meaning was clear enough: if he had to return, he wouldn't come alone.

Now a steady trickle of customers began and, as if they believed they were back inside the walls of the Beauty Queen, people talked more freely. I was surprised at their candour, though they kept their voices low when they discussed the rally. The day had gone well in the main, but there had been trouble from a few of the marchers, men that no one had recognised. Constabulary men in civilian clothes, or thugs hired to discredit the protesters. I listened, looking around me every now and then, alert for new faces.

When Eddie's Mercedes pulled up at the kerb, the conversation stilled and everyone turned to watch him get out of the car. Behind him, I could see Cesar. I slipped through the crowd to return to the boarding house, still too stiff and slow to run properly. Aunt Mary was waiting in the sala, her handbag ready by her feet. She left with me immediately.

When we arrived, Eddie was sitting in one of the salon chairs, his legs crossed, his hands clasped in his lap. He was smiling. Cesar stood beside him, glaring at Lady Jessica, who leaned in towards the lawyer, her hands on her hips, her breathing harsh and rapid. Jaynie reached forward and touched her friend's shoulder lightly. Lady Jessica folded her arms and took a step back. 'We don't want to move across town,' Jaynie said calmly. 'We live *here*. Our customers live here.'

'Here,' said Eddie, 'is going to change.' His voice was affable, dismissive, as if he were making a humorous observation over dinner. A murmur of displeasure snaked through the crowd. Aunt Mary pushed her way through and slid into the chair next to Eddie. Without a word she opened her purse, pushed some notes into Jaynie's hand and said, 'I'll leave it up to you this time, Jaynie.' Eddie looked surprised and then amused. He greeted her and though Aunt Mary nodded in his direction, she didn't turn to meet his eye. Then, as everyone looked on, Mary Morelos' hair was combed and pinned and measured and cut. Eddie looked around at the sea of faces, becoming aware perhaps of the temperature change that Aunt Mary, in her own small, calculated way, had caused. He got to his feet and, with Cesar a few steps behind him, started back to the car. There was nothing to be done about it; despite not having her family's money, despite the years of taking paying strangers into her home, round here Aunt Mary was still *somebody*.

The new haircut made her look younger and even the boys complimented her when we returned home, after the salon furniture had been carried away piece by piece to the apartments and garages and storage rooms of friends and neighbours, after it had been stacked and dismantled, and the Beauty Queen parlour had finally closed for business.

# COCKROACHES

My father stood in the doorway of Jonah's office, cap in hand, eyeing the line of outriggers that bobbed in the surf. The boats were light, the boatmen already asleep under their canopies, legs striped with sunlight. Inside the office, Jonah sat with his feet up on a crate, rubbing his hands back and forth across the top of his head. He was red in the face, his eyes and lips pressed tightly shut, his breathing deliberate. In front of him, his ex-wife Margie paced up and down looking in scarcely better humour. In her pale suit – the jacket still on despite the heat, the line of the skirt tapering towards matching shoes – she looked like she belonged in a skyscraper, behind a glass desk. As I approached, my father said gratefully, 'My boy's here.'

But Jonah beckoned me in and said, 'Joseph! A beautiful day, eh?'

'You never listened to reason, not once in your life,' Margie said, dismissing me with a glance. Jonah frowned at me; like my father, my presence had proved to be no deterrent at all.

'I keep telling you – it's not just about me. What about my boys?' he said.

'I didn't *marry* your boys.'

'You didn't marry *me* for very long,' said Jonah. He looked away, avoided looking back, aware immediately of his mistake. Margie turned round to glare at me and my father. My father took my arm and, darting an apologetic look at Jonah, pulled me away. He kept hold of my arm until we reached the sea wall.

The jetty was quieter than usual and beyond it an empty blue sea fell away. Two of the jetty boys were shifting the last sacks from the sand up to the road; the rest were smoking and playing cards or shooting hoops, but they seemed more listless than usual, even Subong. From the sea wall I could still make out the sound of Margie and Jonah arguing in between the rush of waves against sand and stone. I felt bad about abandoning Jonah when everyone knew there was little that upset him more than Margie. My father must have been thinking the same thing, for he said softly, 'Got no business coming between a man and his wife.' In any case, Jonah didn't have to face her for long. Shortly, we heard the door of his office fly open and Margie's voice say, 'Fine!' We turned to see her snatch her handbag from a chair. The bag was the same colour as her suit and shoes. She stalked to a waiting car, climbed into the back and was driven away.

Jonah came to the door and watched her go, watched until the car had disappeared entirely. Then he walked over to where we sat. He looked weary. 'Construction's started down the road,' he said. 'She figures this place won't be around for much longer. She wants me to go work for her family.'

'A job's a job,' my father said. 'Why not just take it? She's just trying to look out for you. She's still your wife.' He sounded impatient, a tone I hadn't heard him use with Jonah before.

Jonah clapped him on the back. 'I'm not built to sit behind a desk, Dante,' he said. He patted his *pregnancy*. My father raised his hands in defeat; Jonah always escaped into humour if a matter got too serious for his liking. 'Maybe I should ask her to find *you* a job,' Jonah added. 'Now that you've taken on the trouble of a second family.'

My father looked shaken. He evaded my eye. 'What could I do?' he said. 'I never finished high school. You at least started college.'

'Started, never finished,' Jonah sounded almost proud. I'd never known this about him, that he'd come so close to a different life. I opened my mouth to ask him about it but my father said, 'As many endings as beginnings,' and in the time it took me to think about this the moment was lost.

The sight of another of Margie's departures seemed to deflate Jonah and he retreated to his office, closing the door behind him. When he was gone, more for want of something to say than because I was interested, I asked my father about Lorna and the baby. Even as I asked, it irked me that this girl and her child had become the main currency of conversation between us. Lately, when I looked at my father, he seemed more tired to me, older, and I was stung by his willingness to take up the fight again for *her*, when she was little more than a stranger, and at a time in his own life when he might otherwise have rested. 'She's doing well,' he said. 'Missy visits and the child is gaining weight.'

'Great,' I said.

'She went through all the names beginning with L and then decided on Marisol.' He laughed at this and then added, gravely, 'I think she misses her mother.'

There had been no word from the House-on-Wheels since the day after the birth, when the broken cart had rolled off along the coast road towards Little Laguna. My father stared now into the distance, southwards – the direction in which the cart had gone – and I saw that he was worried. I thought it unlikely he was concerned for their safety; Lottie and Lando were street people, wily, alert to every opportunity for survival. Lando had likened his family to cockroaches, able to survive even a nuclear bomb, he'd said. I suspected, rather, that my father believed their return would stamp some final seal of approval on Lorna's entry into his household and he was anxious to show that she and the child were thriving, that he hadn't harmed her in any way.

We set off for his apartment. Since Lorna's arrival and the birth of the baby, my father had simply assumed that I'd want to see them, and so every Sunday afternoon instead of heading for the chapel I accompanied him back home. I suppose I should have been grateful that at least now I didn't have to spend the little time I had with him staring at the carved retablos of a European Jesus or at the gilded altars; everywhere pictures of people kneeling, heads bowed, penitent. Though of course dutiful visits to Lorna and her baby were hardly what I'd hoped for instead. He seemed proud, almost as if he were the father of the child, engaging with it in a way I'd not seen before, a way I didn't remember from my own childhood. Of course it didn't occur to me at the time that he might simply have been grateful for the chance to feel necessary again.

The apartment was tidy and newly scrubbed. A curtain of laundry hung across the main room and I had to duck beneath it to get to a seat. Lorna went to fetch water and cordial and a dish of unshelled peanuts while my father sank down onto the mat next to the baby and removed his cap. The baby wriggled on her back, becoming livelier at the sound of his voice. 'Are you feeling better, Joseph?' Lorna said carefully, and I was afraid for a moment that my thoughts were all too transparent, that she'd guessed how I resented her. She was eager to please and watched our glasses to see when they might need refilling, attentive to the baby lest it make too much noise and irritate us. Her solicitousness made me feel ashamed.

'Marisol's a good name,' I said, 'and she's real pretty.' Lorna beamed at me. The baby *was* pretty. And she had a watchful look about her, like an old woman at a roadside store. My mood softened as I took her in.

My father said very little except to the baby. It was Lorna who eventually said, 'Your father's worried you might drop out of school.' I stared at her. It hadn't even occurred to me that my father might discuss me with her. I looked at him but he nodded as if he was only half listening, though I knew from the way his hands slowed that the conversation had his full attention. Lorna said quickly, her voice appeasing, 'He thinks you could study more. Maybe even college.'

'I didn't think you'd be so interested in *my* future,' I said, but at the same time I was surprised that my father had such ambitions for me at all.

Lorna, undaunted, continued, 'Aunt Bina is already teaching me to sew. There'll be more money.' She sounded apologetic and of course she had to know the money to keep her and the baby came from somewhere, that my schooling was not the only consideration.

My father kept quiet. Eventually, Lorna got up to take the glasses away and to feed the baby in the kitchen. When she'd gone, my father said, 'She knows better than anyone how every opportunity must be grasped.'

'She works hard,' I conceded, looking round the apartment.

'I'm getting old, Joseph,' my father said and his voice was suddenly harsh. 'And things will change around here soon enough.'

'I'll work harder at school,' I said, and I meant it. School-work was easy enough for me anyway.

'You could study to be a teacher or an engineer,' he said, 'get a good job.' I thought of Suelita and the poetry she told no one about. 'She's smart too,' said my father, and his eyes flitted towards the kitchen where Lorna was trilling in a low voice at the baby, enticing it to feed. 'When she's older she'll make a good wife.' I didn't respond, unsure for a moment why he'd said it. And then, appalled, I understood that he might be planning to marry again some time, to replace my mother with this girl. Then he said, 'You will want to marry some day.'

From the kitchen, the sound of the trilling stopped and I remembered how little of what was said could be hidden here. The rooms were small and the walls thin. I felt my resentment bloom into anger. My father had never spoken with me about so much that mattered, yet he talked openly to this girl-child, enough that she felt she could chide me about my disinterest in school. She was smart all right. 'Your mother would have liked her,' he said quietly. That he could mention my mother so casually now, when for years he couldn't bring himself to say her name, even for my sake when I was afraid of forgetting her, finally unhinged me. I chose my words hastily, too hastily. 'I hardly saw Mom before she died because *you* sent me away,' I yelled. My father looked aghast. In the kitchen Marisol started wailing. I lurched to my feet and called out a curt, acidic goodbye to Lorna. She came out of the kitchen, looked first at my father and then at me. I saw her embarrassment, her uncertainty, and saw also that, yes, a marriage had been discussed, if not as something definite, it had been given at least sufficient substance to form a hope for her. I glared at my father and, hesitating as he proffered his hand, I declined to shake it and left.

# WOMAN WITH ROSARY

'You had your hair cut in the street? Like some . . . some *comfort girl*?' Lola Lovely stood over her daughter in the sala, one hand on her hip, the other working mercilessly at a coral-and-pearl rosary that she sometimes wore as a necklace, ready for sudden moments of piety. She had come in to find the familiar sight of her daughter at the piano, the lid still closed, sheet music spread about her as she sorted and reorganised it. In the hall, I paused in my task of polishing the banister, massaged the muscles in my arm. I'd been working fiercely at the wood, still mad at my father. I wondered what might need doing elsewhere. It sounded like Lola Lovely was hankering for a row and I wanted to work at something in peace. 'You can't even play piano in front of your own mother, yet you can have your hair cut in the street like some *cuchinta* vendor?' Aunt Mary placed the score she was holding on top of the pile on her lap and frowned at her mother. 'He said he would never have imagined you there like that.'

'Who said that?'

'Mr Casama. That man who was here the other day.'

'You spoke to Mr Casama?'

'Yes, I just said so. He came by to apologise for his wife

misleading you – he was back in Esperanza earlier than she thought, but just too busy to get home. Or something like that. I didn't care about that. I asked him about Dominic.'

'*What?* What exactly did you say?'

'I asked him outright if he had anything to do with it. You know, he was appalled. Said he knew nothing about it. He seemed genuinely concerned.' Aunt Mary stared at her mother. 'He said there are some big players behind the redevelopment,' Lola Lovely continued. 'A lot of money at stake. Not all as honourable as himself.' Aunt Mary smiled frostily and, seeing it, Lola Lovely snapped, 'What were you thinking? Having your hair cut like that in front of everyone so soon after Dominic? And such a ridiculous little protest. The whole street must be laughing about it.' Aunt Mary was silent but I knew that kind of silence. She might be seething but she didn't want an argument and Lola Lovely's voice was changing, becoming shrill. Neither woman seemed aware of my presence. I thought about moving away, giving them some privacy, but I'd already been there too long. I started polishing again, slowly.

'I may be your offspring but I'm almost fifty. You can't – '

'*Offspring!*' Lola Lovely mimicked her daughter's tone unsuccessfully. 'You think you're so clever. Why do you care about some salon anyway, or this Jennie? Dominic is your son!' Lola Lovely shook her rosary at her daughter. 'I should take them away with me. Back to Manila. Both of them. They are my flesh and blood too, even Benny. Yes, even him!' Aunt Mary cast a furious eye over the piles of music around her feet as her mother continued, breathlessly, 'You think I don't know that I'm not as *good* a person as you? You think I never wish I could go back and change it? I did the best I could at the time and I got it wrong. There! I said it. Are you happy?' Aunt Mary sighed heavily; her mother's concessions were not always a good omen.

'What happened to Dominic wasn't about – '

'The rules have changed, *hija*. These people! They're not gentlemen. They don't respect the old ways, the old blood.'

'It was only a haircut.' Aunt Mary's tone seemed suddenly wheedling, conciliatory.

'No one else in this street has a right to come before your own boys. Least of all this Jennie person,' Lola Lovely said icily.

'I have *always* put them first!'

'Dominic can come to Manila with me. It's about time he stopped this pop-star business. He must go to college. You have to tell him so.'

'I will not order him about. He has the right to run his own life.'

'So *that's* what this is about!' Lola Lovely said. 'Is this why you won't play the piano? Because your horrible mother locked you in the sala and forced you to practise?' Aunt Mary pushed the pile of music from her lap onto the floor and stood up to leave, but Lola Lovely was between her and the door. For a moment, the two women faced each other without speaking and then Lola Lovely said, tiredly, 'Why do you insist on rotting here anyway? You could put on a little make-up at least.' Aunt Mary pushed past her mother and marched out of the sala. Lola Lovely dropped into a chair. I draped my rag over the banister and slipped into the sala to pick up the papers. As I worked, I heard Lola Lovely leave, her footsteps heading for the kitchen, and shortly afterwards the sound of the door opening into the courtyard. I left the music on top of the piano in no particular order and went back to polishing the staircase. On reaching the landing, I glanced through the open door of the nearest guest room and saw Aunt Mary standing over a suitcase, packing her mother's things.

The following morning, in the shade of the flame tree that leaned over the front yard, beside an idling taxi, Lola Lovely hugged first the boys, then America. She patted me on the shoulder and winked at me. Finally, she turned to her daughter. Aunt Mary, stiff in her mother's arms, allowed herself to be embraced. Lola Lovely held her like this for a long time.

# PSYCHIC SURGERY

The Reverend Julio Orenia, World Famous Psychic Surgeon, was to appear in the auditorium of a girls' school on the other side of Salinas. A fortnight before the show, at her mother's insistence, Aunt Mary had procured tickets through a Lopez family connection. But now Lola Lovely's early departure had left an empty seat. America watched me mischievously as she told me I was going. Only the day before she'd listened, bristling, as I denounced psychic healing as unscientific. I turned away to hide my excitement.

The school was an easy walk from the Bougainvillea but Dub insisted on taking his motorbike. Benny clamoured to ride with him but Aunt Mary wouldn't hear of it, declaring instead that I was to go with Dub while Benny went with the others in a taxi. Being around Dub was the last thing I wanted at that moment and I opened my mouth to protest, closing it again almost immediately on glancing at Aunt Mary; she was rarely to be persuaded out of something once she'd made up her mind, and certainly not by me. Her voice was terse as she dispatched me to fetch a cab.

The afternoon sun picked out the planes and edges of Esperanza as I rode back with the cab. The world felt solid, defined. I rolled down the window to disperse the stale air inside the car. A fine breeze blew in from the direction of the jetty, bringing the smell of the sea with it as it stirred the leaves of Aunt Mary's cheesewood hedge. I'd have enjoyed the walk.

Dub smiled sheepishly at me as he handed me a helmet. I felt Benny's eyes on me and, turning, I held his gaze for an instant longer than I might have before. Since the news about his real mother, the household had carried on around him as if nothing had changed, Aunt Mary and America fussing over him and berating him in equal measure as they always did. For my part, I couldn't help but look at him differently now, though I was careful not to betray it. Of course he was the same Benny as ever, but he was half the same substance as I, even if, like his brother, the rest of him was descended from what my own mother had always referred to as *good stock*.

The schoolyard was heaving and it was as much as we could do to stay together as we pushed our way inside. We were early, but most of the seats were already filled and there would be many people standing for the evening. People in wheelchairs lined the walls, crowds streaming slowly past them.

Aunt Mary walked straight to the front of the auditorium and along the first row, counting off with little nods of her head the number of seats for our group. Across the hard wooden back of each seat a strip of paper asserted in capitals: *RESERVED*. I removed mine, studied it for a moment. Next to me, Benny leaned back in his chair, crumpling his paper strip in his fist after barely a glance. He made to drop it on the floor, hesitated as he looked at mine still in my hand. He watched as I folded it carefully into my pocket. His eyes met mine and he flushed lightly. He pushed the ball of paper into his pocket and settled back into his seat.

Beside me, Dub scanned the crowd with a studied casualness. I looked around too, as much to avoid catching his eye or having to make conversation as out of curiosity, but I saw no familiar faces in the packed hall; people had come from far afield to see the reverend's show.

The reverend walked onto the stage late but no one protested, for he was, immediately, a charismatic performer. He was smaller and much younger than I'd imagined and he had about him the impatient demeanour of the city dweller. He wore a suit, the jacket unbuttoned so that when he raised his arms, dark rings of sweat could be seen on his shirt under the lights. 'Welcome,' he said, 'in the name of the Father, Son and Holy Spirit. You know,' he continued, his voice like a game-show host, 'it's through the Holy Spirit that my healing occurs.' Although the flyer had described it as a prayer meeting, his show was flamboyant. He rushed about the stage, his voice booming into a microphone. People continued to arrive after he'd started, sliding in carefully at the back, but he waved them forward without pausing in his speech, as if calling friends to join a picnic.

He led the audience through prayers and we sang 'Holy Spirit, Truth Divine', a hymn I didn't know and mumbled along to. I heard Aunt Mary's voice rise up, clear and sweet over the others, but even she couldn't remember all of it.

Halfway through the hymn, I felt Dub shift in his seat and, turning, I saw Eddie and his associates settle themselves noisily at the other end of our row. They were all in suits. BabyLu was with them and she'd dressed up for the occasion, but demurely, in an outfit that wouldn't have been out of place in church. I wondered how Eddie had conspired not to bring his wife.

On stage, the reverend apologised that he wouldn't be able to treat everyone who had come for healing that day; he hadn't expected such a crowd. 'You make me feel like one of The Beatles!' he said. He announced that he would be hold-ing clinics in a nearby chapel over the next few days where he would see anyone who came through the door. He called on the spirit messengers to guide his hands. The audience quietened. I looked around. People were smiling, swaying, some praying with their eyes closed, some still humming the melody of the hymn. Others were laughing, though noth-ing funny had been said since the Beatles remark. I looked back to the stage. The reverend seemed to stumble, his eyes rolled back so that the whites underneath were stark under the lights. He held his arms out to the crowd and asked who wanted to be healed. The air was immediately full of hands. I saw BabyLu crane round to look at the crowd. She didn't raise her hand and neither did Eddie, but from their group Cesar, his face a little feverish, his lips still moving in prayer, raised his. As BabyLu turned back, she stole a glance at Dub but she didn't hold his gaze, turning her eyes quickly back to the stage.

From near the back of the hall, a man was brought for-ward and helped onto the podium by the reverend's ushers. He moved slowly, though he wasn't particularly old, and he was extremely thin. His delight at being called up was evident and he reached out to grasp the reverend's hand in both of his own, pulling it to his breast. The reverend opened his arms and hugged him. The audience, already far from quiet, stirred audibly at the sight. Even I was moved by it; it was hardly something a regular doctor would do. The man was made to lie on a table in the centre of the stage, his head resting on a Bible. The reverend started praying again out loud, something in Latin or what sounded like it. Overhead, the lights dimmed and flickered awhile before steadying. America cast a fearful look at the ceiling. The reverend seemed to sag and then straighten. He moved confidently now. He rolled his sleeves up, took a bottle from a side table and poured something into his cupped palm. He rubbed his hands together as he spoke softly into them, his eyes closed. He opened his eyes again and pulled the man's clothing aside with one hand to bare his abdomen. Next to me, America hissed under her breath. Under the lights, there seemed hardly anything of the man but stark bony ridges. The reverend started to move his hand as if it were a knife, sawing the side of his palm back and forth in the air, then jabbing downwards with his index finger. He did this a few times, his face intent on the man's flesh as if staring into the core of him, and then his hand plunged downwards and seemed to disappear into the man's flesh. There was a gasp from the body of the audience. It filled the room and subsided again. The air felt electrified, like it did before a storm, and for a few seconds it was as if everything slowed down. A faint scent of coconut oil drifted out across the front of the auditorium. Then the hand was out and he was rubbing the man's belly gently. The reverend held his hand out to the patient. It was stained with blood and clenched around something. He opened his fist, palm up. The audience leaned forward in their seats. The thin man stared at the reverend's hand and then down at his own belly. The reverend slipped the object into a jar and held it up for everyone to see. It looked like a lump of meat. He dipped his hands into a basin of water on the side table, taking the time to clean them properly with soap. I saw America nod her approval; she was always impressed by hygiene. He asked the patient to stand slowly, carefully, in his own time, stepping forward to help him down from the table. He needn't have; the man almost leaped down and beaming, pulled his shirt up to show that there was no wound and no visible blood, nothing in fact to indicate that any kind of surgery had taken place. 'No meat,' the reverend said to him, wagging his finger like a school-teacher. 'No sex, no alcohol, no fizzy drinks and no losing your temper for at least two weeks.' A surge of laughter filled the auditorium.

The patient stepped down from the stage. I watched him walk back to his seat, into a forest of raised hands as people craned forward now to be healed. The reverend's ushers moved through the crowd, selecting people, guiding them into a line along the periphery of the hall. One by one, young and old, they climbed or were carried onto the stage. One after the other, bits of flesh, clotted blood, matted hair, worms, stones, shards of glass were displayed like auction lots. The room grew hotter and the doors and windows were flung open. The sound of night traffic and hawkers drifted into the hall, interweaving with the prayers and chants of the reverend and his congregation. The air felt thick and urgent.

I looked at Aunt Mary. She was sitting upright, her hands folded in her lap. She looked composed, contained. She seemed attentive to what was going on, but her expression was closed; she might just as well have been listening to Benny give an account of a basketball match or America recount some kitchen calamity.

I saw Jonah move towards the stage. The sight of him jolted me. I'd been certain none of the jetty boys, my father included, would have been here; the price of the tickets, though not impossibly high, was certainly the kind of money one would think long and hard about spending. I noticed now how lean Jonah was, except for the increasingly conspicuous bulge of his *pregnancy*. When it was his turn, his belly yielded not the half-expected foetus but a handful of small pebbles the size of beans, which the Reverend trickled slowly into a jar with a sound like rain on an iron roof.

After a while, people started to leave. Here and there across the hall, they rose and moved away like twists of smoke from embers; those who had been healed, those who might only have come to watch and seen enough to assuage their curiosity, those whose children had become fractious or who were distracted by the smells from the food stalls outside. Several times Aunt Mary looked over her shoulder, considering, perhaps, how we might leave unobtrusively from the very front row. When we finally got up I saw that Eddie and his companions had already disappeared.

Outside, the air was pungent and smoky. The barbecue vendors were doing brisk business and, sliding between them, women sold corn on the cob, boiled eggs, coconut cakes from baskets on their heads. In the centre of the schoolyard, a ring of stalls displayed statues of Mary or Jesus, bottles of holy water, votive candles, prayer beads. I saw Johnny Five Course's cart – a new notice taped to its roof read *vegetarian option*. Behind her brother, Jaynie parcelled up food without raising her head.

In front of me, Aunt Mary and Benny fell into animated conversation. I thought I heard Aunt Mary say the word *cellular*. I quickened my step but their voices were swallowed by the noise.

As we came to the edge of the crowd, Dub put his fingers in his mouth and whistled. Ahead of us a line of motorbikes leaned beneath a frangipani tree, slick with light from the school windows. Behind them, a group of men and women sat on a low wall. I recognised Earl.

Dub turned to his mother but before he'd even opened his mouth, she said, 'Don't forget Joseph.' I was disappointed again; I'd hoped to walk back with her and Benny, listening in to their conversation. Benny pushed his hands into his pockets and said sullenly, 'Joseph rode out with him,' but Aunt Mary slipped her arm firmly through his. America, tired and impatient now, pursed her lips at the bikes before turning away.

Earl was the first onto his bike. In ones and twos the group pulled out of the school gates, crawling through the traffic and the mass of people spilling out from the sidewalks. We rode in a line to Salinas and then, as we cut through town, one after another the bikes peeled away again until only Earl and Dub rode on together past the edges of Greenhills to rejoin the coast road several kilometres to the south.

Earlier it had taken only minutes to get from the boarding house to the school. And, despite not having wanted to ride with Dub in the first place, as we'd slowed down to turn in at the school gates, I'd suddenly wanted to pick up speed and keep going, leaving the gates, the crowd, the noise and mess of Esperanza behind. Now, as we rode back, the black sea invisible to my right, the wind smoothing my hair away from my face, I felt an overwhelming sense of freedom, and suddenly I understood something so clearly that it surprised me. I understood that for these brief times of being on the road, Dub was not the son of Mary and Captain Bobby Morelos, the product of generations of *breeding*, in the same way that I too harboured the illusion of leaving my real self behind, far back amid the eddies of road dust, and flying forward to meet a future that was still ripe with possibility.

We rode on through the darkness and, after a while, it seemed as if an uncertain light shifted in the distance ahead. When we drew closer to Esperanza we discovered why: under a thick pall of smoke, the jetty was on fire.

# NIGHT SCENE AT THE JETTY

When I was much younger, the jetty was the furthermost boundary of my world. It was busier then; the ferry terminal along the coast hadn't been built and the jetty was always *full* – of people, livestock, engine noise – a chaos that made it seem far bigger than itself. Along the coast road, small eateries and variety stores flourished, many of which closed down altogether or moved away when the new terminal opened. Then, my father was a giant, or so I thought, and Jonah was a young man, unmarried and flat-bellied.

My mother took me there sometimes after the market and, though my father took his work more seriously than the other jetty boys and disliked distractions, he always looked pleased when he saw us approaching. We'd sit for a while on the sea wall, waiting for him to finish. I have scattered memories from that time: the rush of air as my father swung me up over his head, before frowning at me when the suddenness of it made me cry and my mother scolded him; my sister kicking her dry heels against the stone; my brother running along the top of the wall, jumping down to holler at chickens crammed into cages or bunched by their feet against the front wheels of a bicycle.

For me, the jetty contained these events just as my

father's apartment contained other pieces of my life. And now I could see flames bursting out from along its length and stealing from the roof of Jonah's office onto the canopy of the market.

Dub slowed the motorbike down, and as we came nearer, I saw people running with buckets and pans, even jugs, back and forth from the sea. The air was thick with heat and smoke and beneath the smell of burning, another smell, acrid and familiar. Dub stopped the bike in the middle of the road and we dismounted. From up ahead, Earl turned round and cruised back to join us. 'Feel like being a hero?' he said. His garage was on the other side of Esperanza, but the wind coming from over the sea was restive and it hadn't rained today.

'We've got to do something,' said Dub, but he sounded doubtful. A crowd had gathered but, as the heat built, the onlookers edged back slowly along the coast road while the fire, brilliant against the night sky, crept forward in a thin line along the beams that anchored the corrugated iron plates of the market-hall roof. Within the encircling darkness, the first shops and dwellings of Greenhills wavered like ghosts in the uneven firelight. I thought of the curandero's wooden-frame house, the Espiritista chapel, the countless shacks made out of fruit crates and sacking. Even at this distance, hard, dry waves of heat broke over our skin.

'We've got to do *something*,' Dub said again and climbed back onto his bike. We rode up around the back of the market, through the rough, unpaved alleys and across Esperanza Street to leave the bikes on the garage forecourt. Earl knelt to chain the bikes to the garage doors and then he and Dub started running back towards the jetty. I followed after them.

Earl began to force his way through the crowd and we followed in a line behind him, Dub first, then me. Later, this moment was one that came back to me over and over, the sight of Earl's big frame cutting through the crowd and, when it did, I wondered if Dub, like myself, was relieved that all that was required of him in that moment was to follow or whether, in the end, he really was made of different stuff than I. Like most people, I had, in the safety of my bed or daydreaming as I hung sheets in the yard, imagined myself in acts of heroism: pulling Benny from a burning Bougainvillea, even going back for Aunt Mary's most precious figurines, or dragging Suelita from the sea. But now, faltering amid the smoke, the dense, hot air clamouring around me, I was struck by a kind of paralysis. Like a child, I wanted to be told what to do.

The crowd grew. Handkerchiefs and t-shirts tied across mouths and noses divulged only intermittently the familiar contours of a cheekbone, a jaw. Here and there I thought I heard the timbre of a familiar voice. People brought more containers, anything that might hold water, and cleared empty crates from the far end of the market. But the fire had climbed higher now, out of reach of the men and women who passed vessels back and forth along a line. I heard someone shout nearby, a voice I knew well: Jonah. He sounded shrill. 'We have to bring the beams down or it'll catch the wind.' I looked up at the market roof, the lines of fire snaking further towards its peak. A man pushed out from the crowd and moved towards the market hall. He carried an axe and when I saw him I cried out, the sound lost straight away, even to my own ears. It was my father.

I watched him as he strode forward, his gait resolute, a man who had decided not to wait for others to act. He paused for a moment and looked up, studying the roof, the struts that supported it. And then he ran under the canopy, deep into the market hall, and took up position at one of the beams nearest the centre, under the peak of the roof. Shaking my head, I started after him. I felt Dub's hand on my shoulder pulling me back. Jonah stepped forward now after my father, the long, curved blade of the bolo he held orange in the firelight. The lines of people carrying water slowed now and moved away from the market to concentrate their efforts on Jonah's office and the single line of shacks that ran along the coast road and abutted the market hall.

Dub pulled me forward now and we joined the lines and passed buckets and tins back and forth. Dub pulled his t-shirt up over his nose but it kept slipping. My mouth was bitter with the taste of burning. I looked in the direction of the market hall and imagined I heard over the din the rhythmic sound of iron chopping at wood. I knew that my father and Jonah would be working together, each striking the beam as the other swung back. I craned my head to see what was happening and saw that more men had joined them under the canopy to work at the neighbouring beams. I imagined now the roof giving way and the men running out from under it. Esperanza Street itself had cleared as people moved away from where the roof plates might fall. Some of them moved towards the neighbouring shacks, still untouched by the fire, and took with them more containers of water with which to wet the buildings. It seemed a pitiful effort, the pails and basins of water inadequate to the size of the task, the sheer number of homes.

The evening became artificial, dreamlike, and I behaved automatically, passing containers first one way then another. But something tore at me. The beams of the market hall were slowly being weakened but everywhere people worked in a frenzy, without heed to each other's efforts, and I thought dimly that when the roof came down, who could tell which way it might fall? Who could be certain which beam would give first? And my father stood almost at the very centre of the hall.

When it happened, the night, already shattered by noise, was rent again by the sound of iron sheets tearing from their anchorage. I turned to watch, mesmerised, as the iron roof collapsed in a shower of sparks and a surge of sudden heat. I watched the men scurry out from under it like lice, heads down and backs bent, their shapes as indistinct as spectres in the rush of smoke and dust, and then, as it settled, I saw Jonah. He turned to look behind him and when I saw him start back towards the pile of twisted wood and metal that had been the market hall, I knew in an instant that my father was under it still.

Much of the rest of the night was lost to me, fragmented and hazy. Later, I remembered running, and Dub and then Earl pulling me to the ground. I remembered Dub holding me to his chest, forcing my eyes away from the scene. I remembered also that, after all, the fire did not reach far into Greenhills, for soon after the market roof fell in it started to rain, hesitantly at first and then boldly, the drops heavy, unrepentant.

I remembered the sight of Subong tearing at Jonah's shirt as he cried, 'I *saw* it, I saw who did it,' his face raw with fear, with disbelief. And I remembered, days later, when the confusion of images and sensations had settled to a dull, steady ache, the absence of the fire-department trucks and the smell in the air as we'd ridden up the coast road and seen the first flames licking the jetty: kerosene. And finally, I remembered how the last time I'd seen my father I'd left without shaking his hand.

# FACES AT A VIGIL

My father's vigil was held in his apartment and, like my mother, he rested on the dining table for want of room. More people came to pay their respects than could be accommodated and the visitors spilled out into the hallway and, after a while, down the stairwell into the courtyard. Elisa, on her mother's orders, left the door to their apartment open and pulled her mother's chairs out into the hallway one by one to line up by our front door. People milled back and forth, the children left to sleep in Bina and Elisa's room, while the adults filed through to touch the coffin. The coffin was closed and without the proof of my own eyes, it was hard to believe he really lay in it. When the chanting began, the sound echoed through the passages, drawing out the building's remaining inhabitants. I felt penetrated by it, unable to escape it.

My sister and brother came, of course, though I hadn't called them; I wouldn't have known how to reach them, not having foreseen a time when I'd need to keep such information. Instead, Aunt Bina called Luisa from the telephone in the general store downstairs and asked her to track down Miguel. Perhaps it was Bina that Luisa had expected to see first, for when Lorna opened the door to her my sister greeted her angrily.

Luisa came with two children again, another two I hadn't met before: her third and fourth. The two who'd come to our mother's vigil had been left at home. She looked sourly at me as I struggled to name them. I repeated the names after her aloud, as if committing them to memory, my manner exaggerated slightly for her benefit, but minutes later I'd forgotten again. At that moment I didn't really care; I knew I wouldn't see them again for a long time and, when I did, would barely recognise them and they would not recognise me at all. Luisa had changed, become quite stout, her features coarse. She was in her twenties still, yet little girlishness remained in her face or her gestures. She looked tired from the journey but wore another kind of tiredness too; the kind that is not merely physical, and that often masks disappointment. I'd seen her only once or twice since our mother's funeral, though she'd written to my father in between with news of the children.

My brother, Miguel, had returned twice after my mother died, staying fewer days than he'd intended both times. My father had been quiet and angry for days after each visit. Miguel had talked both times about going to work overseas and now finally he'd come with the news that he was leaving for the Middle East at the end of the month. He was thinner, the skin of his face and arms dry and dark. His forearms were marked with fine scars and his palms were rough and red. His hair, still thick, was shot with grey in places, though the effect was still of youth. When I saw him, I thought of the jetty boys; he wouldn't have been out of place among them.

When he greeted me, my brother smiled and embraced me, swaying gently. On his breath was the faint, sweet smell of liquor consumed the night before. He wasn't drunk, but he too looked tired. He'd come a long way, arriving that morning having travelled all night. He spoke briefly to Jonah and Bina and some of the others that he recognised, but then slept for an hour beside the children – our sister's and the baby Marisol – in Bina's apartment.

Aunt Bina greeted visitors at the door for most of the morning and into the afternoon until Missy arrived and took over the same duties. Elisa said very little to me but watched me from time to time. She sat staunchly next to Lorna. Lorna rocked back and forth where she sat, clutching Marisol so tightly to her that I wondered the baby didn't suffocate. She wore her grief and her fear openly. By comparison I must have seemed cold, but the truth was I was still numb. My father's death made no sense. I pictured him at the rally, at the jetty with Jonah. I still expected him to arrive home, as I had my mother seven years before.

So many people came. Some I didn't recognise at all. The mode of my father's death had elevated him to the status of a hero and it seemed as if everyone in Greenhills wanted to demonstrate some connection with him. I was pointed out over and over again. 'That is his son.'

Jonah and the jetty boys came. Without my father, without Subong in his orbit, for he too was absent, they seemed somehow incoherent. I wondered if they felt it too. Dil was among them but I didn't look at him even when he offered a greeting, pretending to be lost in my own thoughts. 'Subong?' I asked Jonah, but without reproach in my voice; Subong had looked up to my father and today would have been hard for him to bear.

'Never showed up the day after,' Jonah said. 'I sent Dil to

his mother's, but he's not been home.' I stabbed a look at Dil. He was watching me and lifted his chin, raised his eyebrows, his eyes without challenge, as if inviting a friendly remark.

'I heard him say he saw who started the fire,' I said loudly.

'I heard it too,' Jonah said.

'No doubt it was deliberate,' Uncle Bee said from the door. He'd brought Missy, Suelita and Fidel with him. Suelita clung to her mother's arm.

'Maybe he's been taken as a sacrifice for Eddie Casama's building project,' someone said, and there was a murmur of alarm.

'Don't talk such rubbish at a man's funeral,' Jonah snapped.

'It happens though,' a woman said.

'In komik books,' someone else said.

'People like us are disposable. They think of us in the same way as pigs or chickens and you wouldn't have a problem with sacrificing a pig or a chicken,' the woman continued.

I didn't want to listen to this, though at another time, about another person, I might have indulged like everyone else in the same kind of macabre speculation.

Suelita came forward to pay her respects. As she turned from the coffin she embraced me without warning, her eyes unguarded and uncertain. Taken by surprise, I barely embraced her back. Still, she held me for a while, her hand cupping the back of my head. She didn't stay for the entire vigil, leaving perhaps to man the *sari-sari* store or cook the evening meal. Anyway, there was simply not the room. She was still there though when Benny arrived with America and Aunt Mary and she returned later to join in the prayers at the chapel.

Benny, when he came, stood just inside the door and looked at the coffin and around the room, taking it all in. He'd never been inside my father's apartment before, for he hadn't been one of the visitors when Lorna gave birth to Marisol, nor when my mother died, which wasn't long after the loss of his own father. Then Aunt Mary had thought him too young to attend another funeral so soon and he was dispatched, against his will, to a school friend's house and on his return sulked for several days. He seemed plain now somehow, unadorned, and I realised of course that he hadn't brought his sketchbook or his bag full of charcoal and pencils and I was disappointed. After all, what other record would my father's death leave? I looked round the room at all the people and thought, bitterly, that it could have been, *should* have been, any one of them that died under the market-hall roof.

Benny wedged himself against the wall and sat with his feet drawn in towards him. Suelita glanced in his direction and he smiled at her, looking away again without lingering. They caught each other's eyes a few times after that. I was distantly aware of each look. But they didn't speak, and when Benny left it was my eyes that he searched out last.

Mulrooney and Pastor Levi came, with Levi's wife Eveline. I noticed absently that Father Mulrooney's hair still looked good, though it had grown out a little. When he greeted me I found myself saying, 'She did a really good job, Father,' nodding at his hair. He blushed and touched it lightly with one hand. He read aloud from the Bible and Pastor Levi said a prayer over the coffin. The heat blended with the sound of their voices in a dense vibration. I felt as if I was watching everything from a distance, as if it wasn't my father who lay on the table, nor I watching his coffin. I didn't care about God or heaven or the spirits now. All I knew was the hollowness in me, the sense of having been cut adrift.

After a while it was decided that my father would be moved to the chapel. More and more people were arriving and the crowds filled the courtyard, pressing out into the alleyway. He was carried by my brother and myself and Jonah and the jetty boys. I wouldn't let Dil take a place under the coffin and shoved him aside when he tried to help. He moved away without protest. Jonah eyed me silently for a moment and appraised Dil.

Uncle Bee went before us down the stairs, coaxing people to move aside, and slowly, fearful of touching the walls, doorframe, railings with the coffin, lest my father's soul be anchored to the building forever, we manoeuvred him down to the street. The visitors formed a long line behind us. I couldn't recollect seeing such a large gathering for a funeral before. We made our way to the chapel, Mulrooney and Levi walking in front. I moved automatically, stepping in time with the other pall-bearers. My arms and shoulders ached. From behind the coffin I heard Lorna cry out but I couldn't turn my head to look. And so I didn't notice when, in the midst of all this, the House-On-Wheels returned to Esperanza Street and fell in alongside our procession.

We entered the chapel where the vigil continued. People took turns sitting next to me – America, Jonah, Missy and Uncle Bee, even Benny – but I was only dimly aware of them in the soft night, or at least no more aware of them than I was of the shadows and candle flame, of the silence and the chanting, of the muted sounds of grief. Subong never came and I decided, grimly, that he would not return, that no trace of him would be found. I didn't notice that Lorna wasn't in the pew next to me and, truthfully, I didn't really care where she was. I resented her grief; she'd known my father for so short a time anyway.

Dub came late in the night and stayed for a couple of hours. As he stood up to leave he hesitated and, following his gaze into the shadows, I saw that BabyLu was there too, in a corner by herself. I hadn't expected her to come and she didn't look at me but stared straight ahead. She wore a scarf that covered much of her face but it was unmistakeably her. Dub walked out quickly but I knew he would wait for her in the dark outside the chapel. Seeing that my attention wasn't on my father's coffin, a few people glanced curiously at BabyLu. She crossed herself and bent her head so that her face was almost entirely hidden. When I looked again a little while later she'd gone.

When I came out into the bright morning sun, I saw at last Lorna and her baby and, with her, Lottie, Lando, Luis, Lenora, Luke and Buan and the ramshackle contraption that was the House-On-Wheels. The gaming tables still hung awry. The children looked hungry. Lando came over and put a hand on my shoulder. 'We didn't expect to come back and find Dante gone,' he said.

'Didn't expect to find the street half burned down either,' Lottie said. I was annoyed with her for exaggerating. It felt like she was making light of things, like they weren't important enough to be accurate about.

'I don't really care about the street.' I knew as I said it how rude it sounded.

'Everyone's been talking about how he died. He was a hero,' she said carefully.

'How long are you staying?' I asked.

Lottie shrugged. 'Depends on the girl.' I hadn't thought about Lorna, about what she might do now that my father was dead. Now that I considered it, I assumed she'd leave the same way she'd come, in the House-on-Wheels.

But Lorna, her eyes on Marisol, who lay wriggling on a pile of bedding in the House, said sullenly, 'I don't want to come.'

'Where else can you go?' Lottie said. 'Your rich husband gonna take care of you and your bastard child? Buy you a coupé?'

Lorna didn't reply but looked at me, her eyes red, the skin of her cheeks blotched.

'Your father paid up his rent for a few days?' Lottie said. 'Or she has to leave straight away?'

I looked away so that she might not see how her question offended me. 'I don't know,' I said.

'You know?' she said to her daughter.

Lorna stole a look in my direction before replying. 'He always paid to the end of the month.'

'So you want us to wait around till you've considered all your offers?' Lottie said.

Irritably, I cast my eyes about the gathering. I hadn't thought about any of this, about Lorna, about sorting through my father's things, emptying his apartment so that it might be rented again to a stranger. Even his vigil and the burial to come had been organised by someone else. I spotted my brother with Jonah and watched him till I caught his eye. He waved me over and, gratefully, I excused myself and went to join him.

Miguel was smoking a cigarette. He looked pale. 'What's your plan now?' he said. I didn't have one. I told him that we had to think about clearing the apartment, making sure our father's things were in order. 'Not me, man,' he said. 'I can't stay long.'

'Your father lived like a saint,' Jonah said. 'A lot less stuff than most people.'

'Sure,' my brother laughed, 'a saint. That his baby?' He nodded towards the House-on-Wheels.

'No,' I said.

He finished his cigarette and, straight away, lit another. 'Come with me to Saudi,' he said. 'We could lie about your age.' I hadn't considered the possibility of escaping, not just Esperanza and Puerto, but the country.

'Your father would've wanted you to finish your studies,' said Jonah. 'Plenty of time for gallivanting later.'

'Gallivanting!' my brother laughed again. 'Joseph never had *that* in him. Always serious about life, from the very beginning.'

'No sign of Subong?' I asked Jonah.

'His mother went to the police. They filed a report.'

My brother snorted. 'This country's going to hell. He'll be washed ashore in a week.'

'It's a hard enough time, Miguel.' Jonah clapped him on the shoulder gently enough but his words were abrupt and there was iron in his voice.

My brother ground his cigarette out without finishing it. I studied him cautiously. 'You ever think about getting married?' I said.

'Sure, I'm gonna marry an actress,' he said without looking at me.

'Seriously, Miguel. Find someone to look after you.'

'You know any rich women?'

'Just any decent girl.'

'I'm not cleaning up Pop's mess if that's what you're hoping.'

I looked over at Lorna. She was crying now, quietly, her face in profile, lower lip jutting out sulkily. She really wasn't pretty, I thought, yet the baby was cute. 'I didn't mean her in particular,' I said.

'What plan are you boys hatching?' said my sister coming towards us. My nephews trailed after her, squabbling at her heels, but she ignored them.

'Poor girl,' said Jonah, looking at Lorna. 'I guess your father taking her in gave her hope for a while.'

'Who is she anyway?' Luisa said. 'He wasn't her father or her husband.'

'Is that four now, Luisa?' Jonah said.

My sister looked down at her children. 'Yeah,' she said.

'Keep you out of trouble,' Jonah said.

'Married young. Never had a chance to *get* in trouble,' she glanced at Lorna.

'You didn't have a lot but you had more than her,' Jonah said. Luisa's eyes blazed at him.

Soon it was time to take my father to the cemetery, where arrangements had been made for him to lie beside my mother. Luisa and Miguel were quiet through the mass. Lorna cried openly and once or twice I saw Luisa cast a scornful look at her. The Bukaykays all came to see my father interred, as well as Aunt Mary and the boys and America. I didn't look about to see who else came and who didn't, though I was conscious of a crowd. I stared instead at the wall of tombs as my father's coffin was pushed in and the opening sealed with concrete, the cemetery boys balanced barefoot on planks and bamboo scaffolding. The fate of the cemetery was still uncertain but there was nowhere else for him to go. I pushed the thought away for now and started thinking about the reality of going through his things, of understanding more fully, from the minutiae of his life, what kind of a man he'd been. I wasn't looking forward to it, and when I overheard Luisa complaining to Missy that it would take her days to sort through Pop's stuff, I kept quiet.

On the way back we returned home by a different route, snaking in a long line through the alleys of Greenhills, just as we'd done for my mother.

# MAN WITH BOLO

After the funeral Aunt Mary urged me to rest a few days but I was afraid to sit idle and be alone with my thoughts. So after a while she and America conspired to keep me busy instead, sending me out on easy errands so that I wouldn't work away in silence in the subdued rooms of the Bougainvillea. America, quieter in my presence now, shifted her attentions briefly to Dub, specifically to his state of nutrition. And so I found myself once again on the forecourt of Earl's garage holding another of Dub's forgotten lunch packets, having promised America I'd watch him finish it.

It was the first time in a long while that we'd been alone together. I'd intended to leave quickly but he started talking as he took the parcel from me. He looked me in the eye as he said, 'I'm sorry, Joe. For everything.' He told me he'd spoken to her the night of the vigil as I knew he would. 'She was pleased the vigil was moved to the church,' he said. 'She wouldn't have felt she could come to your pop's apartment.' I could see that talking about her lifted him.

'I'm glad she came,' I said, and I meant it.

He looked away, staring along the street into the distance. 'She's leaving,' he said and he tried to sound indifferent. 'She's moving out of Prosperidad. She won't tell me where she's going, but she's going with *him*.' And his voice betrayed him as he said, 'She's keeping it. She still won't say if it's mine or his. Either way it'll grow up calling him Pop.' I imagined then how he must have begged her, in the shadow of the stone church, until eventually she would have grown anxious, looking about her to see who might be watching. He hadn't seen her since, he said, and though he'd stared up at her balcony every day from the garage forecourt, the windows of her apartment had remained closed. Each time he'd gone to knock at her door there was no answer, though once or twice he thought he'd heard movement inside. He looked at me as if I might have an explanation. 'She doesn't love him,' he said bitterly. 'Just his money.'

I didn't know what might console him. I said, without thinking, 'She has to think of the child.' His face coloured.

'She sent something for you. Didn't even ask me to fetch them, paid some kid instead. Told him to make it clear they were for *you*.' I felt a flicker of pleasure. He didn't mention whether she'd left him anything too.

I followed him into the garage. Under the workbenches, against the wall, was a line of cardboard boxes that had once contained coconut oil, sour-sop juice, soap. Each one had already been torn open. Dub knelt down and pulled one out. It was full of books. When I saw them I knew for certain that she wasn't planning to return and I was sorry; I'd have liked to say goodbye, to tell her myself that it had meant something that she'd come to my father's vigil even when everyone knew she was Eddie Casama's mistress.

But there was more to the story, an event that gave shape to her leaving, and Dub told me only a part of it. The rest I constructed later from fragments that by themselves might have been nothing at all: the way he started to cradle one hand with the other, the way he touched his guitar but wouldn't play it, the way he touched his hair, his jeans in the laundry basket wet at the seat from having been rinsed, the t-shirt he never wore again – *Eat My Dust*. No one else mentioned it either, though their eyes carried its reflections for some time. Of course they may not have known much more than I did. When I recount my version now, no doubt I'll have embellished some parts and diminished others, but I hope that in the end I will have told, as far as is possible, the truth, and that I will have given both Dub and BabyLu their fair due.

I didn't pay much mind to Dub's absence during the rally, distracted as I was by so many other things: Dil at my father's side, Suelita's sudden vivacity in Benny's company, the bruises that proclaimed my weakness. I'd assumed that Dub would be at the garage and didn't think otherwise, even when I glimpsed Earl standing alone in the crowd. It was only later when his mother asked me to look for him that it occurred to me he might have gone to see BabyLu, for she would have been alone at home while Eddie was at the rally. I imagined that Eddie, happy enough to be seen with his mistress from time to time in the back of his car, at a local noodle joint, or even on the balcony of one of his apartments, would never have brought her to a protest rally, particularly one where he might have preferred to present a blameless exterior. Dub would have expected to have BabyLu to himself for the rest of the evening too, for Eddie's time even after the rally was over would surely have been taken up by Judge Robello and others of his kind and then, later, with Connie, his wife, to prolong the appearance of propriety.

The morning of the rally, then, Dub helped carry baskets of food down to the jetty office but his mind wasn't on the rally, it was on her; on the memory of her leaning in a corner of her balcony the evening before, the light from inside her apartment glowing on her hair and back, leaving her face in shadow. He'd looked up at her from the garage forecourt and, though she'd barely moved in response, it was enough to tell him that she'd seen him and that perhaps she was ready to talk. Before he could respond he saw a movement behind her and Eddie came out onto the balcony, slipped an arm around her waist, his fingers spread over her belly. Eddie looked down over Prosperidad, at Dub who automatically bent to his bike as if inspecting it. Dub hadn't meant to look away at that moment, to relinquish her to Eddie so easily, and he was never sure later why he did. He looked up again immediately, a challenge in his stance, but they were already turning away, already moving back inside the apartment, the doors swinging partly shut behind them. Dub kicked his bike lightly, gazed up at the empty balcony, then rode slowly home.

By the next morning he'd slept little and thought a lot. His night had been consumed with analysing her slight movement on the balcony, the incline of her head, her glance in his direction though her eyes, like her face, were indistinct in the half-light. He'd decided that if she was on the balcony when he got to work he would go to her the first chance he got. And of course she was there, watering her bougainvillea.

When Earl left for the market hall, Dub bolted the garage door and walked across the street. She was watching him from just inside the balcony doors and counted out the seconds, opening her apartment door to him as he raised his hand to knock.

The sun was low in the sky and Dub and BabyLu were asleep when Eddie's men came. Cesar was not with them of course, for he was with Eddie, and would never have embroiled himself too deeply in his employer's personal matters. Nor was Eddie's chauffeur there, the man who had warned Dub off in the street without a word passing between them. Rico's *barkada* may have sufficed for me but Eddie would surely never have sent them to BabyLu's apartment to deal with Aunt Mary's boy: they were too coarse and of course they were local. The men who came to the apartment were probably not even from Esperanza.

The men, three of them – a fourth waited in the car – knocked at the door, politely, then more firmly, for it took BabyLu some time to answer. When she did, they didn't stop to speak to her, though they nodded respectfully enough and held their hands behind them or out to their sides so that they wouldn't touch her as they pushed past. They walked straight to the bedroom where Dub was already dressed, and even as they pulled him out of the flat, as BabyLu flung her books at them one after another, they still did not say a word.

I imagined at first that he was taken to a place similar to where I was taken by Rico: a patch of waste ground at the edge of Greenhills strewn with piles of trash that nobody would ever clear away, or perhaps a dead-end alley behind Colon Market, the stench of which would bring back the memory of this day in all its clarity; a place where a boy like him would be lost, out of context. But because I didn't like to imagine him there surrounded by Eddie's men – thugs – even if they did wear suits – I pictured him instead being driven around Esperanza, around Puerto, in silence for some time. Then at last the man next to the driver, clean shaven, a few years older than Dub, with the appearance of a clerk or the manager of a small but respectable store, said, 'She's pretty, huh?' as he twisted round in the seat to look at him. Maybe it was the first time this man had ever seen her.

The other men nodded in agreement. 'Anyway, there'll be other pretty girls for you,' one said to Dub.

'She looked real mad, eh?' the clerk laughed, rubbing the back of his head.

'Heavy, some of those books.'

'She reads a lot, huh? That's what you do together? Read? Talk about books?' The men laughed.

'You should really forget about her.' The tone of voice was casual, as if giving advice to a friend.

'Girls that pretty are always trouble.'

'Sure. Find a girl who's not so much to look at and they won't mess you around.'

'You think it's just you? That you're even the first?' the clerk said suddenly.

'That true?' the driver turned to him.

The clerk looked at Dub again. 'Would you leave her alone if you thought it was true?'

'I love her,' Dub said quietly, almost to himself, looking out of the window at the streets moving past, the painted stalls strung with fruit, clothing, lottery tickets. I wondered, when I imagined it, whether he would really have said such a thing. I suspected not, though I hoped he had, for the possibility of him saying it seemed to me the only thread of purity in the entire matter.

'Well then,' said the clerk, 'that's a bit of a problem.' They drove out of town, away from the coast. The suburbs yielded to rice paddies, coconut palms, guava groves. The men stopped the car and pulled Dub out onto the road. In the distance, the twilight was pricked by lights and smoke threaded up between the trees. The air smelled clean. The men pinned him down, his face turned to the side, one cheek against the dirt. They pulled at his right hand, spread his fingers out, palm to the road. One took out a pocket-knife but kept it folded. The clerk took out a bolo, tested the blade with his thumb, whistled. 'My cousin Jaime plays guitar too,' he said.

'You know anyone who doesn't play the guitar?' Pocket Knife said.

'My grandmother.' The men laughed, enjoying them-selves.

'It's nothing personal,' the clerk said. 'It's just that she belongs to Eddie Casama. He's not known for sharing.' He raised the bolo. Maybe at that moment Dub felt a surge of disbelief, before the fear, like I had. But for Dub the blow never came. The bolo hit the ground in front of his hand, in front of his face, and stayed upright, wedged in the dirt at the slightest angle, visible the whole while as the men pulled his head back and cut his hair away jaggedly with the pocket knife. When they'd finished they pulled him back to the car.

'Eddie knows your mother, eh?'

'You have a little brother?'

'You like bikes? You have to be real careful on some of these tracks.'

'Maybe we'll see you around.'

He was driven back. They dropped him on the coast road, within sight of the jetty, where the last boats were already leaving and the scent of roasting nuts and meat and wood smoke filled the air. He walked quickly, not looking around him to see who might notice Dub Morelos without his usual confidence, the stains of old tears and road dust on his face, his hair short, uneven, filthy.

At the corner of Prosperidad and Esperanza he slowed. In the street in front of the entrance to her building: the same car, the same men. They saw him, waved. He looked up at her balcony, then back down. He counted the men, *four*, though he already knew of course how many there were. He hesitated, not wanting to walk away when they remained so close to her, aware all the time that his presence would keep them right where they stood. Her balcony door opened and he saw her come out. The men looked up too and were caught by a cascade from her watering can as she missed her bougainvillea, scattering along the sidewalk as she hurled the empty can down at them. She leaned out over the balcony, picked up a small potted plant in each hand, raised them, ready. The clerk looked across at Dub and in that same moment Dub knew that if BabyLu saw him she would come out to him and then he alone could not guarantee her safety or that of the child inside her. He turned away and ran on up the hill, the sound of laughter, real or illusory, trailing in the air behind him all the way home. I imagined then that she turned, expecting to see him without knowing why, and saw only the emptiness where he had been.

# ASSEMBLAGE

Luisa moved into our father's apartment with her children to sort through his things. I offered, reluctantly, to help, but she picked impatiently through everything I did until I left her to it. At first Lorna and the baby, Marisol, remained in the apartment too, which vexed my sister no end but, aware of how it might seem if she asked them to leave straight away, she decided to ignore them instead. She wouldn't let Lorna help, other than leaving her to tend all the children at once. Luisa's children, sensitive to their mother's dislike of Lorna, were disobedient and made this more difficult than it ought to have been, which Luisa seized upon as proof of Lorna's ineptitude and the reason why she had attached herself so readily to our father. Luisa's only concession was to accept the meals that Lorna presented her with and which, I later found out, had been paid for by Missy. Lorna, without any real claim to the place, was careful around us. Quiet and deferential towards my sister, she fetched and carried as Luisa decreed. I felt uncomfortable seeing Luisa ordering her about like a servant; my father had never treated her that way. But Lorna seemed happy enough to comply.

Outside, the House-on-Wheels took up temporary encampment in the courtyard, but Luisa wouldn't let its other occupants, especially the children, into the apartment, and watched them closely whenever they came to the door. I'd have let them inside to see Lorna at least, but Luisa wouldn't have it. Missy Bukaykay, when she came, clicked her tongue at Luisa from time to time but my sister remained obstinate. Lottie and Lando hung on, uncertain when their daughter would be rejoining them. I wasn't sure what she was waiting for either but I didn't want to ask. More than once I overheard her crying, being comforted by Elisa who said to me later, 'She doesn't want to take Marisol back on the streets.' She said it as if she was asking a question I ought to have an answer to, and I was annoyed at her tone, but I was even more annoyed with Lorna for not crying over my father.

'Can hardly blame her,' Missy said.

'It's what she knows,' Luisa snapped. 'She had her time living off him.'

'She kept house,' Elisa said. 'She kept it real clean.'

'I'd take her back with me as a maid, but then there's the baby. I've got enough to deal with at home,' Luisa said.

Without a purpose in the apartment, Lorna took Marisol outside to be entertained by the other children. 'It's a shame,' Missy said looking straight at me after they'd left.

It was a hot day. From time to time the sound of the children in the courtyard drifted in through the open door and windows. Occasionally Lottie or Elisa or Bina's voice came up, chiding the kids into a briefly sustained order. Inside, we mostly worked in silence. Luisa was brisk and bossed me around but I didn't mind. She spoke more softly to Missy and to Bina when she came in to help. To Elisa she spoke quietly but didn't look at her when addressing her. I was sure Elisa minded but she didn't say anything. Maybe she figured Luisa would be gone in a day or two and, with both parents now dead, she might never return.

When it was time for me to return to the boarding house, Missy got up to leave too. The afternoon air felt thick as we stepped out into the hallway together. In the courtyard the children were flinging water at each other from a pail. Lorna stood by the House-on-Wheels holding Marisol to her and fanning her gently with her hand. She lowered the baby into the cart, wedging her into place on the bedding pile, one side against a sack of rice, the other against the shoeshine boxes. The baby started to whine at being put down. I called a greeting at Lottie and Lando and, leaning over the side of the House, waved at Marisol. At the movement, Marisol quietened, but only for a moment. Lorna picked her up again to soothe her. 'She likes him more than you!' said Lottie to Lando, nodding at me.

'We all know I wouldn't win any beauty contests,' Lando replied.

'I could've married a rich man at least,' said Lottie.

It sounded like the start of an old game but Lorna wasn't playing along this time. 'Babies don't know nothing about looks or money,' she said stiffly. She smiled at me hesitantly. I wondered if she felt she couldn't return to the apartment if Missy or I were not there. But it couldn't be helped; I couldn't stay there all evening to her convenience. Still, I felt guilty, and shot a look at the baby as I turned to go. Missy and I stepped out of the courtyard into the alley. Behind us, Lorna started to croon softly to Marisol, a Rey Valera song, one of my father's favourites.

Missy was quiet as we walked in the direction of the Bukaykay shack. 'Lots going to be changing around here,' she said eventually, looking in the direction of the jetty where the blackened remains of the market hall still lay where they'd fallen. 'People are already talking about leaving.'

'The whole place feels different now anyway.'

She nodded. 'The fight's gone out of people.'

'Maybe they can't win,' and even as I said it I wondered why I hadn't said *we*.

If Missy noticed, she ignored it. 'Why do you think she's not left yet?' she said. I thought about saying *Who?* as if I didn't know she was talking about Lorna. 'If your father was here he'd be hoping you'd give her a reason to stay.' Missy stared at me but I ignored her, concentrated on walking. 'Suelita's off to nursing college soon. She won't wait for no one now. Maybe she'll marry a doctor. Or get work stateside.' I blushed. 'You think I don't know you like my own?'

'If she matters so much to you, make Fidel marry her.'

'What are you saying now?' Missy was annoyed but she didn't say another word after that.

By the time I got back to the boarding house I'd worked myself up into a temper and I was heavy-handed about the kitchen until America reminded me sharply that I could take my bad mood out on my own possessions.

I was still seething when we sat down to eat together after the rest of the household had finished. America looked tired and I wondered if her rash was giving her trouble again, but I didn't ask. She'd made *bibingka*, one of my favourites, and saved a large piece for me. She watched me closely as I ate. 'What are you sweetening me up for?' I said.

'Who says it's for you?'

I didn't reply, which seemed to irritate her suddenly. 'I'm getting pretty tired of this,' she snapped. I stared at her, waited. She always said stuff like that. This time she kept me waiting for longer than usual. 'I'm going home,' she said, 'for good. The end of the month.' She was cunning; she'd waited for me to fill my mouth before she said it. I stopped chewing and she added testily, 'Don't go trying to make me feel bad.'

I thought about being at the Bougainvillea without her. Because of my duties at the boarding house I'd never really had the chance to cultivate friendships to the extent that other boys at school did and, though I was well enough regarded there I suppose, I wasn't popular. I didn't have my own crowd. The other big houses at our end of Esperanza also had houseboys, but none my age, and on the occasions we met they talked lightly about what could be taken from the household that wouldn't be missed or which of their employers' children regularly broke curfew or kept bad company – conversations that made me uncomfortable, as if I was complicit simply by listening.

America looked disapprovingly at my plate, the *bibingka* left half eaten. She got up, leaving me to tidy up the dishes while she went to find Aunt Mary. There was little else to do and I waited in the silent kitchen for her to return before giving up and retiring to my room.

I arrived at my father's apartment block the next morning to find the House-on-Wheels emptied of itself, its contents displayed around it in small, neat piles. Lorna perched on the foot-rail, leaning over the side into the cart. She smiled at me as I walked in and pulled her skirt down to cover the back of her legs, though it hadn't risen particularly high. I felt a stab of scorn; did she think I'd be looking? Her other hand moved up and down rhythmically and I saw that she was fanning Marisol, who was asleep on a mat in the cart. The baby fidgeted as I looked over the side but didn't wake. 'It'll be cooler inside,' I said. 'Anyway, Dante had an electric fan.' In the last couple of days I'd caught myself on a few occasions referring to my father by his first name, as if his death had left us on equal terms. Lorna shrugged and smiled again, glancing up at the apartment window.

On the other side of the House, Lottie was boiling a pan of water over their small stove. 'The Queen of England made them sleep outside last night,' she said. She sounded offhand, as if this was only to be expected. I wasn't sure how to respond, whether to defend Luisa, and I was irritated by Lottie's tone. Yet I could picture my sister closing the door on them, her face pinched and icy. I said nothing. I looked over to where Lando was washing his feet and rinsing his mouth at the water tap. He raised an arm in greeting. The other children were nowhere to be seen. I peered over the side of the cart at Marisol again. Lando turned off the tap and came over. 'Thinking maybe we'll leave today,' he said, looking at Lorna. She ignored him and me, fanned the baby a little faster. I excused myself and ran up the stairs to the apartment.

I was surprised when Elisa answered the door, for just the day before she'd said in a low voice, close to my ear, that she'd only come if she knew I was already there. She was holding a broom and looked in bad spirits. 'She's lucky she's your sister,' she said.

Luisa came out of the kitchen. 'Need to give it an *extra* clean,' she said. 'How long was she staying here?'

'Not long. Why'd you make her sleep outside?'

Luisa looked at me, her lips a thin line. 'What, you're Mother Teresa now?'

'She's all right. And the baby's not used to sleeping out.'

Luisa was twelve years older than me and, though I hardly saw her, she acted like she'd stepped into our mother's role in her dealings with me, even standing the same way with her hands on her hips, the same taut expressions and sudden flashes of displeasure. I hadn't minded it before but now I did. 'You're not my mother, Luisa,' I said. 'You haven't even been home for years.'

She looked away to hide her surprise. 'We should sell the furniture, unless you want to keep it for your *wedding*,' she said.

'You can't tell me what to do!' I was incensed.

Elisa stopped sweeping. Luisa stared at me. 'What are you talking about?' she said.

'Why should I marry her? Why can't Miguel or Fidel marry her?'

'Marry who?' She looked bewildered and I remembered that it had been my mother's line, whenever I wouldn't finish my food: *you want to keep it for your wedding?*

'Missy thinks I should marry Lorna,' I said, 'but I don't want to. I don't love her. She's not even pretty.' Luisa stared at me for a moment and then, unexpectedly, she smiled. I didn't know what she found so amusing and I bristled. Then, behind me, I heard soft sounds. At the open door stood Lorna, the baby held to her chest. She was flushed and looked away as I turned round. She looked almost as if she might break into a run. *She's not even pretty.* I glared at her, unrepentant.

'You can tell her yourself now,' Luisa said, and turned away.

Lorna, without saying why she'd come, walked away again quietly, her back straight, head high, and it was Elisa who went after her, throwing a look in my direction as she left. I closed the door after them impatiently.

Inside, the furniture had been pushed to the edges of the room and the remaining space was ringed with boxes that Luisa had filled with our father's possessions in no particular order, a strip of paper taped to each: *books, cassette player, kerosene lamp, PASTOR L?* It surprised me how little there was, finally. No vestige of him remained, or rather, now that his things were no longer where he had placed them, it felt at last that he was gone. I was struck by how many of his belongings were functional: kitchen implements or tools. Even the books were volumes in an old encyclopaedia. The few ornaments had been my mother's. Most of it was to be given away to the church, Luisa said, with an exaggerated tone of generosity that made me despise her for a moment.

She'd found a small tin containing photographs of us as children and of my mother. We sat on the floor to divide them between us but, except for one picture of her with our mother, Luisa let me have them all. There was one of Miguel squatting on the sea wall, both hands giving a thumbs-up to the camera, his mouth hesitant, tender; in the background, our mother pregnant with me. After the funeral, he'd said that he wanted no mementoes but had left an address for money to be wired if there was any.

In the bedroom my nephews, told to sit still by their mother, were fretful. They were bored, the novelty of the trip having long since dissipated. 'When are you leaving?' I said.

'Soon. Fetch Pastor Levi to help you move this stuff. Or take Elisa.' I looked at the boxes. Luisa hadn't thought to pack them lightly; one contained the entire encyclopaedia.

'The neighbours might use some of this. Or Lottie and Lando,' I said.

'I don't want anyone taking the best stuff and Pastor Levi thinking Pop was cheap.'

'What about the furniture?'

'The landlord's coming to check the place. I told him if he wants to keep the furniture he can buy it. Otherwise we'll have to sell it. We can send the money to Miguel.'

'The rent was paid till the end of the month.'

'I can't stay that long.' She glanced out the door, towards the stairs that led down to the courtyard, where the children of the House-on-Wheels could be heard returning. 'I've just cleaned the place, Joseph,' she said crossly.

She'd left a pile of things on top of her own case: a china figurine of two European children kissing coyly, a photograph, an empty silver-coloured picture frame that had been my parents' wedding gift, a cutwork tablecloth, a set of glass bowls. Her luggage would be heavy on the way back and I thought of her struggling with it, the boys whining at her side. 'What are you so happy about?' she said.

'Nothing.'

Elisa came back in. She pulled a sour face at me, ignored Luisa. 'Let's go see the Pastor,' she said.

'Take a box each,' Luisa said, but Elisa stayed by the open door, staring at me. I followed her out.

In the courtyard, Lorna kept her back to us as we passed. 'You're not responsible for her and her baby,' Elisa said sulkily when we were out of earshot. 'She said that too.'

'I don't want to talk about it.'

'She wants me to ask Pastor Levi about adoption.' There was nothing accusatory in her tone. It was a practical solution that I hadn't considered but, even so, hearing her say it jarred on me.

# BUMPER STICKERS

Pastor Levi and his brother, Cesar, with eleven kids between them, lived together on the same plot: Cesar in the house that had belonged to their parents and Levi in a house that he'd built in the garden. Pastor Levi's house was much smaller and, when he built it, Cesar's wife, Loring, complained about him building all over her rose garden. There was nothing for it though: Pastor Levi's wife was expecting their first child and there was no money to buy another plot. Besides, Levi had turned down the chance to go to medical college and make some real money to follow his dream of entering the seminary, so arguably had God on his side; the rose garden had to go. It worked out fine anyway. The children, close enough in age, played happily together and after a while everyone else learned to get on.

I'd never been inside the Pastor's house before, though I'd passed by it enough times. It smelled familiar, of oil lamps and fried fish. It was dark inside, the windows small and cluttered with things. Those that didn't have the family's belongings heaped against them had stickers of Jesus or the Virgin Mary further obscuring the little light that came through. They were stickers like one might find on a car: *God Is My Co-Pilot*; *Are You Following Jesus This Closely?* Each room seemed to encroach upon the next: the chairs and television were in the hallway, so close to the front door that it didn't open fully; the refrigerator stood just inside the doorway of the bedroom nearest the kitchen. When we entered, Gregorio, Levi's eldest son, got up from one of the chairs, nodded at me, switched the television off and retreated wordlessly to another room.

Pastor Levi sat us down and offered us both a drink. I shook my head. Elisa took a glass of cold water and sipped at it steadily. Levi looked at me gravely and asked how I was. 'Fine,' I said. 'Luisa wondered if the church wanted some of his things.'

'Will you not keep them, Joseph? Dante might have preferred it.' I felt like telling him that I knew better than he did what my father might have preferred but I didn't.

Elisa spoke up now. 'I also need to discuss something with you, Pastor,' she said. 'About Lorna and her baby.' Pastor Levi looked at me, and I pretended not to notice. Instead I stared straight ahead. On the wall above the television was a calendar with his name and his wife's name on it and a small photograph of the two of them holding hands and smiling. The picture must have been taken some time ago because they both looked younger in it and Eveline more slender than I'd ever seen her. Underneath the photograph were the words: *Jesus is the head of this household. He is the unseen host at every meal, the silent listener to every conversation.* I thought about Gregorio's apparent obedience at home, though he had as foul a mouth as any of the older boys at school. I wondered whether he felt that at least at school he didn't have to worry about Jesus eavesdropping on him.

'She wanted me to ask you about adoption,' Elisa said and I could tell from her voice that she knew she had my attention as well as the Pastor's, though she didn't turn to include me. I guess Pastor Levi had already given this some thought because he didn't seem at all surprised and was quick to answer. The church had connections, he said, with agencies that might be able to place the baby with a couple or a family, perhaps even overseas. He talked plainly, looking at each of us in turn, but I couldn't hold his eye. Eventually he said, 'I'll come by later, talk to her and look over your father's things,' and he put a hand on my shoulder, turning away again before I had to acknowledge him. He insisted on saying a prayer for us before we left and when he closed his eyes Elisa began drumming her fingers on the arm of the chair, before stopping and balling her hand when she realised I'd noticed. If Pastor Levi heard it, he didn't falter.

Elisa was quiet when we left. She didn't speak until we were back on Esperanza and then she said, 'It wouldn't be fair on you either, Joseph. She knows that.'

I didn't want to go back to the apartment so we cut through Prosperidad and out onto the coast road and walked along the sea wall away from the ruined market hall and jetty. The charred timbers of the jetty had been knocked away and replaced by makeshift ramps to keep the boatmen and jetty boys in business for a while. I didn't want to speak to anyone there, didn't want to have to behave in whatever way was expected of me by my father's friends and co-workers. Elisa didn't push me to say anything and we sat on the sea wall for some time in silence. After a while I said, 'When we were young, I thought that one day you and I would get married.'

'I'd only marry you if you were rich,' she said, kicking her legs against the stone.

'If Marisol went to a good family that would be the best thing,' I said. 'She'd get sent to school, maybe even college.'

'You talk like it's a *choice*,' Elisa said, her legs suddenly still. She put a finger to her cheek, inclined her head girlishly. 'Shall I wear the red one or the yellow one? Put my hair up or leave it down? Give up my baby or keep her?' Her tone fooled me for a second and, on reflex, I made as if I was going to push her off the wall, like we were kidding around. Then, all at once, her words surrendered their meaning. I looked down at the water, the surface of it skimmed with rubbish and oil from the boats, the water beneath clear. I opened my mouth to defend myself but she wasn't done yet. 'You think poor girls miss their babies less than rich ones?' she said. She didn't want an answer and I didn't want to give her one; anything I said now would infuriate her. Her words anchored us to where we sat. I couldn't get up to leave; it would have ended the conversation and she'd have been doubly mad with me for, even though she said nothing more, I knew from her face that the subject was far from closed. So we stayed put, some distance from the broken jetty but close enough to make out the boats coming in and the figures of the jetty boys, their identities indistinguishable apart from Jonah. My throat felt thick. *So what?* I wanted to say. *What's it got to do with me anyway?* High above us the sun reached its peak, blazing off the water.

Back at the Bougainvillea I followed America round the kitchen. 'She's a hard worker,' I said. 'She kept Pop's apartment real clean.'

'Nothing doing,' America said. 'You can ask her yourself. You're old enough and pretty soon I'll be gone anyway and then you'll have to handle everything without running to me to bail you out.'

Aunt Mary was in the sala, seated at the piano. By her feet were piles of sheet music but on top of the piano was a stack of photograph albums and there was another on her lap. It looked as if she'd started one task only to be distracted by another. She smiled at me as I walked in. 'How are you feeling, Joseph?' She asked me this almost every time she saw me now.

'We're almost done at the apartment. Luisa will be gone soon.'

Aunt Mary's smile deepened. 'We don't choose our family, Joseph.'

I asked if she needed any help with whatever she was doing and she laughed then. I looked down at the album on her lap. The page was half empty. In front of her on the closed piano lid sat a small, neatly squared pile of photographs. On the otherwise empty music stand above it, a solitary picture: the girl under the yellow bell tree. Aunt Mary was making a space for her. I sat down on the mat near her feet and told her then about Lorna and Marisol and our visit to Pastor Levi, about whether there might be a way out that meant she didn't have to lose her baby. 'I could show her how to do everything the way you like it,' I said.

Aunt Mary listened to me patiently, frowning slightly the whole while. When I'd finished, she said, 'I have to think about the boys. Dub will be gone soon, but Benny is only fifteen.' She didn't have to say any more. I understood what she meant. Lorna was only a year younger than Benny and me, but already a mother. I couldn't press her; I knew my place. Aunt Mary was a woman who considered everything carefully, who rarely if ever spoke in haste. Perhaps she'd even considered it already and decided against bringing the unknown, the unknowable, into her house. I didn't blame her for it. It wasn't her problem. It wasn't anybody's.

I didn't return to the apartment that evening as I'd planned. Instead I worked and read at home. I didn't want to be there when Pastor Levi came to pick through my father's things or see Luisa flattering him and offering him refreshments while ordering Elisa or Lorna to fetch them. When I did return it was late the following morning and, as I turned the corner past the general store, I saw that the courtyard was empty. The House-on-Wheels had gone.

# CUTWORK

Upstairs, Luisa was making ready to leave. 'Where were you last night?' she said irritably.

'Did Pastor Levi come?' I said. I looked around the flat. The boxes containing our father's life were still there.

'Yes, he came. Spent more time talking to that girl than to me,' she said. 'Private talk. Quiet talk. Like she can discuss her affairs in my house and it's none of my business.' I imagined Pastor Levi sat in a corner with Lorna, his voice dropping if Luisa made to busy herself nearby. 'Landlord doesn't want to buy the furniture,' she continued. 'I guess you can give it to the Pastor. I can't be bothered with it any more. Miguel will only drink the money anyway. You'll have to move all those boxes when the Pastor's ready for them. I'm leaving this afternoon.' She looked at her watch and then, looking up at me, added, 'No need to look so pleased about it.' She pulled a face but I could see that it was a relief for her too. I suppose we only knew how to be our old selves in each other's company.

Luisa knelt down to pull the boys into their clothes. They were sluggish in the heat and uncooperative. I started to collect their toys. 'Lottie and Lando have gone then,' I said.

'Who?'

'The House-on-Wheels.'

'That junk heap in the courtyard? Yeah, they've gone. The girl was at Bina's just earlier.'

'Lorna?'

Luisa regarded me shrewdly. 'Yeah. Your *wife*.'

I didn't bite. 'And the baby?'

Luisa shrugged as she finished dressing the children. 'With her. Why, you thought maybe she'd eaten it? Or lost it playing Tong-its?' I was surprised at the sudden tempest I felt then, which was as much relief as it was dismay. I pinched my nephews' cheeks gently but they turned away without smiling, pushing their faces into their mother's breast, her neck. Luisa rested her cheek against the youngest's hair for a few seconds. 'I miss him, Joseph. I miss her too,' she said. I was annoyed with her for wanting to open such a conversation now, at the eleventh hour, not knowing what memories she might exhume and leave me to contain on my own. I moved to the door, gathered up her luggage and walked out. I heard her fuss at the children as they started after me, one for walking too slowly, the other for not waiting. I stacked the bags at the base of the stairwell and went in search of a cab.

When I returned she was chewing her lip and she looked away from me as I stepped out of the taxi. She looked sour, her eyes bright, the lashes clumped and wet. She settled the children into the cab, kissed my cheek before climbing in after them. When the cab pulled away, she stared straight ahead, not permitting me even at the last to look into her eyes.

Aunt Bina's door, like most of our neighbours', was often left ajar and, as always, I walked in without announcing myself.

Marisol lay on her back on the mat, her limbs playing in the air above her, her eyes intent on the brightly coloured strips of cloth tied around her wrists and ankles. Beside her, carefully, clumsily, Lorna stitched away at something. She looked up as I came in and smiled. Elisa and Bina came through from the kitchen, dragging between them a large sack. Bina pulled a handful out of the sack and scattered it over the floor: old clothes, offcuts of fabric.

The women sat down to stitch and I sat with them, sorting the fabric into piles of different colours, running the softer ones over Marisol's face to make her smile. I thought how bright her eyes were, how hard she worked at taking everything in. An unwritten story, I thought; in her eyes the clarity of a life rich only with beginnings. I wondered how long it might be before that clarity was lost. And I understood then, quite suddenly, how Lorna and her baby might be for me too, as much as they had been for my father, a second chance. It dawned on me that in some way I'd just been reprieved, for if Lorna and Marisol had not been at Bina's, if they'd already been pulled back into the world of the House-on-Wheels, I would never have found it in myself to pursue them out onto Esperanza and on down the coast road while the sea turned indifferently on one side. Despite my daydreams of heroism, I'd have been struck by the same paralysis that stopped me on the night of the jetty fire, fastening me to the spot while others around me acted, while my father hurried towards his own death. But Lorna and the baby were here and all that was required of me was to make a choice that was being presented to me once again. Yet even as I made my choice, as I decided the kind of man I was going to be, my heart was far from quiet.

Lorna put her sewing down on her lap and stroked Marisol's foot lightly. 'Maybe in a couple of years there'll be enough for you and Elisa to go to college,' she said eagerly. Bina glanced at her but not at me, and I thought how open Aunt Bina's face had always been, how unsuccessfully she hid her thoughts.

Neither Aunt Mary nor America was in when I returned to the boarding house. I attended to my chores taking more care than I usually did, carrying out each task slowly, more purposefully, as if to imprint the textures of each movement, each object. I started to polish the piano, though there were other, more pressing jobs. The house was empty and I lifted the lid, ran a finger lightly to and fro over the surface of the keys before depressing a single key in the centre of the keyboard. The sound, louder than I'd expected, filled the still house and, shutting the lid quickly, I listened to its ghost die away in the afternoon air. It had barely faded when I heard keys in the front door, and Aunt Mary and America walked into the hallway.

I went out to them and took their bags. 'Has your sister left yet?' Aunt Mary said as the women followed me into the kitchen. I was glad she'd asked; it would be easier to turn the conversation to what I had to say.

She was quiet as I told her and for a moment or two afterwards. As I watched her, waiting for her to speak, it occurred to me for the first time since I'd come to her house how lonely Mary Morelos must have been, how losing her money had marooned her. If she was surprised by what I'd said she didn't show it. I thought she looked a little sad. She didn't try to change my mind. 'I'd have liked to see you finish high school,' was all she said.

Later, in my room, I looked about me at everything I'd thought of as mine in the world. Like my father, I thought – no great love of *things*. The room that had contained much of my life for the past five years appeared to me as it really was: small, empty. I would miss it, but only in the way of a bird whose cage has been left open and who hesitates, momentarily, to leave.

# OLEANDER IN BLOOM

When I was six or seven my mother found a mouse's nest in our kitchen, in a pail inside the low cupboard on top of which she often prepared our food. She was surprised, and yelled, and my father came running. The mouse had just had a litter and the three baby mice, blind and naked, squirmed around the mother, who pushed herself up against the sides of the pail, her fur bristling, aware of the threat of us. Seeing the mouse and her brood, my father took off his slipper and raised it over his head, but my mother caught his arm and, pressing it down towards his breast, looked hard into his eyes. My father ran his hands through his hair, uncertain what to do. The mice couldn't stay, my mother knew it and she smiled at me, stroking my head when I asked if I could keep them. Eventually, my father picked up the pail with the mice inside and took it down to the courtyard, tipping them out, gently, behind a white oleander bush. He looked up to where I peered over the railing, my mother's hand on my hair. Afterwards my mother was quiet and I asked her if she missed the mice. She laughed then briefly. My father said, 'They've got a new home under the *adelfa*. They can smell its flowers all summer.' All summer, though I never caught sight of them, I imagined the baby mice growing up in the garden and thought how much better that might be than living in a pail in our kitchen. I laughed softly when I thought about it now and remembered too how my mother had also told me it was bad luck to move a spider away from the place it had chosen to spin its web. 'It won't just spin another web,' she said. 'It will die because it has been torn from its own life.'

# ESPERANZA STREET,
# OCTOBER 1981

I stood at the boarding-house gate looking out over Esperanza Street. The rains had stopped now and the ground was dry. The garden behind me was lush with the green of fresh growth. At the top of the hill, towards Salinas Boulevard, Concepcion, one of the fish vendors, leaned forward on her stool. She rummaged for a while between the folds of her breasts before drawing out her tobacco tin. With her other hand she continued in her rhythm of sluicing the fish with water from a pail at her feet: lines of crab and milkfish and groupers. Nearby, the cycle rickshaw drivers fidgeted in the heat, fanning themselves with newspapers or their palms, pulling the visors of baseball caps low across their faces, settling back on their passenger seats as if asleep, feet up on the saddles.

Further down in the direction of the jetty, Abnor and Primo lounged in the doorway of Primo's store and, across the road, Johnny Five Course swatted the flies away from his bottles of soy and fish sauce. He was doing good business. The boarding houses and inns of the neighbourhood were filling slowly with people from out of town. Architects, engineers, officials with briefcases. And every day more people arrived looking for labour.

At the bottom of the hill the market hall had been cleared of debris and the market was running again, but as a more subdued version of itself. At the jetty the boats were still arriving. Only now, like the haulage trucks full of bricks and steel and lengths of bamboo, many were laden with the materials that would change Esperanza forever.

There was to be a reprieve for the cemetery at least, Eddie Casama having little appetite for conflict with the dead as well as the living, it seemed. He was quoted by the newspapers describing it as a gift, a sign of his goodwill towards the inhabitants of Greenhills, or at least to those who might remain, for people had already started to move away, the first departures coming not long after the fire. A few days later, in the same newspapers, he announced his intention to stand in the coming year's elections.

At the Bougainvillea, Dub was finally preparing to leave for college in Manila to study engineering, at his *grand pater's alma mater*, he said. I smiled whenever I recalled him saying it because it still sounded funny, but at the time I didn't know what it meant. I didn't know then whether I'd see him when he returned, or whether he'd forget that I was ever a part of his life.

I'd moved the few things that were mine to my father's apartment, including BabyLu's books, though these still waited in their boxes for me to fix more shelves. Soon enough, I knew, the apartment would be gone, but until then we would make a life there. I spent every night there now, coming to the boarding house only occasionally to help Aunt

Mary in the garden or to show the new houseboy how she liked things done, though she never asked it of me. Whenever I was there, I took a few minutes to linger, as today, at the gate. She and Dub had made enquiries for me and I'd started work at Earl's garage. If I showed any aptitude, he would keep me on, but I was enjoying it already, and even learning how to ride a bike.

I was standing at the gate, my cheek against the cool part of the stone that lay under the shadow of the cheesewood hedge, when I heard him walk across the verandah and down the driveway towards me. I knew it was Benny without turning, knew by heart his footsteps and the sound of the bag, full of sketchbooks and papers, banging against his legs. He came over and stood next to me, his hands in his pockets, looking out as I did over the street. He leaned in close, trying to see it from my perspective. Already he was so much taller than me.

We stood for a while without speaking. Then he pulled some papers out of his bag and handed them to me. I looked down at them. They were bound together: a komik, unmistakeably his work. I opened them and started to read, but I didn't get very far. My eyes clouded and I wiped them on my sleeve several times. *But, Benny*, I opened my mouth to say. Even if I had been able, at that moment, to find the right words with which to voice the truth, he would never have heard them. For he was already walking out of the gate, his long, loping stride carrying him up the hill towards Salinas. I closed the komik to read it later in my father's apartment, *my* apartment. I ran my fingers softly over the cover. *The Black Riders*, Issue Number One: the story of a man protesting against the destruction of all that is familiar to him; the story of his courage at a fire, his death, his funeral and his son – a small man barely out of boyhood, quite handsome on the page at least – who goes on to become a hero.

# ACKNOWLEDGEMENTS

I am indebted to the following people for providing practical support, critical feedback, and belief and encouragement during the writing and publication of *Esperanza Street*. In (almost) alphabetical order:

Jean Dowton, Vanessa Gebbie, Liat Hughes Joshi, Dnyan Keni, Caroline Maldonado, the late Archie Markham, Pippa McCarthy, John Milne (aka Tom Bowling), Zoe Rhodes, Carl Smith, Euan Thorneycroft, Martin Vaux. Also, particular thanks to my editor, Ana Fletcher, and the rest of the team at And Other Stories: Stefan Tobler, Sophie Lewis, Nicci Praça, Sarah Russo and Deborah Smith. Finally, thanks to the staff of the British Library.

Dear readers,

We rely on subscriptions from people like you to tell these other stories – the types of stories most publishers consider too risky to take on.

Our subscribers don't just make the books physically happen. They also help us approach booksellers, because we can demonstrate that our books already have readers and fans. And they give us the security to publish in line with our values, which are collaborative, imaginative and 'shamelessly literary'.

All of our subscribers:

- receive a first-edition copy of each of the books they subscribe to
- are thanked by name at the end of these books
- are warmly invited to contribute to our plans and choice of future books

## BECOME A SUBSCRIBER, OR GIVE A SUBSCRIPTION TO A FRIEND

Visit andotherstories.org/subscribe to become part of an alternative approach to publishing.

Subscriptions are:

£20 for two books per year
£35 for four books per year
£50 for six books per year

## OTHER WAYS TO GET INVOLVED

If you'd like to know about upcoming events and reading groups (our foreign-language reading groups help us choose books to publish, for example) you can:

- join the mailing list at: andotherstories.org/join-us
- follow us on Twitter: @andothertweets
- join us on Facebook: facebook.com/AndOtherStoriesBooks
- follow our blog: andotherstoriespublishing.tumblr.com

This book was made possible thanks to the support of:

Abigail Miller
Adam Lenson
Adrian May
Adriana Maldonado
Aidan Cottrell-Boyce
Ajay Sharma
Alan Cameron
Alan Ramsey
Alasdair Hutchison
Alastair Dickson
Alastair Gillespie
Alec Begley
Alex Martin
Alex Ramsey
Alex Robertson
Alex Sutcliffe
Alexandra Buchler
Alexandra de
    Scitivaux
Ali Conway
Ali Smith
Alice Brett
Alice Toulmin
Alison Bowyer
Alison Hughes
Alison Layland
Allison Graham
Alyse Ceirante
Amanda Anderson
Amanda Dalton
Amanda Love Darragh
Amanda Jane Stratton
Amber Dowell
Amelia Ashton
Amy Capelin
Amy McDonnell
Amy Rushton
Ana Amália Alves
Andrea Davis

Andrea Reinacher
Andrew Marston
Andrew McCafferty
Andrew Nairn
Andrew Whitelegg
Andy Burfield
Andy Chick
Angela Creed
Angela Thirlwell
Angus MacDonald
Ann McAllister
Ann Van Dyck
Anna Demming
Anna Holmwood
Anna Milsom
Anna Vinegrad
Anna-Maria Aurich
Annabel Hagg
Annalise Pippard
Anne Carus
Anne Maguire
Anne Meadows
Anne Waugh
Anne Marie Jackson
Anonymous
Anthony Quinn
Antonio de Swift
Antony Pearce
Aoife Boyd
Archie Davies
Asher Norris
Averill Buchanan

Barbara Adair
Barbara Mellor
Barry Hall
Barry Norton
Bartolomiej Tyszka
Belinda Farrell

Ben Schofield
Ben Smith
Ben Thornton
Benjamin Judge
Benjamin Morris
Bianca Jackson
Blanka Stoltz
Bob Hill
Bob Richmond-Watson
Brenda Scott
Briallen Hopper
Brigita Ptackova
Bruce Ackers
Bruce Millar
Bruce & Maggie
    Holmes

C Baker
C Mieville
Candy Says Juju
    Sophie
Cara & Bali Haque
Carl Emery
Carole JS Russo
Caroline Maldonado
Caroline Mildenhall
Caroline Perry
Caroline Rigby
Carolyn A Schroeder
Catherine Meek
Catherine Taylor
Cecilia Rossi
Cecily Maude
Charles Beckett
Charles Lambert
Charles Rowley
Charlotte Holtam
Charlotte Ryland
Charlotte Whittle

Chris Day
Chris Elcock
Chris Gribble
Chris Hancox
Chris Stevenson
Chris Watson
Chris Wood
Christina Baum
Christine Luker
Christopher Allen
Christopher Marlow
Ciara NT Riain
Claire Mitchell
Claire Fuller
Claire C Riley
Clare Lucas
Clarissa Botsford
Clemence Sebag
Clifford Posner
Clive Bellingham
Colin Burrow
Collette Eales
Courtney Lilly

Damien Tuffnell
Dan Pope
Daniel Carpenter
Daniel Gallimore
Daniel Gillespie
Daniel Hahn
Daniel Hugill
Daniel Lipscombe
Daniela Steierberg
Dave Lander
David Archer
David Eales
David Hedges
David Johnson-Davies
David Jones
David Roberts
David Smith

David Wardrop
Debbie Pinfold
Deborah Bygrave
Deborah Jacob
Deborah Smith
Delia Cowley
Denis Stillewagt &
    Anca Fronescu
Denise Muir
Diana Fox Carney
Dimitris Melicertes
Dominique Brocard

E Jarnes
Ed Tallent
Eddie Dick
Eileen Buttle
Elaine Martel
Elaine Rassaby
Eleanor Maier
Eliza O'Toole
Elizabeth Cochrane
Elizabeth Draper
Elizabeth Polonsky
Ellen Wright
Emily Diamand
Emily Jeremiah
Emily Rhodes
Emily Taylor
Emily Yaewon Lee &
    Gregory Limpens
Emma Kenneally
Emma Teale
Emma Timpany
Eric Langley
Evgenia Loginova
Ewan Tant

Federay Holmes
Fi McMillan
Fiona Graham

Fiona Powlett Smith
Fiona Quinn
Fran Carter
Fran Sanderson
Frances Chapman
Francesca Bray
Francis Taylor
Freya Carr
Friederike Knabe

G Thrower
Gabriela Saldanha
Gale Pryor
Gawain Espley
Gemma Tipton
Genevra Richardson
Geoffrey Fletcher
George McCaig
George Savona
George Sandison &
    Daniela Laterza
George Wilkinson
Georgia Panteli
Gill Boag-Munroe
Gillian Stern
Gillian Jondorf
Glyn Ridgley
Gordon Mackechnie
Gordon Cameron
Gordon Campbell
Grace Dyrness
Graham R Foster
Graham & Steph
    Parslow
Guy Haslam

Hannah Perret
Hanne Larsson
Hannes Heise
Harriet Mossop
Harriet Sayer

Harriet Spencer
Helen Brady
Helen Buck
Helen Collins
Helen Wormald
Helena Taylor
Helene Walters
Henrike Laehnemann
Henry Hitchings
Holly Johnson &
    Pat Merloe
Howdy Reisdorf

Íde Corley
Ian Barnett
Ian Kirkwood
Ian McMillan
Inna Carson
Isobel Staniland

J Collins
JA Calleja
Jack Brown
Jack Browne
Jacqueline Lademann
Jacqueline Taylor
Jacquie Goacher
Jade Maitre
James Cubbon
James Huddie
James Portlock
James Scudamore
James Tierney
James Upton
Jane Whiteley
Jane Woollard
Janet Mullarney
Janette Ryan
Jason Spencer
JC Sutcliffe
Jeff Collins

Jen Grainger
Jenifer Logie
Jennifer Campbell
Jennifer Higgins
Jennifer Hurstfield
Jennifer O'Brien
Jennifer Watson
Jenny Diski
Jenny Newton
Jeremy Weinstock
Jeremy Wood
Jerry Lynch
Jess Wood
Jethro Soutar
Jim Boucherat
Jo Elvery
Jo Harding
Jo Hope
Joanna Ellis
Jodie Free
Joe Gill
Joe Robins
Joel Love
Johan Forsell
John Conway
John Fisher
John Gent
John Stephen
    Grainger
John Hodgson
John Kelly
John McGill
John Nicholson
Jon Gower
Jon Iglesias
Jon Riches
Jon Lindsay Miles
Jonathan Ruppin
Jonathan Evans
Jonathan Watkiss
Joseph Cooney

Joshua Davis
JP Sanders
Judith Norton
Judy Kendall
Julia Sutton
Julian Duplain
Julian Lomas
Juliane Jarke
Julie Freeborn
Julie Gibson
Julie Van Pelt
Juliet Swann
Juraj Janik

Kaarina Hollo
Kaitlin Olson
Karan Deep Singh
Kari Dickson
Karla Fonesca
Katarina Trodden
Kate Gardner
Kate Griffin
Kate Pullinger
Kate Wild
Katharina Liehr
Katherine El-Salahi
Katharine Freeman
Katherine Jacomb
Katharine Robbins
Katherine Wootton
    Joyce
Kathryn Lewis
Katia Leloutre
Katie Martin
Katie Prescott
Katie Smith
Kay Elmy
Keith Alldritt
Keith Dunnett
Keith Walker
Kevin Acott

Kevin Brockmeier
Kevin Pino
Kinga Burger
KL Ee
Koen Van Bockstal
Kristin Djuve
Krystalli Glyniadakis

Lana Selby
Lander Hawes
Larry Colbeck
Laura Clarke
Laura Jenkins
Laura Solon
Laura Woods
Lauren Cerand
Lauren Ellemore
Leanne Bass
Leeanne O'Neill
Leonie Schwab
Lesley Lawn
Lesley Watters
Leslie Rose
Linda Broadbent
Lindsay Brammer
Lindsey Ford
Liz Tunnicliffe
Liz Ketch
Loretta Platts
Lorna Bleach
Louise Bongiovanni
Louise Rogers
Louise S Smith
Luke Williams
Lynda Graham
Lynn Martin

M Manfre
Maeve Lambe
Maggie Humm
Maggie Livesey

Maggie Peel
Maisie & Nick Carter
Malcolm Bourne
Mandy Boles
Marella Oppenheim
Margaret Jull Costa
Margaret E Briggs
Marina Castledine
Marion England
Marina Galanti
Marina Jones
Marion Tricoire
Mark Ainsbury
Mark Blacklock
Mark Howdle
Mark Lumley
Mark Richards
Mark Stevenson
Mark Waters
Martha Gifford
Martha Nicholson
Martin Brampton
Martin Conneely
Martin Cromie
Martin Hollywood
Martin Whelton
Mary Hall
Mary Nash
Mary Wang
Mason Billings
Mathias Enard
Matthew Francis
Matthew Lawrence
Maureen Freely
Maxime Dargaud-Fons
Meryl Hicks
Michael Harrison
Michael Johnston
Michelle Bailat-Jones
Michelle Roberts
Miles Visman

Milo Waterfield
Monika Olsen
Morgan Lyons
Moshi Moshi Records
Murali Menon

Nadine El-Hadi
Naomi Frisby
Natalie Brandweiner
Natalie Smith
Natalie Wardle
Neil Pretty
Nia Emlyn-Jones
Nick Chapman
Nick James
Nick Nelson & Rachel
  Eley
Nick Sidwell
Nicola Balkind
Nicola Hart
Nicola Hughes
Nina Alexandersen
Nina Power
Nuala Watt

Olga Alexandru
Olga Zilberbourg
Olivia Heal
Owen Booth

Pamela Ritchie
Pat Crowe
Patricia Appleyard
Patrick Owen
Paul Bailey
Paul Brand
Paul M Cray
Paul C Daw
Paul Dettman
Paul Gamble
Paul Hannon

Paul Jones
Paul Miller
Paul Munday
Paul Myatt
Paulo Santos Pinto
Penelope Price
Peter Armstrong
Peter Burns
Peter Law
Peter Lawton
Peter McCambridge
Peter Murray
Peter Rowland
Peter Vos
Philip Warren
Philippe Royer
Phillip Canning
Phyllis Reeve
Piet Van Bockstal
Polly McLean

Rachael Williams
Rachel Kennedy
Rachel Lasserson
Rachel Van Riel
Rachel Watkins
Read MAW Books
Rebecca Atkinson
Rebecca Braun
Rebecca Carter
Rebecca Moss
Rebecca Rosenthal
Réjane Collard
Rhodri Jones
Richard Dew
Richard Ellis
Richard Martin
Richard Smith
Rob Jefferson-Brown
Robert Gillett
Robin Patterson

Robin Woodburn
Rodolfo Barradas
Ronan Cormacain
Ros Schwartz
Rose Cole
Rosemary Rodwell
Rosemary Terry
Ross Macpherson
Roz Simpson
Russell Logan
Ruth Stokes

SE Guine
Sabine Griffiths
Sally Baker
Sam Gallivan
Sam Gordon
Sam Ruddock
Samantha
    Sabbarton-Wright
Samantha Schnee
Samuel Alexander
    Mansfield
Sandra de Monte
Sandra Hall
Sara D'Arcy
Sarah Benson
Sarah Bourne
Sarah Butler
Sarah Fakray
Sarah Salmon
Sarah Salway
Sascha Feuchert
Saskia Restorick
Scott Morris
Sean Malone
Sean McGivern
Seini O'Connor
Sharon Evans
Shaun Whiteside
Shazea Quraishi

Sheridan Marshall
Sherine El-Sayed
Shirley Harwood
Sian O'Neill
Sigrun Hodne
Simon Armstrong
Simon John Harvey
Simon Martin
Simon Okotie
Simon Pare
Simon Pennington
Simona Constantin
Simone O'Donovan
Siobhan Higgins
Sioned Puw Rowlands
Sonia McLintock
Sophia Wickham
Sophie Hampton
Sophie Johnstone
Sophie North
Stefano D'Orilia
Steph Morris
Stephen Abbott
Stephen Bass
Stephen Pearsall
Stephen Walker
Stephen H Oakey
Steven Williams
Stewart McAbney
Susan Murray
Susan Tomaselli
Susanna Jones
Susie Roberson
Suzanne White
Sylvie Zannier-Betts

Tammy Watchorn
Tamsin Ballard
Tamsin Walker
Tania Hershman
Tasmin Maitland

The Mighty Douche
    Softball Team
Thees Spreckelsen
Thomas Bell
Thomas Fritz
Thomas JD Gray
Tien Do
Tim Gray
Tim Jackson
Tim Theroux
Tim Warren
Timothy Harris
Tina Rotherham-
    Winqvist
Tom Bowden

Tom Darby
Tom Franklin
Tony & Joy Molyneaux
Tracy Bauld
Tracy Northup
Trevor Lewis
Trevor Wald
Trilby Humphryes
Tristan Burke

Val Challen
Vanessa Jackson
Vanessa Nolan
Victoria Adams
Victoria Sye

Victoria Walker
Visaly Muthusamy
Vivien
    Doornekamp-Glass

Walter Prando
Wendy Irvine
Wendy Langridge
Wenna Price
William G Dennehy

Yukiko Hiranuma

Zara Todd
Zoe Brasier

other stories

# Current & Upcoming Books

Title: *Esperanza Street*
Author: Niyati Keni
Editor: Ana Fletcher
Proofreader: Bryan Karetnyk
Typesetter: Tetragon, London
Cover Design: Hannah Naughton
Format: Trade paperback with French flaps
Paper: Munken LP Opaque 70/15 FSC
Printer: TJ International Ltd, Padstow, Cornwall, UK